PRA
THE SEC ORY
OF MOSCOW

"Sedia writes prose that begs to be read; pick up this book and you'll find yourself drawn in almost if it exudes the sort of magic it portrays too well. Her characters simply step into your life, no introduction needed . . . [She] sculpts a world that's rich, clear and chock-a-black with charming strangeness."—*The Agony Column*

"Modern blue-collar Moscow is pitch-perfect . . . bustling yet seedy, disorganized and none too respectable."—*Publishers Weekly.*

"Sedia's beautifully nuanced prose delivers both a uniquely enchanting fantasy and a thoughtful allegory that probes the Russian national psyche."—*Booklist.*

"Flavorsome fantasy set in the hidden underworld of newly capitalist Russia, from an ex-Muscovite and current New Jersey resident . . . great character sketches and plenty of magic-realist incidents, all set forth in charmingly Russian-accented prose."—*Kirkus Reviews.*

"A very practical book with a marvelous sense of wonder . . . A highlight of the year." —*Realms of Fantasy continued*

"**The Secret History of Moscow** is a clever cocktail that's one part Bulgakov and one part Gaiman—dark, disturbing, audacious, and wry as only a true Russian fantasy can be." —Gregory Frost, author of *Fitcher's Brides* and *Shadowbridge*

"A lovely, disconcerting book that does for Moscow what I hope my own *Neverwhere* may have done to London . . . the prose and the atmosphere is beautiful and decaying, and everything's grey with astonishing little bursts of unforgettable colour . . . deep, dark, remarkable stuff."—Neil Gaiman, author of *American Gods, Anansi Boys, Caroline, Neverwhere,* and *Stardust*

"Exciting and original! Myth, history and fairy tale meet and mingle with some compellingly real modern characters. Ekaterina Sedia is a very impressive young author, and one I'll be watching with great interest."—Ellen Kushner, author of *Privilege of the Sword*

"Ekaterina Sedia's **The Secret History of Moscow** is a jewel of a book, a dispatch from a mythic tradition unfamiliar to most American readers."—Jay Lake, author of *Mainspring*

"Lavishly imagined and written, as all strong fantasy must be, with a compelling authenticity of detail and psychological insight, Ekaterina Sedia's **The Secret History of Moscow** is a brilliant read, another step taken in what promises to be a long and significant career."—Lucius Shepard, author of *Viator* and *Softspoken*

THE SECRET HISTORY OF MOSCOW

Ekaterina Sedia

PRIME BOOKS

THE SECRET HISTORY OF MOSCOW

Cover design by Stephen H. Segal.
Cover art by Frederic Cayet.

Prime Books
www.prime-books.com

For more information, contact Prime.

ISBN: 978-0-8095-7223-6

ACKNOWLEDGEMENTS

This book owes its existence to many people—my history teachers and my instructors in Marxist theory; the wonderful old professors of the Biology Department of Moscow State University with whom I had the privilege to study; and finally the engineers and the street artists of Moscow who were the inspiration for this book.

I owe a debt of gratitude to the many writers and first readers who helped with advice, support and friendship—Paul Tremblay, Jay Lake, Catherynne Valente, Nick Mamatas, Bill Preston, Paul Jessup, Paul Abbamondi, Sarah Prineas, Hannah Wolf Bowen, Mike Allen, Mike Kelly, Jessica Paige Wick, Darin Bradley, Ivona Elenton, David Schwartz, Jenn Reese, Forrest Aguirre, Barth Anderson and Amal al Mohtar.

Many thanks to the wonderful folks at Prime—to Sean Wallace for having faith in this book and to Stephen Segal for his graphic design and general tolerance of late night AIM pings.

Finally, I am forever grateful to my family: Chris, my long-suffering husband, who puts up with me on a daily basis, and to my mom, dad, my sister Natasha, my dad-in-law, and Connie for their encouragement and love.

Thank you all for being in my life.

Моим родителям, Нине и Алексею, эта книга посвящается

1: *Galina*

She had long pale fingers, tapered like candles at the church. She swiped them through the flame of a match carefully at first, feeling nothing. Then she held them there longer, expecting them to drip and melt. Instead they turned red and blistered, and she withdrew carefully, watching the skin peel and stand in tiny transparent tents on her fingertips. She was already thinking of a lie to tell her coworkers to explain the blisters. Iron. Sizzling, spitting oil in the skillet. Napalm. She laughed at the thought. Napalm is never reassuring, and only reassuring things made for good lies—food, ironing, domesticity.

There was a knock on the bathroom door. "Galka, are you asleep in there?" Masha asked. "Come on, I have to go."

She blew out the match. "Will be right out."

"Are you smoking in there?"

"No," she said, and opened the door.

Masha, pink and sweating, bustled past her, brushing her enormous pregnant belly against Galina, already hiking up her housecoat.

Galina exited hastily. Masha's pregnancy bothered her—not just because she was only eighteen and not because Masha's husband-to-be was still in the army, serving the last of his two draft years. The impending arrival of the squalling pink thing that would steal the remnants of her sister's affection away from her hurt more than she would dare to admit—their mother and grandmother were so excited about the baby. Galina pretended that she was, too, and burned herself with matches when nobody was watching as a punishment for being so selfish. She hoped she wouldn't get into trouble again.

She blew on her fingers and headed for the room she shared with her mother and grandmother; Masha now had a room of her own, all the more reason for resentment and consequent weeping at her own monstrosity. The grandmother was away, at the hospital again and perhaps not ever coming back home, and the mother was on the phone in the hallway. Galina relished the moments of solitude. She stretched on her bed and listened to the familiar noises of the railroad outside, and to the mumbling of her mother's voice in the hallway. Quite despite her intentions, she listened to her mother's words.

Of course she's too young, the mother said. *But better too early than too late, and you know Galina: she's an old maid and I doubt there would be any grandchildren out of her, and really, I wish she would just have one out of wedlock, nowadays who really cares. I know she won't find a husband and I've resigned to that. But if she would just have a baby . . . Oh, I know, I told her a million times. But she's stubborn like you wouldn't believe, and I doubt any man would put up with that for long.*

There was nothing there Galina hadn't heard before—to her mother, men were rare and precious prey that had to be snared with cunning and artifice. Galina couldn't remember when last their conversation hadn't turned into a lesson in making herself attractive—how she should dress nicer, and mouth off less and smile more. Maybe this way she would hold someone's attention long enough to get knocked up. Neither mentioned the premise of these speeches—that Galina was unlovable without artifice and deception. She tried to avoid talking to her mother lately. But the voice in the hallway continued:

I just don't want her to turn into a bitter man-hater, her mother said. *Last time when she came home from the hospital* (she could never bring herself to say 'mental institution') *I had hope for a while. But now—I don't know if she should just go back or if there's nothing they can do to fix her.*

Galina remembered that day, when she had returned home, still swollen from the sulfazine-and-neuroleptics cocktails they had plied her with. The injection sites still hurt, and she resolved then to never do anything that would cause her to go back. She never told anyone about the things that flickered in the edges of her vision—strange creatures, awful sights. The mental institution was an extension of her mother, punishing her every time she disappointed. She chose her mother's dull torment over the acute pain of needles and the semiconscious nightmare of neuroleptics. She still felt guilty about her lies.

She pushed her face deeper into the pillow and pulled the pillow corners over her ears to block out the voice from the hallway. But it was too late—the fear had already kicked in, urging her to run, run far away, to protect herself. Like when she was a child (the only child), and there was a driving fear that the life she saw around her was all that awaited her in the future, and she wanted to run to avoid being trapped in the soul-killing routine of home and work, of TV, of acquiring things for the sake of it. How she longed to escape then; now, the desire was given a special urgency by her adult awareness that there wasn't anywhere to run to. The books she loved, the promises of secret worlds turned out to be lies.

And then there was a scream—she thought it was a cat at first, a neighbor's cat with a stepped-on tail complaining loudly of its bitter injury, and Galina wrapped the pillow tighter around her head. Then she realized that the cry was not feline at all but human. A baby.

She tossed the pillow aside and ran, her socks sliding on the smooth surface of hardwood floors. The cry was coming out of the bathroom, and Galina pounded on the locked door. No answer came.

Her mother, the phone abandoned dangling from the little table in the hallway, banged on the door too. A small woman, her fists struck the door with enough force to shake it. Galina stepped back.

"Don't just stand here," her mother snapped.

Galina ran into the kitchen. There was an old chest of tools their father left before he departed for environs unknown, and she searched for it, slamming the cupboard doors, her panic growing with every little door opened and slammed shut in disappointment. She finally found the chest on top of the china cabinet, and grabbed the largest screwdriver there was. Armed, she rushed back to the bathroom door, where her mother was still banging and the baby still cried inside.

She pushed her mother out of the way and struck the door by the handle, chipping away long slivers of wood over the lock. When the lock was exposed, she pried it open.

The baby, umbilical cord still attached, lay on the floor. A squirming purple thing her mother rushed to pick up and rubbed with a towel. Galina's gaze cast about, between the white porcelain of the toilet and the chipped rim of the tub. Vanity. Mirror. Window. The window is open. But no Masha.

Her mother was too preoccupied with the baby to notice her youngest daughter's disappearance. Galina looked out of the window, as if expecting to see Masha hovering by some miracle eight stories above the ground. The air in front of her was empty, save for a lone jackdaw that circled and circled.

She stood on tiptoes, half-hanging out of the window to see the ground below her, afraid to see it. Through vertigo and the waves of nascent nausea she saw the asphalt below—empty, save for a couple of stray cats and a clump of old ladies on the bench by the entrance. The jackdaw cawed and flapped its wings. It circled over Galina's head, demanding attention; it landed on the windowsill and cocked its head, looking at Galina with a shiny black eye, its beak half-open as if it were trying to talk. Its dull feathers looked like iron.

Galina felt the world careen under her feet, and the incessant crying of the baby and her mother's plaintive voice fell away, the jackdaw's eye trapping her in a bubble of silence and awe. "Masha?" she whispered with cold lips. "Is that really you?"

The jackdaw hopped closer and nodded its head as if saying, *yes it is me. It is me.*

"No," Galina said. "It cannot be. I don't believe you."

The bird cawed once and hopped off the window ledge. It fell like a stone until it almost hit the dead asphalt below; then it took wing and soared higher, obscuring the sun in the pale September sky.

The sounds intruded back, and Galina winced and pressed her fingers—blistered on her left hand but untouched on the right—to her ears, and turned around.

Her mother sat on the floor, the wailing baby cradled in the sagging folds of her housecoat, and cried. Her voice rose to a high-pitched scream, oddly matching that of the newborn infant, as the realization of her loss enveloped her. "Masha, Masha!" she cried, and the birds outside answered in angry shouts and caws.

"She's gone, Mom," Galina said. She never mentioned the jackdaw. She didn't want to go back to the hospital.

THEY CALLED IT THE GOLDEN AUTUMN, AND THAT MONDAY morning Galina could see why. The poplars lining the road on her way to the bus station turned yellow overnight, shining like the gilded onions of the churches in the old city in the slanted rays of the morning sun. The air had just a hint of the autumnal bitter taste to it, and Galina smiled, squinting at the bright colors of the trees and the sky until she remembered.

She did not want to go to work today, not with the misery back home; she felt like a traitor this morning, leaving her mother, who looked startlingly frail, with the bundled baby, among the diapers that needed washing and bottles of formula.

"Just go," her mother had said, her ire visible. "If you lose your job, what am I going to do with you then?"

Galina realized then that her mother was angry that it was Masha who disappeared—the youngest one, the normal one. She got ready for work.

She worked in the center of the city, in the old part of it, where everything was historical and beautiful. Even there, though, new life in the shape of kiosks had sprung up on every corner—they sold magazines, cigarettes, books, Tampax, pins, film, booze, eyeglasses, school supplies, handbags and T-shirts, and were manned by loud people who wouldn't leave the passersby alone.

To get to her place of employment, a small science publisher, she had to navigate the underground crossing that used to be so wide and free but was now crammed with endless kiosks and beggars. In all her life Galina hadn't seen beggars until recently; she wondered where they came from, and left whatever money was in her pockets in paper cups extended to her by thin hands, on the homemade trolleys—board and four wheels taken off a child's abandoned toy truck—that carted about old men with no legs, dressed in torn, disintegrating army fatigues, as if they had existed like this since 1945. Some of the cripples were younger, and she guessed them for Afghan vets; she avoided meeting their eyes, as if the things they'd seen could pour into hers somehow, travel to her heart, and freeze it forever. She averted her face and tossed the loose change blindly, in a vain effort to assuage her guilt.

She emerged on the other side of Tverskaya and ran to the two-storied old building in the Gazetniy Pereulok. The trees turned yellow and orange, and the first fallen leaves rustled under her sneakers. She could've made this trek with her eyes closed—she had worked for this publisher for the last three years, translating medical articles from English and German. She congratulated herself on having a job. Nowadays, there was simply no certainty in finding gainful employment. She frowned when she perused help-wanted ads in the newspapers—every time anyone mentioned foreign language skills, they also required that the owner of said skills doubled as a secretary and looked good in a miniskirt. It seemed that every day hundreds of new businesses sprang out of nowhere, like the beggars in the subways, and none of them were interested in a translator, just a good-looking entertainer for the eventual foreign investors. Yes, she was lucky to have a job; it didn't pay much, but she enjoyed it and, as a bonus, kept her dignity—a hard thing to find nowadays.

The cool entrance greeted her, the old stone breathing with the conserved cold of winters long past.

"Galka!" the voice of the senior editor named Velikanov, a man of gigantic stature matching his name, boomed. "Do you know what time it is?"

"Yes," she said. "My sister gave birth last night, and now she's missing."

"Wrong order, huh?" Velikanov grinned through his beard. He noticed her face and the grin faded back into the tangles of his facial vegetation. "God, you're serious. I'm so sorry. What are you doing at work then?"

She shrugged. "There's nothing else to do. I notified the police. My mom is taking care of the baby. I get to earn the money, I guess."

Velikanov patted her shoulder, careful not to crush it in

his meaty paw. "I'm sorry. I know you were close. How much younger was—I mean, is she now?"

"Ten years," Galina said.

Velikanov nodded and ushered her through the office to the kitchenette, where the kettle boiled perpetually. "Have some tea. Three sugars?"

She nodded and blew on the hot surface of the cup Velikanov handed to her. "Thanks. Anything urgent today?"

"Just a couple of news items from *Lancet*," he said. "Nothing urgent. You can take the afternoon off if you want."

"Thank you," Galina said. She wanted to add something else, to say that she was lucky to have Velikanov as her boss, but thought better of it. The giant man always looked at her with such helpless eyes that she worried that any kind word would make it worse. What was that story she used to love as a kid?

She sat at her desk and riffled the papers in a feeble ritual. She spotted the *Lancet* articles—two pages each, no big deal—and put them on top of her pile. She opened her notebook and thought of the story.

A children's book, large format, thin, with pictures on every page. Pictures of two children—a boy and a girl—cowering before an old, deformed woman with a large nose and a cruel cane in her hand. Then there were talking rabbits and fairies, and for the life of her she could not remember the plot; but she remembered the ending. On the last page, the old ugly woman stood transformed to her former youth and beauty, smiling at the eager children, as she explained that there had been a curse on her. She had been transmogrified into an ugly misshapen creature, and if she as much as breathed a kind word to them or offered the barest of comforts, the children would have turned to stone.

Galina raised the pages to her face to hide her tears from her coworkers—their desks crowded close together in this old room; Galina was the nearest to a large radiator by the window, so she would always be warm. Another one of Velikanov's many kindnesses that she could not return—she was afraid that if she did, his heart would be eventually turned to stone and be shattered by a false hope.

The picture stood in her mind and refused to be chased away by a valiant attempt to concentrate on the English words in front of her. When she was little, that story made so much sense—she was the only child, but the rest fit perfectly. Her haggard, angry mother who wanted to love her but was prohibited to do so by a curse, a mortal fear of expressing her love because it could kill.

When Masha was born, the curse theory went out of the window—their mother doted on the newborn, and nobody turned into stone, not even Galina. As Masha grew, Galina also learned to appreciate the affection her sister showed and that she missed so badly now. She swallowed her tears again, as she thought of her mother with Masha's baby in her lap, crying and rocking, and no radiant Masha around to comfort all of them.

Galina finished her tea, shook her head as if forcing out the devastating thoughts, and read the articles—a review of the new book on goiter (goiter? Did anyone even get that anymore?) and a conference report. She quickly jotted down a longhand translation, and tossed it on the typist's desk. "I'm taking a few hours off," she said, and left.

It was strange being out of the office during the day, and she walked across Tverskaya teeming with tourists, and let her feet meander until she found herself on Herzen Street. Old like everything in this part of the city, the street was lined with old stone buildings, and Galina stood a while, trying to remember that one house she used to love as a teenager. She spotted the three-storied brownstone, and prayed that the tenants hadn't installed the security lock at the entrance.

They hadn't, and she ran up the stairs, guilty and quiet on her feet. She hoped that none of the tenants would emerge from their comfortable, expensive apartments with steel security doors and question her right to be here.

This stairwell was one of her treasures, one of the secrets nobody knew about—she collected them obsessively, and reveled in the knowledge of her riches. Few of them were tangible—a convex piece of green bottle glass, buried in a sandbox with a perfect autumn leaf and a dried daisy underneath it, so one could unearth it slowly, grain by grain, and revel in the miraculous crystalline beauty; others were less so—a hidden eddy on the river, a particular angle at which sunlight struck the gilded onion of a church, and that house on Herzen Street, which had an unguarded roof exit, where one could sit on the slanted metal roof, warm from the sun, and be in awe of the old city curled in a cradling embrace of the river.

There was no one else on the roof, nor had there been in all the years she came here. There was trash by the chimney, and she surmised that others came here too; perhaps some of the beggars in the underground tunnel slept here, away from the stray dogs and police patrols in the streets. She rested her back against the chimney and pressed her toes against the gutter, lest she slid off the steep incline, and looked.

There is a reason they call it the city of forty times forty churches. Splashes of gold dotted the landscape before her, unobscured by the tall modern buildings. Yellow of the poplars and gold of the churches and blue of the sky made her sigh happily, forgetting for a moment her acute misery. Then she noticed a dark cloud in the sky, and shielded her eyes from the sun. The cloud grew larger and closer, and Galina realized that it was composed of birds—jackdaws, crows, owls. Owls? She stared up at the soft soundless beats of softly feathered wings, and round yellow eyes stared back. The birds circled over her head and one of the jackdaws kept dipping lower, its wings almost brushing against her face, the wind of their beats ruffling her hair.

"What do you want?" Galina asked. There was no one around who would care that she talked to birds, who would decide to send her back. Alone, she did not have to fake normality.

The jackdaw landed on the edge of the gutter, tilting its head.

Masha, she wanted to say, but bit the word back. She might be ill, but she knew well enough to recognize a hallucination. Birds appearing out of nowhere and trying to talk to her, owls not at all bothered by the sunlight—it wasn't true, it wasn't happening to her. A good schizophrenic—a brave schizophrenic—knew that she was ill and that things that she saw were not necessarily there. A good schizophrenic should ignore a hallucination once she recognized it as such.

"Go away," she whispered fiercely. "You do not exist, so leave me alone."

Her spirit in shambles, she rose and headed back to the hatch that would take her back to the world below. The birds grew agitated at her departure, and all of them drew closer, their wings raising a wind so strong she almost lost her footing. They mobbed her like the crows mobbed the cats who got too close to their nests, diving low, their claws pulling at her hair, their beaks opened wide. She fled to the safety of the hatch, her sneakers slipping on the suddenly too-smooth and dangerous metal. She grabbed at the boards framing the black square opening of her exit, splinters lodged in the weeping wounds on her fingertips, panicky, half-blinded by the black-and-gray movement in the air. She pulled herself into the dusty attic and ran for the stairs, the cawing and hooting finally left behind.

Too shaken to return to work, she walked along the New Arbat, recently converted to pedestrian traffic only and taken over by street artists. She looked as she passed; most exhibited landscapes of the city around them. She recognized the features as one would the corpse of a loved one—with features devoid of sparkling life and motion. Sketch artists called out to her, offering to draw her portrait, but she shook her head and watched the neat rectangles of the pavement. She passed several artisans exhibiting matryoshkas and painted jewelry boxes, imitating, more or less successfully, the traditional Palekh and Gzhel art. Several tourists haggled over the prices via their interpreter, and Galina shot the hassled man speaking in two languages at once a sympathetic look. She could never do that, she thought, to work for those people who descended upon the city like a plague—demanding, condescending, rude. But she wondered what it would be like, to believe that the world was created just for your pleasure and amusement.

She looked away, and stopped. A large painting propped against a storefront caught her eye and she stared at it, willing it to disappear. But it remained, the only painting that captured the spirit of its subject—the view from the roof she had just left, dotted with fat vivid strokes of gold and yellow, capped by a pale blue expanse of the sky. Worse, several birds, all beaks and claws, hung menacingly in the empty vastness of the sky.

The artist slouched by the painting, a dead cigarette in his slack lips. He eyed Galina with indifference and detached himself from the storefront. Unshaven, red-eyed, dirty. "Are you going to buy it?" he said.

Galina shook her head. "Sorry, no. But these birds . . . Can you see them too?"

The artist smiled, the stubble on his concave cheeks bristling. "Since last Friday. How about that! I thought it was the DTs."

Galina smiled. Great, she thought, a schizophrenic and an alcoholic saw creepy birds together. "Have you seen the owls?"

"Since Sunday," he confirmed.

"Where did they come from? Why are they here, now, during the day?"

The artist stretched and yawned, blasting Galina with the stench of stale smoke and alcohol. "Who the fuck knows?" he said philosophically. "But if you want my opinion, it's probably the gypsies' fault."

"Gypsies?"

"Or some other damn magic," he conceded. "If you really want to know, come by some other day, after it gets dark, and I'll show you."

"My sister's missing," Galina said. "I think it has something to do with the birds. Can't you explain now?"

"There ain't no explaining it," he said. "And I can't show you until it's dark."

He spat out his cigarette, shoved his hands into his pockets, and indicated that he wasn't going to say anything else.

Galina sighed, and turned to leave. "I'm Galina," she said in the way of goodbye. "I'll see you tomorrow."

"See that you do." He gave a short nod. "Fyodor, that's my name."

2: *Yakov*

YAKOV NEVER LIKED THE WAY HE LOOKED—HE SEEMED too prosaic, with not even a whiff of the Englishness he expected himself to possess. But from every spare line of his small square body to the last bristling hair on his head his appearance screamed 'Russian peasant' at the world. The world acted indignant in response and shoved him away. Moscow was especially violent in regards of shoving.

"Limitchik," that's what they called people like him—housing in Moscow had always been for the native Muscovites, and a limited number of out-of-towners. Native Muscovites viewed the out-of-towners with condescension and contempt that surprised Yakov when he moved here, all of ten years old. Twenty years later, the hatred did not seem to lessen. He started to suspect that he would never grow into a native.

Yakov stood in front of the window, in his boxers and wifebeater, looking at the poplar that didn't quite reach his sixth-story window. There was a crow's nest on top of it, and the nascent wind whipped it around; Yakov worried for the safety of two young crows in the nest. Their parents were nowhere to be seen, and the young birds squawked as the mass of twigs and branches and accidental fluff swayed back and forth with the windblown treetop. Yakov wondered if the baby birds felt nauseous. He wondered what they were still doing in the nest in September.

"Yasha!" his mother called from the kitchen. "Breakfast!"

He pulled on a pair of track pants stretched at the knees, the red stripes down the sides faded with too many washings. Too many faded red things in his life—another one of them, in the form of his mother's housecoat, dashed from the stove to the kitchen table and back, with the desperate energy of clockwork.

"Calm down, Ma," Yakov said, and patted the old woman's shoulder. He always thought of her as old and felt startled on her birthdays, when he remembered that she was barely fifty. "It's Saturday, no need to rush."

"I was going to meet Lida to go to the cemetery," she said. "To visit your grandparents, and the grave needs cleaning, what with all the leaves."

"It's fall. There'll be more falling tomorrow."

"Graves have to be clean," she said, stubborn and small. "Eat."

"Don't wait on me. Just do what you have to."

She sighed. "You'll be all right?"

"Of course." There was no need to get irritated. She always worried, a habit that wasn't going to go away. Be patient, he reminded himself. You're the grownup now, even if she doesn't realize it. "Go, do your thing. Have fun. Enjoy the graves."

Her face pinched. "The dead need to be taken care of."

He knew better than to argue. There was no point in

telling her that she was the only one comforted by the endless, thankless, pointless labors at the cemetery, that the dead didn't care. Yakov drank his tea.

His mother retreated to her room and slammed the wardrobe doors and shuffled polyester. He buttered bread and sliced thick slabs of cheese, fragrant and full of holes. He waited to be alone, and felt guilty for it.

She came into the kitchen, armored in flowered fabric and stern black shoes. "It wouldn't kill you to visit your grandparents."

Grandparents. He remembered his grandmother vaguely, and grandfather—not at all. His mother didn't remember him either. They knew only that he was an Englishman. Then there were half-remembered stories and conjectures, but his nationality was the only certainty. That, and the fact that he had worked on the radio for six months, between May and November of 1938, as an English-language correspondent. During this short time, he married grandma and got her pregnant, and was promptly executed—or, as they called it during Khrushchev's times, repressed. Nobody was quite sure what was buried in the grave with his name on it, and how it got there, but no one was curious enough to find out.

"I'll stay home today, Ma," he said. "Next weekend, maybe. We can go to church too, if you want." Throwing pacifiers at her, trading a small present inconvenience for a larger delayed one. Smart.

"We'll see, Yasha." She softened. "I'll be back soon."

He finished his tea, now cold, and found his binoculars. Through them, he could see the wide beaks of the baby birds, fringed with yolk yellow, opened in a silent scream. The wind was picking up.

The wind was blowing the leaves in yellow eddies and swirled them upward, then let them fall back to the ground. The wind blew through the dry grass in the empty lot behind the day care center visible from Yakov's window and whistled in the empty bottles strewn between the peeling benches, tugged on the fur of the dogs running across the dry mud and clumped dead grass in the no-man's land, and their owners lifted their collars up and lit up, cradling the tiny flames of matches in their palms, expertly buffeting the wind with their shoulders.

Yakov watched a young man chasing after a Scottish terrier; the dog, a blurry caterpillar of motion, ran in circles, easily outpacing its owner, even though its legs were so short they were hidden under the shaggy fur. The young man's jacket flapped around him as he ran and chased after the dog, plaintively calling out his name. A gust of wind pushed the young man in the back, forcing him into an awkward hobble, and threw the jacket over his head. As the man struggled to free himself from under the jacket, twisting and flapping his arms, another gust came and picked him off the ground. Yakov leaned closer to the window, not quite believing his eyes but too content with a Saturday alone to truly feel surprised or panicked. The man's arms flapped faster, the jacket grew longer; his feet shrank away from the ground, closed into tiny bird fists, and he hovered, half-human, half . . .

Yakov looked at the other people and dogs, but no one seemed overtly concerned or even cognizant of the young man's strange behavior. Only his terrier stopped running and sat, its head tilting quizzically, following something high in the air. And then Yakov realized that the young man was gone, and only a large crow flapped its wings above the empty lot, chased by the howling Scottish terrier dragging its leash through the mud.

MONDAYS BROUGHT THE UNEASE AND TUGGING IN HIS CHEST, and a desire to dig deeper into his pillows and just sleep. Instead, he rose at five A.M. and went to work. The bus was populated by sleepy citizens, unwilling to meet any-one's eye in this ungodly hour, when the soul, still tender from sleep, was vulnerable to any assault of light, noise, or an unkind word. Yakov, like the rest of his compatriots, feigned sleep and hid his face in the upright collar of his uniform.

The moment he closed his eyes, wind blew and coats upturned, dogs barked and crows cawed. He could not find a way to reconcile the scene he had witnessed, and decided to consider it a hallucination or a strange optical trick. He pushed it out of his mind, and got himself distracted by attending to one of the crows—he fell out of the nest, and Yakov spent Saturday night and all of Sunday alternately tending to the bird and trying to convince his mother that crows did not peck people's eyes out. He smiled now at the memory of the circular argument.

"He's a wild bird," his mother had said. "Let him go."

"I can't, Ma," he had answered. "There are stray cats out there, and he can't fly yet."

She had sighed and gone about her business, knocking

on his door an hour later and repeating her entreaties. Yakov shrugged and fed the bird with ground beef and boiled fish.

Now on the bus he worried a little about the little crow. He kept peeking into the messenger bag that held his new pet and a supply of food. The sleeping crow felt almost like a talisman, a handy distraction from a nagging memory he avoided, feeling only its general shape—that of a man with wings. He cringed and squeezed his eyes shut, and almost missed his stop.

The police station where he worked was located in the ground floor of an older apartment building—only seven stories tall and built of brown bricks. The stairwell smelled like every stairwell in this city—of tobacco smoke and cat piss, of cooking cabbage whose insidious smell seemed to creep from under every door, and abandoned old age. He glimpsed an old man exiting the building as he entered, not even seven in the morning.

"Good morning," Yakov said to the old man's back.

He didn't answer, his back in a well-worn jacket painfully straight, seized forever in a single position. The old man walked stiffly, leaning on his homemade cane, and Yakov felt bad for the old-timer—probably a vet; was there an old man who wasn't? It had to be hard to pick up the empty bottles off the streets and playgrounds where they were abandoned by the careless young. It was probably a good thing that there were so many bottles, so an old man didn't have to starve half to death on his pension. Still, it wasn't a good way for an old man to live—a war hero, an old man had to be respected and deserved some rest. If he was Yakov's grandfather, he wouldn't have to.

Frowning, Yakov walked up the flight of stairs and into the office. He settled at his desk, and positioned the crow, whom he had named Carl, in a comfortable nook between the radiator and the window. His desk was in the back, where actual work was taking place and no petitioners were allowed. The front room, bisected by the glass partition with small semicircular windows, was dominated by the passport desk, which was always doing brisk business.

He longed to be at the passport desk—although boring, the work there was familiar, and one could go through the motions of looking up vital statistics and stamping and filling in the blanks while thinking about something else entirely. Other police work suddenly lacked the familiarity.

Their station always used to be a quiet one, and Yakov had resigned himself to going through his life and retiring without ever investigating a homicide, without ever solving anything more serious than a domestic dispute or a drunken confrontation. It suited him fine, and the recent increase in crime, racketeers that came out of the woodwork, the territorial disputes, the murders, the torture—all of it was too much for him.

He shuffled papers in his desk, hoping that he would remain unnoticed, that no one would unload a petitioner on him and make him listen to another bitter tale of misery he could do nothing about. He would give them the usual speech of how they would do everything in their power, not mentioning that it wasn't much, that they lacked funding and morale, and that retirement seemed like a distant paradise to the young among them, and a nearby oasis that would finally quench their thirst to those who were older, but none of them really wanted to be here, and all regretted going into this line of work, except maybe the girls at the passport desk.

He managed to spend the morning pretending to be busy, and surreptitiously feeding the little crow every time he opened the bright glass beads of his eyes, his yellow beak gaping expectantly. Yakov shoved bits of raw hamburger into the hungry mouth, worried that the chunks might be too big. But Carl swallowed, and waited for more. Then Yakov worried about overfeeding.

"Richards," the voice by his desk said. "I need your attention for a bit."

Yakov looked up to meet a steely gaze of his lieutenant, who despite Yakov's seven-year tenure at the station still had trouble with his last name—he pronounced it carefully, as if the foreign word would burn the roof of his mouth if he weren't vigilant about it. "Just be a moment, Lieutenant Zakharov," he said.

Zakharov couldn't wait, of course. He ushered in an older woman, an obvious provincial covered with headscarf and shod in the gleaming hooves of orthopedic shoes. She had been crying, but her mouth formed a tight pucker, to ward against any impending emotion. Yakov knew that look well.

He sat the woman in front of his desk, and shoved Carl out of the way. She studied the chipped composite wood and a stack of papers Yakov kept there just to appear busy. The woman then turned her suspicious attention to Yakov. Her furrowed face betrayed her thoughts—she considered Yakov too young, too uneducated, not someone who should be in position of authority, making decisions that people's lives depended upon.

"What can I do for you?" Yakov said, derailing the unpleasant train of thought.

Carl squawked, and the woman frowned. "My name is Anna Chernina. My son-in-law is missing. He went to buy cigarettes and never came back. My daughter's been crying for two days straight now."

Yakov wrote down the address of the woman and her daughter, and the description of her son-in-law—eyes: brown, hair: brown, beard: none, height: 1 m 81 cm. He promised to call as soon as they heard anything.

The woman left unconvinced that Yakov was going to help her. He was pretty sure that he wasn't.

When lunchtime rolled around, Zakharov reappeared and straddled the peeling vinyl-upholstered chair in front of Yakov's desk.

"Yasha," he said, more familiar than Yakov ever remembered him, "we have five disappearances reported today."

Man. Wings. Scottish terrier abandoned in the empty field. Yakov banished the thought. "Racketeers," he said.

"It's happening all over Moscow. Thirty people in the last week."

"Racketeers are all over Moscow."

Zakharov rested his aristocratic skull on his hands folded over the back of the chair, his gaze traveling up the freshly whitewashed walls and to the ceiling blinking with naked bulbs. He sighed. "I suppose. God, why me?"

Yakov shrugged and reached for the bag with his little crow.

"Neat," Zakharov said. "Where'd you get it?"

"He fell out of the nest Saturday," Yakov replied. "It was windy." *And there was no man turning into a bird.*

"I can keep an eye on him," Zakharov said.

"Oh? And I will be doing what exactly?"

"You'll be visiting the families of the missing persons and finding out whether they were involved in any sort of commerce."

"Who isn't nowadays?"

"My point exactly. See who they worked for, see if any Chechen gangs were involved."

Yakov looked up. "Chechen?"

"Yeah. Armenian, Georgian—whatever. Caucasian nationals."

"Most thugs I see are Russians," Yakov said.

The lieutenant frowned and tossed a notepad with names and addresses at Yakov. "Go see to it."

Yakov went.

HE COULDN'T UNDERSTAND WHY HIS MOTHER HAD DECIDED to move to this city. Sure, the center, the old city, was beautiful. But they lived in the suburbs, which were dreadful and empty and grey, all natural vegetation twisted and starved by overturned dirt, by too many people, by the incessant burrowing of new construction. One couldn't cross a yard without accumulating great clods of clay on one's boots, and their weight inevitably dragged down the spirit. By the time Yakov reached the well-paved streets and the bus stop, he would usually lose the desire to live anywhere, let alone this place. The anorexic poplars bent in the persistent wind given free rein in this neighborhood, rarely more than corridors between tall flat buildings that begat drafts and winds; Yakov hoped that one day the confluence of air streams and accumulated depression in the air would create a tornado. He pictured it in his mind, a perfect whirlwind picking up the discarded garbage, the construction bricks carelessly left in sloppy piles, cars parked by and occasionally on the sidewalks. Just clearing out all the trash which hard life had deposited here and forgotten about. He went back and forth on whether he wanted the people gone as well.

His first visit took him into the heart of this desolate labyrinth. He imagined himself a Theseus in a police uniform; only a thread and an Ariadne attached to it were missing. Sweat trickled down his neck and cooled in the hollow between his shoulder blades as he imagined a minotaur waiting for him—a terrible creature brought forth by the upset of the world's order, born from the chaos that ruled the land and the pungent dreams of the new Russians, a misshapen embodiment of lawlessness and despair.

The hoodlums hanging out by the building gave him oblique looks but didn't heckle. He was grateful for that, for being able to go by without being called names. He ducked into the entrance and ran up two flights of stairs to the second floor where his first appointment waited.

He rang the bell and waited. He pushed the door and it swung noiselessly, admitting him into a crammed one-bedroom apartment, where pride masked poverty with knick-knacks and imitation wood furniture. He saw a cockroach, scuttling away shyly, and called into the empty place, "Hello?"

"Over here," he heard from the kitchen.

A young girl, maybe seventeen, sat at the kitchen table, her hands folded in her lap. Her gaze never met Yakov's, and remained directed toward the single window. "When we first moved here," she said, "there were apple orchards. This house was the first to be built in this district, and all the rest was just gardens, and the woods past the railroad tracks. There were owls there—I could hear them hooting every night. The trains whistling and the owls hooting, this is how I remember it. Especially in the summer."

"I'm with the police," Yakov said. "We got a report of a missing person?"

"My mom," the girl said, stubbornly staring out of the window. Her voice wavered a bit, and with a sinking heart Yakov realized that she'd been crying.

He never knew what to say to the crying people, especially the younger ones. It made him panic and make promises he couldn't possibly keep, just to stem the tears and the heartbreak. "Please," he said. "Don't cry. We'll find your mom. But you'll have to help me there, all right?"

The girl rubbed her face with her palm angrily, and shot him a smoldering look, furious that he'd seen her like this, red-eyed and snot-nosed. He pitied her for her grief and for her plain face and sharp nose, for her thin mousy braids, for her obvious awkwardness.

"When did you last see her?" Yakov asked, and sat down at the table though no invitation was forthcoming.

"Friday morning," the girl said. "She went to work but she didn't come back."

"Where does she work?"

"At the meat processing plant across the railroad tracks." The girl pointed. "Where the woods used to be. They say she didn't come to work Friday."

He wrote it down. "Do you have any relatives you can stay with meanwhile?"

"No." She gave him a dark look from her eyes reddened with recent tears. "I can take care of myself."

He nodded. "We'll call you if we find anything. Your name is . . . ?"

"Darya," the girl said. "And you?"

"Yakov," Yakov said. "If you call your local police station, just ask for me, all right?"

"All right," the girl said, and turned back to the window.

Yakov headed for the door. There was a yelp, and he spun and ran back into the kitchen, imagining something horrible happening to the girl. Instead, he found her unharmed but pale as she pointed at something outside the window. He looked at the flock of birds winging their way toward the building, not understanding at first. And then he saw.

The birds were owls, squinting in the luminous sunlight, but circling nonetheless.

"Where did they come from?" Yakov muttered, looking over the expanse of asphalt and construction.

The owls seemed confused as well. They remained silent, and their wings, soft as down, made no noise; they were phantoms, not birds of flesh and bone, he thought. They were not real because they were not supposed to be here, had no right to exist, had no reason to fly about in daylight. Yet Darya saw them too and waved at the birds, shooing them away or inviting them closer, Yakov couldn't tell.

One of the owls split from the flock and headed directly for the window. Its eyes, huge and round and yellow, set in a white triangular face, gripped Yakov's. The bird screeched once and slammed into the windowpane, its speckled feathers erupting at the impact and showering down, falling just seconds before the dead owl's body hit the asphalt below. Darya cried.

It was dark when he arrived at the last address, not too far from the station—he planned it that way. An older woman opened the door; her eyes were haunted. A stained and wet housecoat clung to her spindly legs, and the buttons were missing, showing a yellowing slip underneath. The woman motioned for him to come in, and he heard water rushing into the bathtub and a baby crying.

"Doing the laundry," the woman explained. "My daughter's missing. This is her baby."

"I can wait a little," Yakov said.

The woman nodded and disappeared down the hallway, muttering to herself and sighing. Yakov felt for her, left like this with a double burden of a missing child and care for the grandchild. He didn't dare to venture inside the apartment and waited by the door, resting his back against its smooth surface, until a lock clicked and the door shoved him into the hallway.

"I'm sorry," the woman who entered said, and eyed him suspiciously. She was taller than Yakov and about his age; she carried grocery bags. "Are you with the police?"

"Yes," Yakov said, resisting the impulse to sarcasm. "I'm sorry it took me so long—I'm interviewing many people today. A lot of folks seem to be missing. I think I just spoke to your mother?"

The woman nodded. "My sister disappeared two days ago."

"Where did she work?"

"She was a student, at the Pedagogical Institute. Started last year. She just had a baby."

"A boy or a girl?" Yakov asked.

The woman looked at him with a strange expression in her dark eyes. "I don't know," she said. "I was so shaken, I never thought of asking."

The old woman reappeared, wiping her hands on the housecoat. "It's a boy," she told Yakov, pointedly ignoring the woman with grocery bags. "Come on in, son. I'll tell you all about it."

She led him into the living room, where he sat on the collapsed couch, a spring digging into his thigh, and asked questions. Just like everyone else, the missing girl had no criminal connections and led a startlingly ordinary life. The only unusual thing was the circumstances of her disappearance—giving birth in the bathroom and then melting into thin air.

"And you haven't heard or seen anything?" he asked. "And are you sure the bathroom door was locked?"

"I'm sure," the woman said. "And there wasn't anyone else, except myself, and Galina."

"And a jackdaw," the tall woman said from the doorway where she apparently stood for some time, silent.

Man. Wings. Scottish terrier.

The old woman shook her head in exasperation. "Excuse her," she told Yakov. "She's not—right."

There didn't seem to be anything wrong with the woman, except that at her mother's words she shrank and retreated into the hallway.

"Wait," Yakov called. "Did you say a jackdaw?"

The woman peeked in again. "Yes. Other birds, too. And I think I know someone who can help you look. Only . . . "

"Stop that," the older woman said. "You're embarrassing me."

And Galina faded from view, silently disappearing into the darkness of the apartment. She reappeared once, when Yakov was leaving, and shoved a crumpled note into his hand. "Call me at work. There's a street artist who knows something," she whispered and fled under her mother's withering stare.

3: Fyodor

Fyodor was afraid of gypsies; when he was little, his mother used to warn him of straying too far away from the house. "Gypsies will get you," she said. "They steal children and sell them."

Fyodor played by the porch, in its cool shadow smelling of rotting wood, and rarely wandered past the outhouse and the fence discolored by weather.

When his stepfather came to live with them, he was much less aware of the gypsy problem. "Go play outside," he would tell little Fyodor. "What are you, stupid?"

"But the gypsies," he tried to explain. "They'll get me."

The stepfather laughed, and gave him a shove away from the porch. "Gypsies are not dumb. Why would they steal a kid who'd fetch no more than a quarter?"

Fyodor went then, sobbing silently to himself. He hoped to run into some gypsies and to be stolen away, both to get away from the stepfather and to prove him wrong. He wandered past the fence and down the only earthen street of Vasilyevskoe, the village where he was born and lived all his life. It was just a row of one-story wooden houses and a gaggle of filthy geese fraternizing with a few disheveled chickens. He passed the only store, and then the road led him out of the village, to a small clump of pines overgrowing sandy dunes—the Barrens, too grand a name for such a little place. But it smelled of fresh pine resin, and the sun shone, and wild strawberries stained his fingers with their sweet blood.

He spent all afternoon lying on his back, melting into the heated sand and pine-scented air, swallowing sweet melancholy tears as he thought of the gypsies that would come by to steal him away into some magical and sinister land, and how sorry his mother would be—perhaps sorry enough to tell the stepfather to go away forever since it was his fault.

The sun stretched over him, touching the tops of dunes in a sizzling white flash, and sank behind them. The shadows of the dunes grew blue and touched his face; the sand chilled him, and the strawberries grew indiscernible in the dark. He hated the gypsies then, for scorning him as defective merchandise. It was time to return home, to look into the stepfather's smug face and admit that he was right—there was no value inherent in Fyodor, and even gypsies knew that.

Fyodor's family moved when it was time for him to go to school. Like pilgrims, they took trains north and west until they arrived at Zvenigorod. Fyodor did not sleep on the train and just repeated the word—Zve-ni-go-rod—in rhythm with clanging of the wheels. A twinkling city, a happy city, he imagined, animated by the merry ringing of a thousand church bells, a city promising happiness and sunshine. It turned out to be covered in asphalt, and even the trees were dusty. Seven-year-old Fyodor felt the familiar sting of disappointment as he discovered that the name was a lie.

However, there were gypsies here. They were just leaving the train station as his mother and the stepfather bickered about whether the trucker they paid to transport their belongings to the new residence had arrived yet, when his stepfather paused and spat. "Fucking gypsies," he said. "I don't believe this."

Young Fyodor traced the direction of his gaze and stared at the colorful group—men and women, brightly dressed, sat on sacks and rolled-up blankets, talking loudly in a language Fyodor didn't understand—a secret Gypsy language, he surmised. A few half-naked toddlers played in the dust. All of these people had dark skin and shining black eyes, and the women wore long flowered skirts and jangling earrings and necklaces. The men's teeth shone white in their bearded faces. It was the first time he'd seen real gypsies, and he stood entranced until his mother tugged his hand and dragged him along.

"Don't stare," she said, irritably, and turned to Fyodor's stepfather. "Both of you. They'll see you looking at them."

It was too late—one of the women rose from the bundle she sat on and approached them calling out in a smoky accented voice, "Wait up, beautiful, I'll tell you your fortune if you gild my hand."

"No, thank you," Fyodor's mother said firmly, and turned away to leave. "We don't believe in this stuff."

The gypsy woman was not so easily discouraged. Her dark fingers grabbed Fyodor's mother's wrist, and she spoke so quickly her words blended into a threatening chant, "If you don't gild my hand, your eyes will burst, your womb will wither, your child will suffer . . . " All the while, she held her other hand palm-up, as if offering something invisible.

Fyodor's mother stopped and rifled through her handbag.

"Here," she said, and put the money—not coins, real paper money—into the woman's open hand. "Just leave us be."

"Tell me it wasn't our grocery money," the stepfather said. "I can't believe you just did that."

Fyodor's mother did not answer but shot him a fierce look and pulled Fyodor closer to her in a protective gesture. Even though she did not believe in hexes, she preferred to pay them off rather than dare to prove them wrong. Fyodor was too young to verbalize his new knowledge, but he was now dimly aware that even the most remote threat is too much when it is directed against someone one cares about. His suffering was worth actual paper money. He had never forgotten that.

Young Fyodor's life was quiet, and as the result his formative experiences were few. Later in life he marveled that he could count them all on one hand. First, there were gypsies, a vague threat, and his mother's protectiveness and the stepfather's indifferent malice; then there were watercolors his mother brought for him as a gift for his first day of school. He remembered the first of September, he in his new school uniform—a blue jacket with matching pants—in file with the multitude of other children in the schoolyard. The girls were wearing white ribbons in their hair, and brown dresses with white aprons. All children carried flowers to present to their teachers; gladioli predominated. He did not remember the rest of the school day, but he remembered the set of twenty-four paints, neatly arranged in tiny wells sunk in the ornate wooden case, which his mother presented to him when he got home. She also gave him an album of porous, fibrous paper, which drank the paint thirstily, absorbing it.

He painted so much that he ran out of colors, and only the black well retained a sliver of paint, like a curving strip of dirt under a fingernail. He went through a brief black period, until his mother grew worried and bought him another set. He dreamt of painting and daydreamed about it during the interminable school days. When the winter came, he left the pages blank to depict snow that covered everything, and punctuated it with sets of lonely footprints, of birds and humans. He wanted to draw the gypsies but resisted, fearful that the act of art was magical enough to attract their dark attention. But they hid in the edges of his paintings, hinted at by shadows and an occasional flash of white teeth and gold jewelry. He struggled to keep them out but still they found their way in.

During the summer, students descended upon Zvenigorod, coming from Moscow for their summer practice. They were future biologists, and Fyodor watched them shyly as they marched from the train station to the bus stop, where the bus took them to the mysterious Field Station. They carried knapsacks, laughed loudly, and smoked, and acted as if they owned the city. The stepfather disapproved of them. "Look at those kids," he would say. "Damn Muscovites. Act as if they own the place, like their shit smells of lilacs."

"Are Muscovites worse than gypsies?" Fyodor dared to ask.

The stepfather spat, his rough face furrowing. "Thieves are thieves, however you paint them."

Fyodor watched the receding backs with knapsacks, jeans, canvas sneakers. They didn't look like thieves, and he shared the observation.

"Moscow is privileged," the stepfather said. "See this?" He pointed at the cracking asphalt and stray dogs sleeping in the shade of the storefront that hadn't ever sold anything worthwhile. "We don't have anything so all the party bosses in Moscow can eat and drink and do what they want. They rob the rest of the country and take it to Moscow. Whoever lives there is a thief, plain and simple. Just like those gypsy pickpockets, God help us."

As Fyodor grew, he continued to paint, and he also started to see his stepfather's point. At the same time, he wanted to go to Moscow, to the land of plenty and the carefree students who came every year, like migratory swallows, and left again before the summer was over. Fyodor wanted that freedom to pass through as he pleased, and when he finished school, he applied to the Moscow State University, biology department, even though he had little interest in the subject. He just wanted to return to the town he lived in for the past ten years as a visitor, just passing through.

HE FAILED THE ENTRANCE EXAMS, BUT DELAYED RETURNING home. He called his mother and lied about unexpected complications, and spent the night at the train station. The next morning, he left his suitcase in the locker and went sightseeing—he visited the requisite Red Square and the Mausoleum, and gawked a bit at St Basil's Cathedral. He meandered through the streets and stood on bridges, watching the green-brown river below. Everywhere he went, he carried his album and watercolors, and took quick sketches, mostly just blurs of colors with only hints of shapes of everything that caught his fancy.

"You're pretty good," a girl said next to him.

He looked up and realized that she was a gypsy—long skirt, black as soot hair, soft eyes and mouth. A panic struck him, and he babbled. "Please don't hex me," he begged. "I don't have any money, honest. I'm out of town."

The corners of her mouth dimpled as if she were holding back a smile. "I won't hex you, handsome," she said, clearly enjoying her power over him. "Just paint me a picture, and we're good. I'll even give you a talisman that'll protect you from any gypsy curse."

"I don't believe in talismans," he said.

She laughed. "But you believe in curses? Come on, paint."

"You can have this one." He proffered the sketchpad with his most recent view of the river and the Alexander Garden—splotches of green and light—on the other side.

She shook her head, and her earrings and necklaces jangled. "I want a picture of me," she said.

He obeyed the woman, not quite sure why he did so. He painted in quick strokes, not waiting for the watercolor, barely diluted by the dank river water, to penetrate the paper, slathering it thick like oil. He poured on blacks and blues for the cloud of her hair, he painted gold and silver on her thin wrists, carmine for the lips, greens and yellows for her shawl and wide skirts. He painted with abandon, with catharsis—finally, finally, he had given in, unable to keep the gypsies out. Now he would be stolen away for sure; he felt relieved at the thought. When everything you had ever feared happened you didn't have to fear anymore.

The girl looked at the picture and smiled. "I like it," she said. "Here." She unwrapped a thin chain with a copper circle from her neck and handed it to Fyodor. "Here's your talisman. Now no gypsy could harm you."

He studied the dull circle that looked like an old coin polished into obscurity. "Does it really work?"

"No," she said, "but neither do hexes. Come on, put it on."

He obeyed.

"Now," the girl said, "do you have anything to do?"

"No," he said, and followed her when she beckoned. On the way, he told her about the failed exams and the dusty asphalt of Zvenigorod growing soft under one's feet in the summer heat. He told her that he had no plans and no desire to go back.

"You can stay with my *tabor*," she offered. That's what a group of gypsies was called, he remembered. A *tabor* of gypsies—like a murder of crows or a pride of lions, a special word just for them.

"No, thanks," Fyodor said. "I don't think I'm ready for that yet. Where are we going?"

She pointed ahead, at the squat gigantic building with arched windows, which he recognized as a train station.

"Paveletzky Terminal," she told him. "We're staying there, for now at least. They have a very nice waiting hall, and the courtyard. We need the courtyard for the bear."

"The bear?" he repeated.

She nodded. "Uh-huh. I think we're the only *tabor* in this city that does bear shows. Only he's getting old."

"Oh."

The station bustled with travelers, and the din of voices and sharp sounds of children's crying assaulted Fyodor; he hugged his sketchbook to his chest.

"There are the Roma." The girl pointed.

They were not like Fyodor remembered them. Instead of bright colors they were dressed in drab city clothing, dirty with neglect and age. Only their dark faces indicated that they were truly alien. "Their clothes . . . " Fyodor faltered. "What about you? You're dressed like a proper gypsy."

The girl laughed. "What, this? I'm coming from a party. This costume is something we wear when we have to perform."

"And you pickpocket in the regular clothes."

The girl gave him a long look. "Pretty much, yeah. Want to see the bear?"

He nodded and followed her through the hall of the train station to a small grass-covered yard in the back. Furtively, he made sure that his watch was still attached to the wristband, and that the band still circled his wrist.

The bear chained to a wooden stake thrust carelessly into the ground was old and arthritic, and his rheumy eyes watched Fyodor with indifference born of old age and a lifetime of oppression. The fur under his eyes was sticky with gunk, and his chin was bare, as if he rubbed it too much. There were also large bald spots on his sides, gray skin amid mangy brown fur, like patches of lichen on the stone. The bear smelled strongly too, of wet dog, iodine and bad teeth.

"Poor thing," Fyodor said.

"Poor Misha," the girl agreed. "He's so old, my mom says he won't live through the winter."

The bear sat on his haunches, his sides rising and falling, his pink tongue hanging out among the broken teeth; Fyodor doubted he would survive the summer. "You call him Misha?"

The girl laughed. "Yeah, I know. Original, right? By the way, I'm Oksana. You?"

"Fyodor." He thought a bit. "Why did you drag me here?"

"You said you had nothing else to do." She still smiled, but the look in her eyes was crestfallen.

Had he been older or not so preoccupied, he would've understood that she was showing kindness to a stranger, looking for a friend or just offering a hand. If he had not been so scared of being stolen in all these years, he would've known better than to scoff, and say, "Look, I told you I don't have any money. None."

Oksana just stared at him. The bear moaned.

"I better go," he said. He had sense enough not to add, *I wouldn't have fucked you anyway*, but he thought it, and suspected that Oksana could guess his thought.

He never went back to Zvenigorod—another gypsy encounter, coupled with the presence of the amulet and the image of the old and ailing bear convinced him that going back would mean stagnation and death. As the formerly solid structures and ideologies crumbled and the social services collapsed one by one, he learned how to live the life of the street artist. He squatted when he couldn't find other options, preferring the attics of the apartment buildings downtown, not too far from Arbat where he sold the watercolors and bought art supplies and booze; Herzen Street was the reliable favorite. Sometimes he stayed with the hippies who liked Arbat and the artists, and a few of whom didn't mind his overnight presence on one couch or another. Winters were hard but he survived; if it got too cold in his attic, he dragged himself down the stairs, into the streets, into the flashing lights of ambulances who had the good grace of collecting indigents on especially cold nights and taking them to hospitals and shelters, wherever there were beds and food. Sisyphus' labor if there ever was one, because the winters kept returning, the indigents grew in number, and the ambulances got their funding slashed time and time again.

He was not looking forward to the winters, and come September he started to drink and worry more and paint less—nowadays, he stuck with the views from the roofs and attics he frequented. Every time he saw gypsies, he searched for Oksana, but she was either not there or he failed to recognize her in her street clothes—he remembered her earrings better than her face. He painted her occasionally, hoping to summon her by sympathetic magic, which turned out to be as useless as the defaced coin hanging on the chain around his neck.

The tourists liked buying Oksana's portrait—they liked anything colorful and exotic, like magpies. They were also as loud as magpies, talking at Fyodor in slow, loudly enunciated syllables. He just smiled and gave no sign that he understood English; he didn't have to—exchange of art for foreign green money was a silent transaction. Moreover, if he played dumb, he got to hear them talking about him—terrible, did you see how drunk he was? This is the problem with this country, communism really fucked them all up. Now hopefully things would get better. They'd still drink though.

Like hell they will, Fyodor thought. Although still young, he had learned that things did not get better but worse, that entropy was winning, that despite the appearance of order the universe had one direction—toward heat death, the second law of thermodynamics said as much, and who was he to disagree with Herr von Helmholtz. Everything sought its lowest energy status, and Fyodor had found his.

It was only a matter of time before he discovered he was not the only one finding stable equilibria in low places. Everywhere close to the ground time slowed down, and if he pressed his ear to the pavement, not caring if passersby took him for a drunk, he heard voices, quiet as the whispering of the growing grass, complaining and crying in an unceasing susurrus. The coin around his neck grew cold when it touched the ground, and afterwards the metal burned his skin with the collected cold it retained far longer than was prudent.

When his heart grew too heavy with the whispers, he went to the roof, to get away from them. But sooner or later they called, and he descended back into streets wet with the first September rains, and sold paintings, and listened to the ground talk to him.

It was a surprise when the birds appeared—he expected things to come from under the ground, to buckle the cobbles of New Arbat and reach up, up, consuming the world, pulling it down to the lowest energy state. But there they were, flapping; he followed them as they circled over the hungry, troubled city.

As his fascination grew, he ate less and drank more; he hardly ever slept. And when the woman asking about them showed up, he wasn't quite sure what he'd seen and what he'd dreamt or imagined. He desperately wanted to show it to someone, just to make sure he wasn't going crazy. He wanted a confirmation, a witness who would stand with him and watch the birds emerge from closed windows reflecting nothing but the night sky; he wanted someone else to see doors reflected in puddles open and admit small, weak creatures into the world.

When night fell, he danced with anticipation, the only seller remaining after the ghastly pink streetlights went on, he and his lone painting. The crowd of buyers and gawkers thinned as well and he slouched against the storefront, in the shadows.

"Where is he?" a man said nearby.

"Right here." The woman he met the day before stepped into a warm puddle of light and out. "I hope you don't mind that I brought Yakov along."

"Mind? Why should I mind?" He gave a sideways look to a squat short man with a messenger bag over his shoulder. The bag squawked.

"It's my bird," the man explained. "He fell out of the nest."

Fyodor took his time looking over a young crow. Something about the man made him uneasy—the way he moved, so crisp, almost robotic, as if he worked on keeping in shape. Short hair. Fyodor cringed and hoped he wasn't one of those iron pumpers who, a few years back, used to beat hippies and forcibly cut their hair, but had now graduated to racketeering.

"You wanted to show me something?" Galina said.

"Yeah." He motioned. "Come on. It's not far away."

He found his way by memory rather than street names; he couldn't remember the street names if he tried, but he remembered turns, uneven sidewalks, the calm faces of the old buildings. He meandered, but finally found the place he was looking for—an arch spanning between two buildings, leading into a courtyard dominated by a large puddle.

"There," he said, and pointed at the black surface of the puddle marred by a few oil slicks leaking from a beat-up car parked nearby.

The puddle reflected the faint halos of streetlights, diffuse in the misty air, and the front of the nearest building. A small lamp mounted above the door illuminated its surface, and in the reflection the door glowed with a milky light.

"Watch," Fyodor said. They did, until their eyes weren't sure if they were looking at the reflection or at the real door—the still surface of the puddle completed the illusion of absolute darkness surrounding an upside-down door, hung in empty space for no particular purpose. Then the door started to open, slowly.

"Don't look up," Fyodor said. "Don't look at the real thing. Watch the reflection—this is what's important."

The door swung open and blackened with a multitude of starlings—they came screeching from the door in the puddle into the night air above their heads, with no transition and no trace of water on the glistening feathers.

The crow in Yakov's bag cawed in recognition and flapped its wings. The thing couldn't fly, but that didn't stop it from trying. Before Yakov could stuff him back, the crow strained and flapped, and fell. It made no ripples on the surface as it fell through the door in the puddle and disappeared from view.

4: Entrance

Galina looked at Yakov who stared, slack-jawed, at the puddle that had just swallowed his crow. She made a shallow gesture of poking in the puddle, but felt only water and muck on her fingers, and no crow. The reflection of the door bobbed on the waves she raised, and broke into slivers sharply outlined in the moon-white, rippling across the surface.

"Maybe you should go after your bird," Fyodor told Yakov. His dark eyes reflected the burning ember of his cigarette, and as he dragged on it the flashes of orange light lit his hollow face.

"Go where?" Yakov said.

Fyodor motioned at the puddle, it surface calm again. The door in the puddle was closed.

Galina looked from one man to the other. They were all at an impasse—it seemed equally absurd to deny the crow's disappearance or the reflected door's ability to admit things *somewhere else*. Galina was used to strange happenings, but having someone to share them with her was a new experience. She felt exposed, defenseless without the comforting blanket of madness that would hide her from things she didn't want to see, explain them away—much as people with cats had no reason to fear the night sounds haunting their houses. *It's just the cat*, they would tell themselves even when the feline was sleeping peacefully at the foot of the bed. *There's nothing to worry about.*

There was something to worry about, Galina thought. She waited for Yakov to say something—of the three of them he seemed the most balanced, the most normal. Perhaps this is why he still remained transfixed, his eyes panicked. "You said he would know something about the disappearances."

"You don't think this puddle has anything to do with people turning into birds?" Galina said.

"People don't turn into birds," Yakov answered. "It was just an illusion, a trick of light—it was so windy out."

"You saw it," Galina said. "You saw it too."

Yakov didn't answer, and Galina stared at the upside down door in the puddle. Still closed, she realized with a pang. The same twinge of disappointment she felt when she would spend hours sitting in a subway station, watching the dark hole of the tunnel, waiting for something to happen. She didn't know what it was about the subways—perhaps the fact that they were carved into a dark wet heart of the earth—that made them so magical. But she used to have an unshakeable conviction that they were the way to a hidden world where she could escape.

Maybe she didn't try hard enough, waited long enough—she left the station when the subway closed, instead of hiding and waiting overnight. She headed straight home instead of wandering through the night city until the sky pinked and the long stationary clouds grew translucent. She didn't want it bad enough.

The desire was bled out of her over time, from one hospital to the next, from one diagnosis to another, until she was convinced of her own insanity for even thinking that escape was possible. And now, when the insanity became comforting and dulling, it was yanked away from her, and the old dreams of escape stirred, terrifying and inviting.

"We better go," Yakov said to her.

She smiled. "This is how you investigate things? 'Come on, let's go'? No wonder so many murders are never solved."

Yakov shrugged, and looked away.

The barb hurt, and she immediately felt sorry for him. "I didn't mean it like that. I'm sorry, my sister is gone, and I just think that perhaps we should look into this."

"Look into what?" He barked a nervous laugh. "People turning into birds? Doors leading into puddles? Crazies?" He indicated Fyodor with a toss of his head. "How do you propose we investigate something like that?"

"We could try and go through that door," she said.

Yakov shook his head. "It's just a reflection."

"Your pet would beg to differ. Are you just going to abandon your bird?"

"He's a wild bird," Yakov said. "In any case, suppose you're right. What the fuck could be behind that door?"

Galina thought for a bit. Her childhood imaginings of unicorns and fairies seemed far-fetched—why would there be unicorns and fairies under this dark city that towered over them, surrounded them from all sides with its suffocating stone and metal? What good could hide under it? "I don't know," she said. "But I'm sure it'll shed some light on what happened to Masha."

Yakov threw his hands into the air and paced around the

puddle. "How do you even know that this has anything to do with your sister? Because this lunatic told you so?"

"I'm not a lunatic," Fyodor interjected.

Galina ignored him. "There are two very strange things happening at the same time and you don't think they have anything to do with one another?"

"It's possible," Yakov said. "But—"

His words were interrupted by a soft whistling that came from every direction at once. A second later, a great cloud of birds entered the yard, their wings beating against the thick night air. Galina covered her face and hunched over—the birds on the roof were too fresh in her memory.

The birds gave her no notice, and flew straight through the puddle, disappearing without a trace; only a few crows still hung in the air, their voices harsh.

"Now what do you think?" Galina straightened.

"All right," Yakov said. "They're connected. But we can't go in there—when you reached into the puddle, nothing happened, remember? It was just a puddle."

"Exactly," Fyodor said. "You reached into the puddle. You saw it, not the door. But anyway, this one would be too small for us."

Galina looked over the reflection. "Where would we find a bigger one?"

"I know a place," Fyodor said. "It's big. Only I never saw anyone going in or out of there."

"Where is it?" Yakov asked.

"Not far," Fyodor said. "In a subway station—Arbatskaya, I think. Or Smolenskaya, who the fuck knows the difference."

"On the dark-blue line, or the light-blue?" Galina asked.

Fyodor only shrugged and headed out of the courtyard, under the arch, his back lopsided in the wind.

Subway, Galina thought. She always knew it would be a subway, and once again she lamented her lack of persistence. All this time she thought she was delusional, while in reality she wasn't delusional enough to keep the hope alive.

Yakov caught up to her; the flap of his messenger bag gaped open, as if distraught. "It was just a crow I found," he said. "Not a pet."

"And the puddle was just a puddle," she replied. "Do you always backpedal like this? Every time something significant happens you just tell yourself it isn't important?"

He thought for a bit. "Yes," he admitted. "It's easier that way."

Galina nodded. "It is. I do it too, sometimes. Sorry."

"I am here in the middle of the night, ain't I?" he said.

His defensiveness surprised her. She was used to the police as enforcers, at least in the old days. Now, they seemed superfluous and helpless, struggling against the tide all of them were struggling against, with little success. How could things change like that? How could the world go upside-down overnight? They were promised a future, and having it yanked from under everyone's noses just didn't seem fair.

And now, this. They walked across the cobbles of New Arbat, the pink glow of its streetlights too pink, too sick. Voices came from the side streets—drunken and rowdy, and Galina quickened her step instinctively. There was no smell of leaves in this part of the city, just smoke and gasoline that singed the back of her throat. The pink light painted long ugly streaks across the facades, and occasional gusts of wind brought with them a faint smell of the McDonald's restaurant that has just opened downtown. It was the death smell of the world she used to know, and Galina frowned.

They approached the subway station, and Galina recognized the building of the Ministry of Defense the station was built into; Arbatskaya, then. Fyodor led them inside, deftly hopping over the turnstile. Galina and Yakov exchanged a look but paid. They passed under the giant circular candelabra hanging from the ceiling like an underground sun, and headed toward the escalator. Galina paused, transfixed by the sudden light and the white marble of cupped ceiling, and stepped onto the escalator with the trepidation of someone entering a waterfall; they paused for a brief second at the highest point, and plunged downward, in a dreamlike, dignified descent.

The underground portion of the station waited for them with its low ceiling, cold and ornate like a sarcophagus. The columns, leaning away from the train tracks, met the ceiling in soft arches, like the ribs of an upside-down funeral barge. Galina tilted her head up, to better take in the station closing softly around her. The train roared in the tunnel, getting nearer; a few passengers on the benches stirred and stepped closer to the tracks, as if fearful that the train wouldn't see them and pass them by.

"Where's a reflection?" Yakov asked Fyodor. "I thought we needed a reflection."

"The train is coming." Fyodor stabbed out his cigarette on

one of the columns; in the cold fluorescent light his face appeared even more angular and wild, with sharp shadows jutting under his jaw, the stubble bristling, the eyebrows drawn over the red-rimmed eyes. He stepped closer to the platform, to the center of one of the arches that connected the station to the platform, and motioned for Galina and Yakov to join him. They flanked him silently, and Fyodor's shoulder's tensed. No wonder, Galina thought; she didn't like being surrounded like that either, crowded by pretend kindness.

The train pulled into the station, its sleek shape hissing to a stop. The door opened, letting people out and others in.

"Are we getting on?" Galina asked.

Fyodor shook his head. "Watch the glass," he said.

The doors sighed closed and the train came into motion. In its windows and doors that went by quicker and quicker, Galina saw the reflections of the arches and her own wide-eyed face, distorted by the streaks of light and shadow, the concave glass. She stared into the arch—as the train sped up, the reflection blurred and solidified, sliding from one pane to the next with barely an interruption. She watched the faces of people inside blur and disappear, subsumed by growing darkness between white marble arches.

"Here goes nothing," she heard and felt a strong tug on her hand. She flailed, lost her balance and fell forward, cringing in anticipation of impact with the quickly moving train or a third rail, but keeping her eyes on the wobbling white arch. Cool air blew on her face, and she finally fell on her hands and knees, something warm and wet under her fingers.

"Are you all right?" Yakov asked. He crouched down next to her, the whites of his eyes gleaming in the dusk.

"Yes." The moisture was seeping through the fabric of her jeans and she stood up, her knees wobbly and her stomach queasy.

Fyodor caught her elbow, steadying her. "Took a spill, there."

Both men fussed over her, as if to avoid having to look around and notice the white arch cupping above them and a dim road stretching in every direction. She fantasized briefly that it was just an abandoned tunnel, a secret subway station compartment she had fallen into, and she laughed. "We're actually here," she told both of her companions as they looked at her, worried. "This is real."

"If we only knew where 'here' was," Yakov said.

"Underground," Fyodor said. "Isn't that obvious?"

The road they stood on stretched before them, a single dirt lane worn deep in twin ruts. Tents, wooden shacks, abandoned haylofts lined the road non-committally, sometimes tucked back under the clumps of gangly black bushes with twisting long branches, sometimes crowding it.

"It looks like my home village," Fyodor said.

Yakov laughed. "No offense, but congrats on getting out."

Fyodor's gaze lingered over the road, and a slow smile stretched his lips, black in dim underground. "Thanks. Same to you, limitchik. What, you thought no one noticed?"

Yakov's face darkened, and his fists grew large and heavy. "Don't you talk to me like that. I'll fucking arrest you."

"Oh, a cop." Fyodor laughed. "What, you think if you bark louder than everyone else and protect their shit they'll treat you like a man and not a dog? Keep dreaming, mutt."

Galina frowned. "What are you talking about? Who are 'they'?"

Both men whipped around. "You," they said in unison.

"You have something against Muscovites?" she asked, surprised. And laughed before they could answer. "And why are you discussing it now?"

"As good a time as any," Yakov said. "But this ain't Moscow, so we can leave it for now."

Fyodor shook his head. "You're sure we're not under some KGB dungeon? This road probably leads to the Lubyanka or a secret prison or something."

"I thought you blamed gypsies," Galina said.

Fyodor lit another cigarette. "I blame everyone."

Galina quelled another argument before it broke out by starting down the road. "I wonder if it leads to a river," she said. "Like the Styx."

Yakov walked next to her, pointedly leaving Fyodor to bring up the rear. "I'm expecting more of a hovel on chicken shanks situation," he said. "You know, like in the children's tales."

"I don't," Galina said. "All my childhood books were translated—English stories. Jack the Giant Slayer, and others I can't remember."

"Huh," Yakov said. "That's weird. I also had a bunch of English books when I was little, from my grandfather. When we left Serpuhov, my mom threw them out."

The shacks and tents gave way to trees, a park of sorts. The trees stood tall and bare, their skeletal branches phosphorescing with a weak light. They crowded the road and the branches touched above their heads, forming a lacy canopy against the black backdrop of non-existent sky.

"Definitely Baba Yaga territory," Fyodor said. "I'd like to see you try to apprehend her."

"Simple. Citizen Yaga, you're under arrest," Yakov responded, and all three snickered uneasily.

The road meandered and almost disappeared, thinning to barely visible tracks in the fat white grass the sight of which filled Galina with irrational disgust. White birds—starlings and rooks—studded the trees like pimples. Galina wondered if they were different from the birds outside, or if the regular birds gradually changed color underground, shedding their dark feathers and growing new ones, white like shrouds.

A faint noise that grew for some time finally crossed into her awareness, and she listened to the quiet but powerful throb. It sounded as if it came from a great distance, and she guessed that close by it would roar, deafening. Like a waterfall, she thought, the waterfall of the escalator that brought her down to the overturned skeleton of the funeral barge—the subway station had foreshadowed what was concealed below, and she had to wonder if it were intentional.

People outside, the people that used to run things back in her remote pioneer childhood and who still seemed to be running them now, must have had a hand in the identical design of the above and below ground; suddenly, Fyodor's words about the secret KGB dungeons did not sound as ridiculous. It made sense that the communists would find and harness the river

Styx, perhaps turn it around and plop a hydroelectric station on it, squatting like an ugly cement toad and polluting cold black waters. Charon was dead, rotted to nothing in a labor camp some years ago, and his barge, raised to the surface, was cynically used as the skeleton of the train station below, and nobody ever knew. They probably still charged for the crossing though, and she dug through her pockets.

"What are you looking for?" Yakov said.

"Coins," she answered. "In case we need to pay to cross Styx."

"I have it covered," Fyodor said from behind. "Don't worry about coins. But why are you so hung up on Styx?"

"Listen," Galina said. "Doesn't it sound like a waterfall?"

They listened. The thrumming and the distant roar were growing louder.

"That doesn't sound like a river," Yakov said. "It's—mechanical."

"Hydroelectric station," Galina said.

"That's a station all right," Fyodor said, and pointed at the clearing before them. The trees stepped away from the path, clearing the view of something huge and undoubtedly manmade, gray and low to the ground. It looked like an abandoned construction site, with irregular planes and smokestacks jutting upwards and covered with sailcloth in places, as if to protect the impossibly large thing from rain.

They approached the construction cautiously; in the gray underground light, it seemed especially dead. They circled around the base, all the while looking for people. The thing shuddered with some internal torment, producing a hum so loud they had to yell to hear each other; fortunately, there wasn't much to say except an occasional exclamation of surprise.

The walls of the contraption were cracked with age, and thick white grass stems had invaded the fissures; a black shrub hung out of an especially large crack, and its roots, thick as ropes, crumbled the cement around it trying to reach the ground.

Galina circled the foundation as the sailcloth flapped over her head like a pair of sluggish wings. She looked away from the construction, and called to Yakov and Fyodor to come and see. Previously concealed from their view, a town hid in the shadow of the humming monstrosity—the first wooden buildings and pavements started just a hundred meters away or so. More importantly, there were people in the streets.

They entered the town; at first Galina thought that they had stumbled upon a secret underground prison, but the people seemed too well fed and lacked that haunted spiritual look she usually associated with political prisoners.

Except one man. Dressed in a thick sailcloth jacket, hollow-cheeked and old, he stopped in the middle of the narrow street, his deeply-set eyes catching Galina's. "New here?" he asked in a low rumbly voice.

Galina was about to answer, but Yakov interrupted her. "Yes," he said. "We are searching for missing people . . . "

"My sister," Galina interjected quickly.

"Yes. People turning into birds—do you know anything about it?"

The old man chewed the air with his empty mouth. "Birds,"

he said. "Don't know about them. Sovin's my name. I can show you around." He looked over Galina and the rest, as if appraising them. "Funny we don't see more young people around here these days."

"Here?" Yakov said.

He motioned around him, vaguely. "Yeah, here. Where the fuck else? You're underground, and that's all anyone ever needs to know. As I was saying, not many young people come here these days; I'm really surprised."

"Why?" Galina asked.

"It's always more when things turn shifty on the surface," Sovin said. "I hear in the thirties and forties we were getting refugees in droves. In the sixties it was better for a bit, but then in the seventies and eighties, there's always been a steady trickle. We were taking bets on how much the traffic will increase in the nineties, what with all the fucking insanity that's going on. But nothing, imagine that."

"What about birds?" Yakov said.

"That's the errant magic, and I really don't know much about it. Don't care about that shit—I'm a scientist."

"Who can we ask about them, then?" Galina asked.

Sovin spat a long stream of foul, brown saliva. "Ask David Michaelovich, the pub owner. He sells booze to everyone, even the freaky things."

Galina turned to Yakov to ask his opinion on what those freaky things might be, but was struck by the sudden change in his demeanor. He swallowed repeatedly, as if there were a fishbone stuck in his throat. "That's an unusual name," he finally said. His voice came out stilted, unnaturally calm.

"Yeah," Sovin said. "His last name is Richards, a naturalized Englishman—not many foreigners here all and all, but some. He used to live in Moscow, worked as a radio announcer or something. The stupid ass moved here in 1937, to help build communism, of all things. Guess three times how long until he was accused of espionage."

"That's dumb," Fyodor said.

"Yeah," Sovin agreed. "Still, the man had ideals, and you gotta admire that."

"He's dead," Yakov said suddenly. "Dead and buried."

"That's what we all are, in a sense," Sovin said. "We *are* underground."

"Do you know him?" Galina whispered to Yakov.

Yakov nodded, still swallowing the nonexistent bone. His Adam's apple bobbed up and down. "He's my grandpa, I think."

"Well, come along then," Sovin said, and moved with great speed and decisiveness down a side road, his rough military boots clanking on the wooden pavement like charging cavalry. Only then did Galina notice that he had a pronounced limp, which didn't seem to affect his agility.

Galina thought that the town looked surprisingly normal, if one was willing to ignore the glowing, weeping trees, and the buildings designed by fancy rather than a robust engineering sense. The houses, coquettishly hiding behind wild tangles of weeds and brambles, winked at her with the warm buttery eyes of their windows, all different sizes. "You have electricity?" she asked Sovin.

"Of course we do; what the fuck do you think it is, the Middle

Ages?" He spat again, but this time a small blue skeletal shape scuttled from under the wooden planks of the pavement and licked the brown, lumpy spit clean with its feathery tongue. "We have electricity," Sovin continued. "You must've passed the station on your way here, haven't you?"

Galina remembered the cement and sailcloth monstrosity. "So that what it was. What does it run on?"

"Whatever falls from the surface," Sovin said. "Never you mind that; now, go talk to David Michaelovich."

He stopped before a low brown building, sprawled like a giant starfish; one of its rays jutted into the street, halting any passerby on his way. The building bore a terse inscription made in bright yellow paint. "Pub" it announced to the world in Russian and English.

"Come on in," Sovin said. "Don't be shy. It's like a fucking Casablanca in there, only with more beer and less music and pointless talk and shit."

Galina thought that for a scientist Sovin cursed an awful lot, but followed him through the heavy door, with Yakov and Fyodor behind her. On the threshold Galina turned to Yakov and whispered, "It's going to be all right."

"I know," he said. "It's just . . . I've never even met my father, but here I am, about to be introduced to my grandpa who's been dead for fifty years. My mom comes to his grave every weekend."

Galina struggled for words, but failed to find anything appropriate. She followed Sovin inside, stepping carefully on the thick carpet of sawdust.

There were wooden tables and stools, and a few people

drinking and talking in low voices. She thought that the place looked just like an English pub imagined from an occasional bootlegged movie and Dickens' novels.

The low bar, covered in round traces of glasses forming a complex fractal pattern, held up an impressive battery of variously shaped and sized bottles, bearing homemade labels with careful handwriting and simple but expressive ink drawings.

The man behind the bar looked young—no more than thirty-five; his muscular forearms shone with droplets of water from recent dishwashing. He wiped his hands on the towel tucked into his belt, and smiled at Galina. He had a thin face, and his eyes looked at the new guests attentively through a pair of wire-rimmed round spectacles perched on a long arched nose. He nodded at Galina and smiled wider, showing white uneven teeth. "New recruit," he said in strongly accented Russian. "Welcome home, dear. Can I get you anything to drink?"

"Stop flirting with the broad," said Sovin, and pulled Yakov, suddenly shy and blushing, in front of the bar. "That's your relative, or so he claims. I'll leave you to your tender reunion as soon as you get me a beer on the house."

David watched Yakov over the rim of his spectacles as he poured Sovin a generous glass of amber beer from one of the bottles. "All right," he said after Sovin shuffled off in the direction of one of the tables, where two old men played checkers. "And who exactly are you?"

5: *David*

"I am your grandson," Yakov said. "I think." He couldn't quite accept that this man, barely older than Yakov, was removed from him by two generations.

David's eyebrows steepled sharply and his face paled. "Oh no," he whispered. "Tanya was pregnant?"

"Grandma Tanya." Saying these words brought to memory a tall stout woman with the strong voice of a schoolteacher and long-held suffering in her eyes. "She was pregnant with my mom. When you didn't come home, she thought that the NKVD got you. She packed a bag the same night and caught a train to Serpuhov; she had relatives there."

David nodded. "Smart. How is she?"

Yakov was not very good at telling people that someone they cared about died. No matter how much practice in bearing bad news his line of work threw at him, he still stammered and averted his eyes. "Dead," he said, studying the patterns on the surface of the bar. "Twenty years. I remember her though."

"So do I," his grandfather said. "I am so sorry."

"She thought you were dead. She wrote to the NKVD, but they wouldn't tell her anything. In the sixties, they finally sent her a letter of apology—the standard form they sent to all families of those repressed." Yakov chewed his lip, remembering the letter his grandmother kept in a small cigar box with happy Cuban women on the lid. Photographs and letters, somé yellowed, some new. Photographs of baby Yakov and his mom, passport photographs of his grandmother looking resolutely into the black eye of the camera as if it were a gun. One photograph of his grandfather, making a silly face, smiling. So yellow and brittle, she didn't let Yakov touch it, especially since his fingers were usually covered with sticky goo of one origin or another. But she let him look. And letters from her grateful students, birthday cards from relatives in Serpuhov, diplomas, dry flowers, and that one letter on government letterhead. Posthumously cleared of all charges, it said. Rehabilitated. Even now, Yakov tasted the bitterness of the word on his tongue, doubly now, when the man exonerated in the letter stood before him, absentmindedly wiping a beer glass.

David nodded. The glass clanked out of his hands and rolled across the rough surface of the bar, obviously whittled from the trunk of a glowtree. He caught the glass and straightened it. "All right," he said. "Let's sit down and talk."

Yakov made an apologetic wave to Galina and Fyodor, who sat at the table with Sovin and his ancient friends. They waved back, probably glad to have the relief of sitting down with a beer and not worrying for a bit.

David settled at a small table tucked away in the remote end of one of the pub's arms, by a triangular window that allowed in some light from the trees outside, and the view of a row of backyards, overgrown with pale weeds. He brought two glasses and a bottle with him, and poured as soon as Yakov sat down. "Well," David said, "let me start with my version of the story."

David was born in 1900 in Lancashire, outside of Manchester, in a place not so different from the underground town—there was little light, and coal dust hung in the air, giving everything a dusty, black-and-gray look. When it rained, black water slid like sooty tears down the windowpanes of the cotton mill where David's mother worked; he started when he was ten, and by fifteen he was involved with a trade union.

By the time he turned seventeen, the cotton industry had finished its migration overseas, and David left Lancashire to look for a job. He worked as a laborer at the docks and at the hops farms; at night, he read. His connection with the labor unions continued, and by the age of twenty-two he developed an over-inflamed sense of adventure and social justice.

He traveled to Melbourne, Australia—not entirely voluntarily, as he hinted. There, he joined the nascent Communist Party of Australia and started a socialist newspaper, which caught the attention of the authorities somewhat earlier than he believed just, and that of his intended audience—not at all. His link to the illegal Industrial Workers of the World led to criminal charges.

"You have to understand," he told Yakov and touched his hand with tentative warm familiarity. "In those days, it took a lot to be considered an undesirable person in Australia. A *lot*. And I only wished that my political activity had done someone some good, for all the trouble it caused me." He sighed. "Anyway."

The socialist newspaper landed him in jail; by the time

he got out, he was a persona non grata in a large segment of English-speaking world.

"So, what brought you to Moscow?" Yakov asked.

"I decided to go to the source, to the place where it actually existed. To learn, so I could understand it better, to explain to people—look, I've seen it, I know. I thought after I had seen socialism, with some first-hand knowledge, I'd be able to persuade them better. And if I were good enough, it was only a matter of time before capitalism in Britain toppled."

"It sounds—naïve," Yakov said.

David nodded. "That's what everyone here said. Jackdaws have more sense than I. Even the bloody fairytale things laugh at me. So be it. Maybe I am stupid. But if I weren't, I would've never met your grandma. What do you have to say to that?"

Yakov had nothing, and David continued.

Tanya, he said, was the only woman, the only person who interested him more than reading *Das Kapital*. He first saw her on the bus he took to work every morning, and he threw himself into courtship with his usual single-minded sense of purpose that always got him into trouble. Ironically, for the first time in his adult life he stayed away from politics; but politics wouldn't stay away from him.

Poverty in his new country did not faze him; he was used to poverty, and found that it seemed less tolerable when it was coupled with the wealth of a few. The language barrier, however, presented a challenge. He got a job at a meat-processing facility—it required minimal talking, and the physical exertion helped him think. At night he read as usual, switching for the time to Russian textbooks. And he waited for the mornings, when he would get on the bus and watch the girl with serious eyes and a high ponytail, until she got off a few stops later, by the school. She usually read textbooks on the bus, and he guessed that she was a schoolteacher; one day, he worked up the courage to sit next to her and ask about the pronunciation of a word in the Russian grammar text he carried with him.

"Which word was it?" Yakov interrupted. It seemed suddenly important, to know what was the word that brought them together.

"Saucepan," David said. "I know, not terribly romantic, but it is a difficult word."

It was spring when they first spoke; by the beginning of summer, they saw each other every day off the bus. By fall, they were married.

Tanya kept her maiden name. David was progressive enough not to mind, but he wondered since it was certainly not traditional. He finally asked her.

She looked at him with her deadly serious dark eyes. "Understand, David. This is not a safe time for foreigners. He (she never mentioned Stalin by name, out of real fear or a superstitious reluctance to attract the attention of malevolent forces by summoning them by name) is insane. Do you know how many people disappear every day? Do you know that you're a suspect just by being a foreigner?"

"But I'm a communist," he argued.

"You're a fool," she corrected. "If you want me to, I'll take your last name. Just know that sharing the last name usually means sharing the fate."

"I thought you'd die for me," he joked.

Her face remained serious, and he wasn't certain that she got it. "No. I would promise to you that I would, if there weren't a real risk of that coming true."

Now he couldn't decide whether she was joking.

He moved to her apartment, shared with a messy middle-aged man, with a propensity to mutter to himself and leave his saucepans soaking in the communal kitchen. Tanya never said anything to him, but David was not so tolerant. "Please clean up after yourself," he told the neighbor in his best Russian.

The man only scowled and mumbled something. "I do what I want," he said out loud as he was exiting the kitchen. "You raise stink again, I'll make sure that you're gone."

He told Tanya about the incident, but instead of laughing with him at the crazy neighbor, she cried. She sat on their bed with the nickel headboard, covered by her mother's quilt, and wept. "David," she said. "You have to understand. You have to be nice to people. You can't afford a single enemy."

"Why me?"

"Because you are a foreigner. He gave power to the worst people, don't you get it? You're too good to rat someone out, and you think that everyone else's the same way. Even the Russians turn each other in, but with you—Maybe we should go to my aunt, to Serpuhov. It's easier to hide in the provinces."

David was not inclined to hide; soon after, he learned that an English-language newspaper needed correspondents, and he applied and got the job by virtue of his ability to read and write English. To his surprise, there weren't many takers for that job, and he admitted that his wife's paranoia seemed commonplace. Worse, the cold feeling in the pit of his stomach told him that she was right.

It was winter when they came for him. He worked at the office until late, and the long blue shadows of the street lamps stretched across the street. He walked home from the bus station—a five-minute walk, but that day it was cold enough to make him hasten his step and rub his ears as he hurried home. The snowdrifts, their delicate blues accented by deeper purple shadows, flanked the street, and the windows in the apartment buildings glowed with yellow warmth.

There were two men waiting by the entrance and he would've paid them no mind if it hadn't been for the scattering of cigarette butts in the defiled dirty snow—they'd been there a while. Then he noticed their black trench coats and a black car with no plates idling by the curb. His heart spasmed in his chest and he forgot about the cold. He only had mind enough to thank the God he didn't believe in for keeping them outside, away from Tanya. He couldn't bring them in, but he wasn't ready to surrender. He kept walking past, his hands shoved deep into his coat pockets. His face grew numb from the stinging cold.

"Hey!" he heard behind him.

He ran, his thin-soled shoes slipping on the long ice slicks, treacherously hidden under the fresh snow; the pursuit panted behind, and he couldn't look back. He only hoped to gain another block, to lead them further away from home, and yet realized that it was an empty gesture—they knew where he lived. Still, his legs pumped, his feet slid, and his throat burned from the chilly air he gulped by the mouthful.

A shot rang out in the crisp air, and he ducked and careened, not slowing down. His spectacles slid off his face and he had presence of mind enough to catch them and shove them into his pocket—he couldn't risk trying to put them back on while running.

He rounded the corner, and almost fell but caught his footing. There were lights and frozen trees, hazy, haloed against the glow of the streetlamps. He could not see very well without his glasses, and when he saw the gaping doorway, dark, promising safety, he ran toward it. His arms outstretched, he was almost in its safe embrace, when more shots tore the air. He felt a sting in his back and a dull tearing pain in his shoulder blade; he made a desperate dive for the doorway when it fractured in front of him, and as he went through he realized that his poor eyesight had fooled him—he had mistaken the storefront window for the door. The window showered jagged glass on his face and hands, stinging them like a million bees. Then a cool air blew into his face, and a tree glowed above, and twelve white jackdaws descended upon him, cawing.

Yakov finished his drink. David looked at him, as if expecting something.

"She never remarried," Yakov said. "Grandma, I mean."

David nodded. "Neither did I. Still, I wish I knew . . . About your mother."

"There isn't much to know," he said. His mother was ordinary—not a sort of person who lived an exciting life; even her hardships lacked exoticism. She was born three years before the war, and remembered it vaguely—the hunger, the fear, the dull torments of ordinary souls who were never offered a chance for heroics. She was someone one needed to know to appreciate, and David lacked that. "She's a good person," he finally said. "You would've been proud of her. Like grandma was. Her name's Valentina; she's going to be fifty-three. She works all week, and on weekends she goes to take care of your and grandmother's grave. She made sure to bury her in Moscow, next to you."

David looked perplexed. "I have a grave? Why?"

"I don't know," Yakov said. "I never asked."

David slumped, his head resting on his folded arms. "I suppose I shouldn't be surprised. Only it is strange. To learn that you have a grave and a daughter who's fifty. I heard about men finding out that they had kids they didn't know about—only not fifty years later. I wish I could talk to her, to tell her . . . "

"Tell her what?"

"That I'm sorry. I'm sorry it happened this way, and I'm sorry I survived. I know I wasn't supposed to. If only I had had my glasses on—I wouldn't have tried to run through that window."

Yakov understood what his grandfather wanted—forgiveness. "You've done nothing wrong," he said. "You were fucked either way."

David shrugged, unconvinced. "I suppose."

Yakov didn't know what else to say. He'd seen this before, people who survived catastrophes. They could not enjoy life knowing that others had died—survivor's guilt, they called it. He'd seen it in his grandmother—she left Moscow, saving her unborn child. Yet, the guilt of abandoning her husband was never far below the surface. The letter on the government letterhead made it worse.

Perhaps there was a reason for it, he thought. Those who ended in this no-man's land underground: perhaps they were allowed to live for a reason. "You were spared," he said out loud. "Surely there is a point to that."

"Perhaps. But if there is, I sure don't know what it is. Nobody here does, and some have been around for centuries." David sat up and shook his head, smiling. "Listen to me babble. Why don't you tell me about yourself?"

"I was born in Serpuhov," he said. "We stayed there until the eighties, and then moved to Moscow. After grandma died. Now I'm a cop."

David seemed amused. "Indeed. Interesting choice. Are you in the Party?"

Yakov shook his head vehemently. "No way. They told me I'd never get promoted, but so be it."

"Married?"

"I was. Didn't work out." He tried to think of something to say, but he had trouble baring his soul to strangers, even if the stranger in question was his own grandfather, unaged since 1937. "Look, we just got here, and the whole thing is a bit much."

"I understand," David said. "You'll get used to it. Anything I can help you with?"

"Yes," Yakov said. "See that girl?" He indicated Galina with a subtle tilt of his head. "Her sister's missing. And a bunch of other people. That crazy guy led us here, and I was just looking for those who are missing. They turned into birds."

"Ah," David said. "Birds? That would be one of the old ones messing around. Berendey is your best bet. He's usually in the forest, but you can't go there—he has a strict no-people policy. But stick around—he comes by every now and again to get a drink. Meanwhile, go to your friends, and I'll ask Sovin to answer whatever questions he hasn't covered yet."

Yakov obeyed. He felt a little relieved that his grandfather didn't offer him to stay with him, to talk more; both needed time to absorb the meeting.

"All right," Sovin said and looked over them, as if surveying troops. "All ready? Come with me, and I'll put you up for the night."

"I'm not tired," Yakov said.

"You will be soon." Sovin clapped his shoulder. "Buck up, son. Tomorrow's a new day, and we'll find your bird-people."

When the young people left with Sovin, David worked the bar until it was time to close, going through the usual movements of opening the bottles and pouring beer and an occasional glass of mulled wine for the habitually cold rusalki. The denizens of the underworld noticed his subdued state, and knew better than to attempt bantering.

His mood cast a pall over the Pub's ambience, and he wanted to apologize to everyone, but resisted. The guilt was his alone and he had no right to fish for reassurance with his apologies. He waited for the place to clear, and put away the glasses for the domovoi to clean. He spread a thick layer of sawdust on the floor and left a saucerful of milk for the kikimora and whatever other house spirits breathed shyly behind the dark paneling of the walls and the wainscoting. He used to be annoyed at the absence of brownies or other English spirits, but with time he grew to love their Slavic equivalents, as pointless and skewed as they usually were. "Seriously," he muttered. "What sort of culture invents a spirit whose only purpose is to throw onions and shriek at night? It's just stupid."

A blood-curdling shriek answered him from somewhere behind the pipes.

"Oh shut up," he said. "Bloody banshee wannabe."

The cries sputtered and stopped in an uncertain whine. David shook his head and unlocked the back door leading to his quarters—a sparely furnished, cavernous room that retained the stone chill despite the brightly burning big-bellied woodstove on bent legs. He sat on the narrow bed with a nickel headboard, his head in his hands, and thought about the death of his wife.

It didn't matter that he hadn't seen her in over fifty years; it didn't matter that she was dead; he had said goodbye to the idea of her years ago. He never stopped loving her, but rather the memory was sequestered away deep in his heart, surrounded by calcified layers of regret and guilt, isolating it from the rest of his mental landscape—like a clam, he surrounded the irritating grain of sand with pearly layers, not to create beauty but to protect the tender mantle from irritation.

Now, the protection was stripped away, and the image of her face tore at his heart like a splinter. He reminded himself that she had grown old, that she raised a daughter and watched her grandson grow big while she aged, something he didn't think much about—everyone underground remained like they were when they first got here, until eventually they faded away, all of them, except the old ones. He tried to imagine how she would look after the years of war and privation, but the image in his mind's eye remained the same—a young woman with serious eyes and a stubborn chin, the woman who tried to keep him alive despite his best efforts, and in the end denied any knowledge of her success. Then it occurred to him that he hadn't seen her in so long that he doubted the accuracy of his recollection. For all he knew, he had constructed the face from his vague dreams and longing. With the doubt, the image in his mind wavered, fell apart, and disappeared.

He lost her again that night, as he lost her every night, ever since he had fled underground. Belatedly he felt regret for never trying to find her or send a word; then again, what good would it do? His mind went over and over the familiar track, each rut honed by fifty years of the same old regrets. And yet, tonight he knew for sure—even though he had a daughter and a grandson, Tanya was dead. Alone in his room, David wept.

6: *Sovin*

FYODOR COULDN'T SLEEP—HE THOUGHT ABOUT HIS childhood in Zvenigorod, about long and dusty provincial summers he usually spent riding his bicycle down local roads. The smell of heated asphalt and tar became forever associated with those summers, when the cheap tinny bicycle bell drowned out the singing birds.

The summers when everything but the road and the bicycle disappeared, and he could ride it downhill, the pedals spinning so fast he sometimes had to lift his feet off them, to the sun, orange and huge, that waited for him at the bottom of the slope. In those days, he half believed that if he rode fast enough, gained enough momentum, he would catch up to the sun and sizzle and become one with the angry red semicircle that set faster than he could pedal.

He was pleased to recognize this old belief in his current adventure—apparently, the ability to ignore reality and to take things for what they appeared, not what they were, was the key to entering the underground kingdom. Everyone here, Fyodor learned from Sovin, had been desperate enough or confused and hurt enough to believe that the doors appearing on solid objects would open and admit them inside, that the reflections were the same as their originals. This is why there were so many madmen here, Fyodor decided. He wasn't sure he should count himself among them. But certainly not Sovin—that man, as Fyodor learned, was stone cold sober, and it was really a miracle that he had managed to make it in at all.

Fyodor could not sleep, even though Sovin's house was comfortable in the way of an old-fashioned wooden village house, with its warm dark walls and low ceiling, each beam distinct and blackened with soot. He lay on the bed (a straw mattress covered with a blanket), and thought about their host, the stories he told while Yakov was yammering away with his youthful grandfather.

SOVIN HAD FOUGHT IN TWO WORLD WARS, EARNED THREE PhDs, and spoke five languages fluently. He was born in St Petersburg into the family of a fur merchant, studied philosophy in Germany, and returned to Russia in 1914, to fight. The world war quickly graded into the civil one, and Sovin chose the red side, surprising even himself. It wasn't any shrewdness in the face of soberly weighing his circumstances; it wasn't the realization of the inevitable victory of the proletariat. It was a desire for fairness, for equality. He tried to like his comrades.

After the war, he went back to the Petrograd University to get a degree in agricultural science. He traveled with Vavilov, he collected seeds; Fyodor could not even imagine the sights he had seen and asked about Tibet and the Himalayas, but Sovin was determined to stay on the subject of seeds. "You have to understand," he said. "There's that thing, a grain of rice or wheat, and it's *small*. But everything, everything every stalk of wheat or rice has ever known is packed inside it. It knows where it lives, it knows whether it's cold or warm; it is perfect in how it suits the place. And every one of them is the same yet different—Asia, East, West, the Andes, any given place. How can you not love such a thing?"

Fyodor recognized that the question was rhetorical, and kept his indifference to grains of anything to himself.

"Anyway," Sovin continued, "you probably know what happened after."

"Repressions?" Fyodor said.

"Lysenko," Galina offered.

Sovin seemed amused by their answers. "You're both right," he said. "But before all that, there was the Genofond and Vavilov's Institute."

Sovin went home to Leningrad, where he worked on cataloguing and classifying the seeds, studying their genetics, crossbreeding strains. His philosophy training not forgotten but rather dormant, he focused all his energy on understanding the seeds and the plants that grew out of them, on defining and describing their traits. The collection of the seeds, the Genofond, embraced all of the variety of cultivated crops and held great promise. Until Vavilov was arrested.

Sovin and others continued their work, apprehensive about the war and Lysenko's crusade against genetics and other sciences with a suspicious foreign whiff about them. Sovin confessed that it was the fear of the labor camps that compelled him to join the army again—he was over the draft age, but they took him. His division was just outside Leningrad when the siege started.

Sovin was tormented by the visions of starving people and the precious grains from all over the world, and their close proximity worried him. He felt deficient when he prayed at night that the Genofond survive. "I didn't want anyone to die, understand," he said. "It was just—I wanted the grains to survive too. To the people, it was just bread. But it was the entirety of human history in there. Even as we moved East and then back West, I kept thinking about it. Some things are just too important."

"It mostly survived," Galina said.

Sovin nodded. "Mostly. But not the people."

He wasn't inside the city under siege, but he had nightmares about frozen streets littered with corpses, snowdrifts building over their hollow faces. He started thinking about whether the present was worth sacrificing for the history.

When the war was over, he could not go back to Leningrad. Instead, he joined the faculty of Moscow State University, teaching introductory biology and plant science; he experimented with plant genetics in secret—Lysenko had already labeled it the bourgeois pseudo-science, and Sovin had to mind his own bourgeois origins. Nonetheless, in 1948 he was sent to a labor camp in Kolyma.

When Fyodor was young, he met some of the men who went through the labor camps—they were recognizable, those craggy old men with gunpowder prison tattoos, foul language, and incessant smoking. No matter how mild-mannered and educated a person had been when they first went in, by the time they emerged they had been transformed by the harsh living and hard labor, by the life stripped to the essentials of survival, its most basic formula: if you work, you eat. The fact that they emerged alive meant that they had worked hard enough not to starve, and Fyodor tried to imagine how he would do in such circumstances. The unavoidable conclusion was that he would perish, and he respected those who were better at living than he. Maybe even envied them a little.

Sovin was released in 1958, after ten years of hard labor, and returned to Moscow. His reputation as a geneticist prevented him from working in his former position, and he realized then that the world as it existed did not have a place for him and, the letter of rehabilitation notwithstanding, he felt hollow and wrong, somehow. He took a job as a night guard in some vast and empty warehouse.

He did not concern himself with what it was supposed to be warehousing, and paid no mind to the miles of razor wire surrounding the perimeter of the empty lot in the middle of which the warehouse sat like a monstrous toad. It felt familiar, especially in winter when the winds howled and the flat lot froze and grew humped with snowdrifts, save for a single path that led from the locked gates to the warehouse and a small cabin, heated with a woodstove and illuminated by a naked bulb hanging from the ceiling like the lure of an anglerfish—his home.

He spent his days sleeping and reading—he became interested in physics and electrical engineering—and his nights pacing under the echoey corrugated roof of the huge warehouse, empty save for the piles of refuse in the corners. There were rats and he left them be, wondering how they survived in the empty frozen place.

The rats grew bold and invaded his cabin; when he woke up in winter, after the early sunset, he heard their scrabbling and the howling of dogs somewhere outside, and thought that he still was in the camp, and had to wait for his heart to stop thumping against his fragile ribcage.

The rats ran free, and he shared his modest food supply willingly. He knew from his time in Siberia that feeding them prevented theft and wreckage of flour bags and other delicate groceries, even though the other prisoners and the guards never believed him; it was their loss, Sovin thought. He was the only one whose stuff the rats left alone.

In his new home it was the same, and the rats behaved. He gave them names, and they learned to come when he whistled gently; they took stale bread from his hands. The rats were cunning and mistrustful, and he felt somewhat proud of having won their benevolence. They watched him from the corners, silent, whiskers a-twitch, as he read or soldered. He put together radios and other small appliances, but never used them.

He was rather isolated in his warehouse and his cabin, and only came into contact with the outside world when he went to pick up groceries—he had developed ascetic tastes, and only bought unrefined flour which he mixed with water and fried into heavy flat pancakes, an occasional carton of milk, rice, buckwheat and canned pork. At the store, he picked up on what was happening to the world—what they called "Khrushchev's thaw" was in full swing, and young people talked about changing times and the unprecedented freedoms of the sixties. Sovin did not believe that; he had learned that the world was not friendly, and any freedom was just an illusion. He heard about the dissidents who moved west, but he knew that their new lives and freedoms were illusory too. He envisioned the world as a giant machine, bloodied fragments of bones stuck in its monstrous wheels, and the only periods of happiness or perceived freedom were just a pause while the cogs swung around, nearing the next bone-crunching turn. He knew better than to be lulled by the temporary silence and to stick his head out.

He bought what he needed and headed back, never talking to anyone. He brought day-old bread for the rats. They waited for him, their eyes twinkling in the shadows.

He never listened to the radios he built, but the rats seemed to enjoy the static and the voices and somber music that occasionally broke through it, and he placed small radio sets along the walls of the warehouse and the corners of his room. He supposed this was why the rats made him a gift.

They labored in secret, and he only found out when they decided to reveal that the back wall of the warehouse had been gnawed through—they pushed away the sheet of corrugated metal, and he saw a hole with ragged edges and distant wan stars shining in a black expanse of frozen sky. He stood a while, looking at the snowy plain, listening to the distant dogs and occasional laughter the wind brought from somewhere far away, from the world he knew about but wasn't a part of. The rats gathered together and nudged him along.

He took one step and realized that the hole, clearly leading outside, did not take him onto his empty lot—instead, he found a dry path under his feet, slightly powdered with dry crumbling leaves, and a distinct smell of autumn and smoke. The rats gathered behind him, chittering excitedly, and he sighed. We can run away together, he told the rats. No one will miss us, we're the unloved children of the world. We are the corners which time sweeping by never touches, and leaves us clogged with our dust and useless memories. Let's run away.

The rats indicated that this was the idea, their idea from the beginning. Uncertain of what lay ahead, he stepped back into the jagged hole and packed a bag with a thermos of strong sweet tea and enough food to feed himself and the rat army. And then they left, he leading the way, the rats close behind. He did not turn around but with his back he felt the rats following him, the weak phosphorescent spots of their eyes bobbing on the wave of brown fur and sharp claws, their long yellow teeth bared in giddy smiles.

FYODOR DOZED A BIT AND WHEN HE WOKE UP LONG BEFORE dawn he discovered a large rat sitting on his chest, watching his face with an intent but inscrutable expression.

"Hello," Fyodor said. He guessed the rodent for one of Sovin's rats, the ones who showed him the way underground, and he smiled. "You're still watching over him, huh?"

The rat twitched its nose and bared long dangerous incisors.

"It's all right," Fyodor said. "We are friends."

The rat sniffed and twitched and skittered up to his neck on its pink nervous feet. It sat up, its paws, disconcertingly similar to human hands, reaching up to Fyodor's neck.

He froze, scared now, but reluctant to do anything that would upset Sovin or his pets.

The rat grabbed hold of the chain around his neck and

pulled it out from under his T-shirt. The faceless coin dangled in its paws, catching light from the glowtrees outside. The rat studied the coin while Fyodor held his breath; finally, the rat was satisfied. It jumped off his chest, hopped across the floor, and disappeared through a cleft in the wall.

Fyodor breathed; this incident disturbed him even more than jumping through the windows of a moving train and finding himself in an underground world. Perhaps Galina was right, he thought; perhaps they did die in the fall, and this was the afterlife. He fingered the coin on his chest, warm from his body heat. Perhaps this coin was meant to weigh down his eyelids; perhaps the rat was just assessing his ability to pay for the passage.

His train of thought was interrupted by a quiet scrabbling at the door.

"Who's there?" he whispered.

"It's me." The door opened and Galina looked in. "I couldn't sleep."

"Rats?" Fyodor asked.

"No, haven't seen any." She tiptoed inside and closed the door behind her. "Yakov's sleeping like a log."

"Figures," Fyodor said.

Galina sat on the floor by his makeshift bed. "Did you hear what David said? About Berendey?"

Fyodor nodded. "Berendey's Forest. I remember; it was a movie or something."

"I saw it too, when I was a kid. How can it be real?"

"It probably isn't," Fyodor said. "Or at least different. Do you think anything here's real?"

"Feels real," she said. "What else do we have to go by?"

Fyodor had to agree with that assessment—once one started doubting one's senses, the subsequent reasoning led straight to a brain in a jar. "Nothing," he said. "It is real. Sovin certainly is."

Galina laughed, covering her mouth with her hand to keep it down. "Yeah. I couldn't have dreamt him up." She grew serious. "Can I ask you something?"

"Sure," Fyodor said, and propped himself up on his elbow.

"How did you know to jump through that reflection? I mean, how did you know it would work?"

"I didn't," he said. "It was a literal leap of faith."

She eyed him cautiously. "But you dragged us along."

"I had to. If I were by myself, I would've doubted. When I had two lives on my conscience, I had to believe in it. Otherwise . . . "

Galina shook her head, as if chasing away doubt or harsh words. "It worked, so that's all that matters. Do you think Berendey will show up tomorrow, or are we just going to hang out in the pub again?"

He shrugged. "Don't know. But if you ask me, I don't mind the pub that much. Seems like a lot of interesting people."

"Yes." Galina sighed.

"I know that you want to find your sister," Fyodor said. But sometimes you just have to wait."

She nodded. "Let's hope I won't have to wait too long. Thanks for talking. I'll let you rest now." She stood and left as silently as she had appeared.

Fyodor lay awake. He felt as if he was the only one who

was a tourist here, with no particular agenda or heartbreak, and no tragedy to run from. He felt dirty and thought of the loud foreigners that crowded New Arbat, haggling over mass-produced matryoshkas repulsive in their cheery colorfulness and floridly red cheeks. They bought the dolls and thought that they were somehow authentic, and that by carrying the little wooden monstrosities home they better comprehended the depressed souls of the drunken natives.

Fyodor wondered if the suffering he had found underground was the same, slightly obscene, mass-manufactured by the cruel system, with as much thought as a matryoshka artisan cooperative that slathered paint and varnish on the light pear-shaped birch husks; perhaps his curiosity had the same sordid taint to it, the illusion of comprehension. His ignorance of real life was now patched up by the images of Sovin's unshaven hollow-cheeked face, dark like a Byzantine icon; still it remained ignorance but armored now with the arrogance of delusion.

He kept an eye out for the rats but they didn't manifest again. He was still wide awake when the morning came—the light changed imperceptibly underground, with the glowtrees flaring up brightly, and the shimmer of golden dust that remained suspended in the musty air, as if millions of butterflies had shed the scales of their wings in midair.

Sovin knocked on the door and called for Fyodor to get up and get some breakfast. Fyodor obeyed, and brushed his jeans to get rid of the hay that covered them. Galina and Yakov already waited at the table, with an old-fashioned copper samovar lording over the rough kitchen table, chipped mugs, and a sugar dish. Sovin hunched over the stove, making pancakes.

"Sorry," Sovin said. "Didn't expect visitors, so I don't have any cheese or meat."

They reassured him that it was quite all right and thanked him for his hospitality.

"Anyway," Sovin said. "Stay as long as you need to. Eventually, we'll fix you up with houses of your own; they're pretty low-tech, but land is not an issue here."

Fyodor traded looks with Yakov. "I'm not going to stay here," he said. "Are you?"

Yakov and Galina shook their heads.

"Huh," Sovin said. "I don't really know about anyone who left."

"You don't think it is possible?" Yakov said.

The breeze outside caught a hold of white curtains on the window and tossed them about. Sovin watched their frantic dance. "I don't know," he said. "I never asked. Although if you consider why this place was made, you'll doubt leaving here is easy."

"Could you explain that?" Fyodor asked. "You told us yesterday about who lives here but not why."

Sovin slammed a clay plate heaping with misshapen flapjacks onto the table, and sat down. "Eat," he said. "Have some tea, and I'll tell you all about it."

It started as the place for the pagan things to go, Sovin said. Back in 980, when all of Russia was christened with fire and sword; there was no Moscow then, and the forested, hilly spot was perfect for spirits and their human allies to seek refuge.

When Moscow was built, the things that inhabited the forests and the swamps, the things that hooted in the night and laughed in the haylofts were buried under the foundations of the first buildings—pagan blood was spilled under every stone, and a spirit was interred under every foundation. Or so they said, the old things, who hollowed out the ground in which they were buried.

"Did anyone know about them?" Fyodor asked.

"Of course," Sovin answered. "This is why they sealed the underground off , and it's not as easy to find an entrance as it once was. As for going back—I suspect that those who created the barrier took care of it. Don't know if it applies to people, but some of the old residents are itching to get out, only they can't, at least not for long. So they have to meddle indirectly."

As he talked, Sovin picked up a flapjack and tossed it on the floor. Immediately, a pack of several large, glossy rats appeared as if from thin air, quickly followed by a tiny bearded man, dressed in traditional Russian costume, of the sort one expected to see on the male lead of a touring troupe of folk dancers; in other words, a fake.

"Cute," Galina said. "You actually have a domovoi."

Sovin nodded. "Everyone does; they appear the moment you build a house. Can't keep them away, but they do the dishes and dust occasionally."

They watched the little man and the rats engage in a brief standoff; the rats decided that the domovoi posed no danger and ate the flapjack, tearing off chunks with their front paws. The little man looked forlorn until Galina took pity and tossed him one of her own flapjacks. The domovoi grabbed the treat and ran toward the wainscoting, pursued by one of the larger rats.

"Yeah," Sovin said thoughtfully. "So we live."

At the pub, there was no news of Berendey. Galina grew angstier by the minute, and soon rose and said that she was going to look around, ask the natives about the birds and what they knew about the world above. "You can't just isolate things from each other," she said. "I'm sure there are more influences and interactions than Sovin tells us."

"Suit yourself," said Fyodor, and settled deeper into his chair. "The cop will probably want to reconnect with his long-lost grandfather, and I'm going to people-watch. And god-watch."

"Have fun," she said and left; the door slammed behind her with uncalled-for force.

"Women," Fyodor muttered into his glass. Like she expected him to drop everything and go traipsing through the narrow streets and vast no man's lands of the underground. He would much rather choose a good vantage point and wait for the world to come by. Eventually—if one stayed put long enough and picked the right spot—he would see everything he needed to see; he remembered reading it in a book.

The Pub was rather empty at this early hour, but he spotted a tall man, covered in blue mottled skin and naked save for a few strips of fish scales running along his arms and spine. He guessed him for a vodyanoy, a water spirit; his suspicion was confirmed when he noticed that the blue stranger continuously dripped water. It soaked into the sawdust on the floor, and a dark saturated spot spread like an especially slow ripple from a dropped stone. Then there was a cold wind from the door, and Fyodor watched, delighted and entranced, as the dark water froze into fine crystals, and a stout man in a red coat walked up to the bar.

"Gimme a shot," he demanded from a small domovoi who operated the home-whittled beer taps and opened the bottles. "It is freezing."

Now it was, and Fyodor shivered in his windbreaker and T-shirt. "You're Father Frost," he called to the stranger. "Right?"

The old man turned around and scowled. "Oh, look at that, another bright young thing. 'Father Frost, will you bring me a New Year present next time?' Fuck you, young man. I'm no Santa Claus, and don't you push your foul Western influences on me."

"I just wanted to buy you a drink," Fyodor said.

Father Frost grinned. "Ah, you've got your head on straight. All right, sonny." He stomped his boots, shaking off imaginary snow, and sat at Fyodor's table.

The domovoi brought over two shots of moonshine, the foul liquid with a strong undertaste of gasoline.

"That's the stuff," Father Frost said. "Warms you right to your bones, doesn't it?"

Fyodor nodded; he indeed felt warm. "You won't freeze me, will you?"

"Not as long as you keep buying me booze." Father Frost motioned to the domovoi bartender. "Keep them coming."

Fyodor searched his pockets, and came up with a roll of several rubles.

Father Frost looked at them skeptically. "Paper money is no money at all," he said. "What about your coin?"

Fyodor found it disconcerting that everyone was suddenly interested in his talisman. "It's against the evil eye," he said. "I need it."

Father Frost laughed with such deafening glee that the beams in the ceiling shook, spooking several barn owls who were apparently nesting there. "That's a *nerazmennaya moneta*," he said once he stopped laughing. "Changeless coin."

Fyodor smiled. "Really?"

"Come on, I'll show you," Father Frost said. "Clueless folk on the surface, gods forgive me. Everything needs to be taught and if it weren't for me you'd be all speaking French now. Assholes." He beckoned the domovoi, and urged Fyodor to take off his coin. When Fyodor gave it to the domovoi, the coin underwent a metallic mitosis, one remaining attached to the chain, while the other was clenched in the domovoi's tiny and slightly dirty fist.

"Cool," Fyodor said. "Does it work like that on the surface?"

"Sure does," Father Frost said. "Only the coin is useless. That's irony, isn't it?"

"Not really," Fyodor said. "What was that about French?"

Father Frost heaved an exasperated sigh. "Have you dumdums ever noticed that the moment there's a foreign invasion, you get a record cold winter? Who do you think is doing that, huh?"

"You?" Fyodor answered, and threw back another shot of the foul liquid. "Why?"

"Because I care," Father Frost said, drunken sincerity coloring his deep voice. "I care about you surface motherfuckers, unlike your stupid wimpy god."

"We were atheists for a while there," Fyodor said. "Materialists, even."

"So am I," Father Frost said. "A materialist, I mean. Berendey is too, but the gods are all solipsists. Especially the one you've picked; those who are here are all right, even though they're mostly big fish in a small pond, demigods and such. And you, you . . . you stupid surfacers, all of you either depressed or melancholy." He cast a wild gaze around, finally focusing on the bar. "Hey, what did I just say? Keep 'em coming."

Fyodor paid with the changeless coin again, and the domovoi dutifully took the spawned copper, as if he saw nothing at all unusual or wrong with being paid with the same coin again.

"As I said," Father Frost continued. "All you know how to do is to wreck what the others have built and mope around as if you were the ones wronged." Father Frost spat, and the gob of saliva froze in the air and shattered as it hit the floor.

"Not all of us," Fyodor said. "So, why do you help us if we're so worthless?"

"It's not about you. It's about the land. It is mine, and I am keeping it that way. No matter what you do and how much of it you sell, bit by bit, until you have nothing left. And then, there would be no one left but us, those who were here before you, holding on to it like a handful of sand in the river, feeling it wash away grain by grain, but never letting go. We hold it together, stupid, so don't you ask me why."

Fyodor tossed back another shot, and waited for the familiar alcohol fog to drown out his sense of loathing of the world. Father Frost was right—the surface world had failed its denizens. And the underground world was a mystery, hidden from the majority, affecting things in an oblique and uncertain way. Their saviors hid underground, exiled and forgotten. It did not surprise Fyodor—Moscow was not kind to those who cared about it.

7: The Decembrist's Wife

Galina left the pub, her feet leading her restlessly away. She just could not bear the thought of wasting another day, and instead decided to find by herself either Berendey or any of the old ones Sovin and David mentioned. How large could this place be?

It turned out to be quite large. She got lost in the labyrinth of convoluted streets—they were clearly not planned, and wound back and forth, often doubling on themselves and petering out in unexpected dead ends. These streets had been built with little forethought as the town grew, and she quickly lost any idea of where she was. There were people in the streets, but she didn't feel quite ready to ask for directions.

She looked for an opening between houses that would lead her to a wooded area; her feet were starting to hurt by the time she found a road that didn't turn around abruptly, but instead led her out of the crisscrossing streets, straight and true. The houses soon disappeared, and the path grew paler, as if from disuse, and often got lost in the tall pallid grass and the uncertain flickering of the glowtrees.

The air smelled of mud and river, and the path soon led her to a swamp. Black trunks of fallen trees rose from dark pools of water like dead fingers, and the hummocks seemed too uncertain to step on. She turned around to find another way.

Someone was there—a tall woman in a long shirt of unbleached linen stood on the path. Her face was hidden by long ragged locks, darkened with water.

"Hello," Galina said. "You're a rusalka, aren't you?"

The woman did not answer, just bobbed her head—the motion was so quick and slight that Galina wasn't sure if it was a twitch or a sign of agreement.

"Can you tell me how to find Berendey?" she asked. She tried really hard not to think that the woman in front of her was a ghost, a soul of a drowned girl.

Another quick movement, this time in the negative.

"Do you know someone who will?" She thought of the mythical beings one might find in a forest. "A leshy, perhaps?"

The girl nodded again, and beckoned Galina to follow her.

She sighed. These creatures, as far as she remembered, were not to be trusted; they stole children and tickled men to death. To her relief, she could not remember any stories of rusalki attacking or harming women. Leshys, however, were indiscriminate, happily confusing and turning around any traveler. Galina was starting to regret her request, when the rusalka took a side path, and led her through a grove of weeping trees—tears rolled down their bark in a constant stream—and a small calm lake with water as black as pitch.

"Where are we?" Galina asked.

The rusalka pointed at the small pavilion rising at the far end of the lake, and Galina sighed. The pavilion was covered with ornate woodcuts and tracery of vines, and did not look like a dark forest where one would expect to find a nature deity who could answer questions about people turning into birds. She was about to ask the rusalka about who lived there, but the woman gave her an impatient shove and dove into the dark waters that closed over her without a ripple or sound.

Galina approached the pavilion, her feet sinking into the rich loose soil of the path. The irises and the cattails fringing the lake nodded at her, and she was surprised to see that their stems and leaves were not completely white but pale green.

The latticed walls of the pavilion allowed her a glimpse inside, and she saw a woman—a young woman in a black evening dress—reclining on a low wicker chaise, reading a book and smoking a long cigarette, the mother-of-pearl cigarette holder wedged between her white teeth.

The woman looked up and smiled at Galina. "Come on in," she said. "I'm Countess Vygotskaya. New here?"

Galina found the entrance—just a simple arch—and sat on the proffered stool.

The woman reached for the ashtray and stubbed out her cigarette, still exhaling long twin snakes of smoke through her narrow nostrils, exquisite like the rest of her. The black strap of her dress slid off her too-white shoulder, and her black curls seemed too black, almost blue. Galina felt intimidated by this woman—not just the aristocratic roots or her beauty, but the way she carried herself. The air around her grew cold and clear, studded with tiny ice crystals, and Galina's breath caught, as if in the middle of a January night. "You've heard about me, of course," the woman said.

"No," Galina admitted in a quiet guilty voice. "But I'm sure that—"

"Of course you have," the woman said. "The Decembrists' wives. I was one of them."

Galina nodded. "I hadn't realized."

"Neither had I," the woman said mysteriously. And added, noting Galina's perplexed look, "How difficult it is to be an icon."

Galina thought of the story. The Decembrists' Revolt left her cold in high school, when they covered that part of Russian history; the Byronic appeal and the misguided liberalism of their useless gesture never quite did it for her. But now she supposed she had a reluctant admiration for the young officers who rode into the Senate Square of St Petersburg to challenge Czar Nicholas and the absolute monarchy, and were greeted by cannon fire. On the back of her mind she always wondered what happened to the soldiers under their command—dead, she supposed, cannon fodder. Only the officers were important enough to secure a place in the history books. They were exiled to Siberia except the five executed outright. Galina dimly remembered something about ropes that gave and broke, and the unprecedented second hanging.

And this is where their wives came in—she imagined them often, those beautiful rich ladies who abandoned everything to follow their husbands into the frozen woods and summers ringing with mosquitoes, to the place away from civilization and any semblance of everything they knew.

It occurred to her only later in life that the women were held up as an example of selfless devotion and obedience—at first, she could not realize why they went. She had been too young for the notions of love and tragedy inextricably linked to it then. Now she was too skeptical of both. In that she differed from her classmates who usually listened to the stories of the revolt and the Decembrists' wives with an expression of almost religious fervor.

"Did you ever regret going to Siberia?" Galina asked.

The woman lit a new cigarette and breathed a slow bitter laugh. "Me? I never went. That is, I went to Moscow. The shame was too much." The gaze of her large dark blue eyes lingered on Galina's face. "But you wouldn't know shame, would you?"

"I do," Galina started. "I—"

"Guilt is not the same thing," the Decembrist's Wife interrupted her again. "Shame is something that is done to you from the outside."

"Why didn't you go then?"

The woman shrugged her shoulder. Voluptuous, Galina thought, that's the word they used to describe women like her. "Because they expected me to, I suppose. Because I was just an appendage. Because it didn't matter what I wanted. The men always ask me, 'Didn't you love your husband?' Women never do—fancy that."

Her languid eyes fixed on Galina for a moment before looking away, at the burning tip of her cigarette. "What do you think?"

"It's not about love," Galina tried to explain and stopped, short of words.

"Those who went abandoned everything," the woman said. "Those who stayed abandoned their husbands. I had abandoned both. A friend of mine went, and she could never write to her family. She left her children behind, and her family loathed her for it. Mine loathed me because I didn't."

Her name was Elena, and she ran away from her home in St Petersburg suddenly filled with empty echoes after her husband was put in stocks and shipped somewhere unimaginable. She realized that she could not win. No matter what she did she would be either a bad daughter to her father, the widowed Count Klyazmensky, or a bad wife to her husband Dmitri. The truth was, she was tired of both men in her life, and she packed two modest trunks with clothes and knick-knacks she couldn't quite dispose of yet, handed the keys to her house on the Neva embankment to her housekeeper, and told her coachman to take her to Moscow. Everyone assumed that she was going shopping, and out of the corner of her eye she saw people—even servants!—shaking their heads with disapproval.

In truth, she wasn't sure what she wanted to do in Moscow. She could visit some remote relatives, but her heart wasn't in it. She could take rooms and cloister herself from the world. Instead, she wandered down to the Moscow River embankment and watched the frozen river, green with crusted ice, with black cracks showing the sluggish black water underneath. She shivered in her furs and wondered if the water was as cold as the air that clouded her breath as soon as it left her lips. She stayed there until the stars came out.

The night had a different color here—farther south, the blue of the sky had grown deeper, more saturated, and the stars had become large and yellow, not the white pinpricks she remembered from St Petersburg. She missed the aurora borealis.

A movement on the ice caught her attention—she squinted at the dark shapes, worried that some clueless peasant children had wandered onto the ice, thick but liable to split open every time a smallest child set a lightest foot on it. She was about to call out, to tell them to get back, when her breath stopped fogging the air; she forgot to breathe. The shapes crawled out from under the embankment on which she stood, covered in mud and raw sewage, and they were not children at all but grown women. Pale filthy women, dressed in nothing but thin linen shirts.

They crawled on all fours like animals, until they reached the first patch of open black water. They slid into it, one by one, noiseless as seals. Before Elena could break her stupor or call for help, they re-emerged, sleek and clean, the linen clinging to their young bodies, their wet hair plastered to their faces and necks. As she watched, they gathered on the ice where it seemed more solid and held hands, forming a circle like peasant girls did at weddings. And they started dancing—moving around in a circle, faster and faster, until Elena felt dizzy. And then their bare feet left the ice, and the women danced in the air, water on their shirts and faces frozen. They looked like ice sculptures come magically to life.

Elena leaned over the embankment, her heart racing. In the back of her mind she knew who these women were—rusalki, spirits of drowned girls, but she wanted nothing more than to join them. There was nobody around, and she climbed over the parapet, awkward in her heavy skirts and coat, but eager.

She could not remember the last time she had such a longing to join people.

She stepped onto the ice; the women seemed oblivious to her approach. She skirted far around the black dizzying splotches of open water. The ice creaked under her shoes. She was close to them now. Just as if someone had given a signal, all of the faces turned toward her, and she heard a thundering, roaring noise as the ice cracked under her feet, opening a black rift across the river. Her feet slid from under her, and the black water reached up, seizing her chest in its icy embrace. It flooded her mouth opened in a scream, washed over her eyes, twined her hair around her neck. She felt hands on her shoulders and arms, and grabbed at them. But instead of pulling her to safety, the women laughed and pushed her down, down, deep down into the black water where even the wan starlight could not reach.

Her lungs burned and her chest heaved, rebelling against the dead heavy embrace of the ice-cold water. She swallowed and breathed water, feeling it churn in her stomach, waiting for the inevitable darkness. She felt hands dragging her along, under ice, where the starlight did not reach and where she could not hope to reach the surface.

Her skin was so numb from the cold that it took her a while to notice a change in temperature—the water had turned balmy, and the glow on the surface signaled escape. She lunged toward it and did not believe her senses when her head emerged into musty stale air and her lungs convulsed, expelling the ice-cold water of Moscow River into the unknown warm lake. The girls that dragged her there surfaced too, laughing and lisping gentle nonsense. She didn't know where she was, but she knew that her former concerns had fallen away, like crust from the eyes of a cured blind man.

"It's all the same with everyone here, isn't it?" Galina said. "You wanted so badly to escape."

"And we didn't fit in anywhere else," Elena said.

Galina nodded. "You know, I always hoped that there was a place for me, a promised land—and I could never find it, until someone I love disappeared."

"You know," Elena said and took a long drag on her cigarette, "people are notoriously bad at discerning what it is they really want. Besides, this is really no promised land—funny you would think that once you stick all the misfits into one place, it would somehow magically become a paradise."

"It seems like one," Galina said.

Loud splashing and cries turned her attention to the lake, and even Elena stood up and looked over, squinting. The rusalki, several of them at once, wept and cried, and shied away from something in their midst.

"What are they doing?" Galina said.

"No idea." Elena carefully picked up the hem of her dress, exposing a pair of small but sturdy combat boots. "Let's go see."

The rusalki left the water, and stood on the shore, dripping wet, fear in their eyes that showed no whites. Elena moved among them as if she were at a party, working her way toward the plates with canapés, and Galina followed in her wake. On the bank, they both stopped, looking.

Galina could not quite understand it at first—dark fabric

flapped in the water, concealing the outline of its contents, until she saw a hand. And like in a brainteaser where one was supposed to find a hidden figure, everything fell into place—there were two hands and a leg, and a pale face with wide open eyes. She was about to call to the man bobbing in the waves when she realized that his hands were lashed together with blue electrical tape, and that the deep blue shadow around his eye was a bruise, spreading slowly over the left half of his face. A dark smear at the corner of his mouth was undoubtedly blood, but at this point Galina did not need any confirmation of the man's dead state. "Who is it?" she asked Elena, unable to look away from the corpse that neared the bank on which they stood, certain as death. "Why is he here?"

"I don't know." Elena bent down to tear out a long and stout cattail stem, and reached out, pulling the body closer. "Never seen him before. And his clothes—do they look familiar?"

Galina looked over the sodden leather jacket and track pants, at the buzz cut. "He's a thug," she said. "What they call a racketeer. There're plenty of them on the surface now."

"I see." Elena grabbed the lapels of the dead man's jacket, and heaved the body ashore. "Never seen a corpse making it here." She turned to the rusalki, still huddling in a disturbed clump, like deer. "Did you drag him here?"

They all shook their heads in unison and cried, wringing their hands—it almost looked like ritual mourning, Galina thought.

"Now, this is really strange," Elena said, looking over the man at her feet thoughtfully. "What, the surfacers don't think they're good enough for us and dump their garbage here?"

"They don't even know about this place," Galina reminded her.

Elena sighed. "I know. I just don't understand."

"There have been strange things happening on the surface too." Galina told her about the birds and her sister.

"This *is* strange," Elena agreed. "There's magic on the surface and corpses down here—it shouldn't happen. I think someone's breaching the barrier. We better talk to one of the old ones."

"I was looking for Berendey when the rusalka led me here," Galina said. "Do you know where we could find him?"

Elena snorted. "Berendey? To be sure, he makes things grow; he even steals sunlight from the surface for my plants—see how green they are? But he wouldn't do something like that; he couldn't if he wanted to. Nor Father Frost, no any of the others—they have a link to the surface, but it is subtle. No, we need someone who actually knows what this is all about."

"And who would that be?"

"The Celestial Cow Zemun," Elena said seriously. "Don't even think of laughing."

Galina didn't feel like laughing, with a dead body almost touching her sneakers. "Can we talk to my friends first? One of them is a cop, and maybe he would know something about this body."

"What is there to know? He's dead." Elena prodded the corpse with the toe of her boot. "But suit yourself. Go get your cop and come back here as soon as you can."

Galina found Yakov in the back room of the Pub. She paused on the threshold, breathing in its sweet smell of pipe tobacco and fresh sawdust. Yakov and David talked in quiet voices, the silences often stretching between them like clouds of smoke.

Galina hated to interfere with their conversation—she could not make out the words, but the obvious comfort between them clung with the warm air of familiarity, and she sighed to think that she wasn't a part of anything like that. She cleared her throat. "Yakov, there's something I want you to see."

He startled with a guilty look on his face. "I'm sorry," he told David. "I guess I better go—we did come here for a reason."

"It's quite all right," David said, and smiled at Galina. "Did you find Berendey?"

"No," Galina said. "Just a corpse."

Elena waited for them by the lake. On the way, Galina explained the situation to Yakov, and he kneeled by the body, examining it. It struck her that this policeman who always seemed so unsure and so defeated actually knew what he was doing—he examined the cuts and bruises on the face and wrists of the body, and turned out the pockets of the leather jacket.

The passport was sodden and unreadable, but there was also an address book and a wallet with a laminated library card. Yakov grunted and placed his hands behind the corpse's ears. The muscles on his arms tensed, and Galina stepped back instinctively—Yakov's usually placid demeanor had prevented any thought that he was capable of violence. Now, as she watched him wrench the corpse's lower jaw, she grew worried. "What are you doing?" she asked.

"Trying to get his mouth open." Yakov pointed at the dry

trace of blood staining the corner of the dead man's lips and smearing his chin. "He was tortured, I think, and I'm looking for bite marks on his tongue and cheeks, and maybe some broken teeth. Those usually occur with torture."

Galina looked away as the face under Yakov's hands crunched and collapsed. She stared at the calm black water, at the rusalki who still minced at the edge of the lake, at the rustling cattails. Anywhere but where Yakov was doing something to a dead man, something wrong. Galina understood the necessity of such procedures in the surface world, but here it felt almost sacrilegious. Then again, she thought, this was what people did. No matter how remote and magical a place was, there would always be corpses and brutish people with ropy arms messing it all up. No matter how beautiful the view from a rooftop was, there would always be empty bottles and squashed cigarette filters, dirty rags and smells of sweat.

"It's all right," Elena whispered to her. "He's almost done."

"It's not all right," Galina said. "You know how they say the grass is always greener on the other side? It is greener, because you're not there. And if you go you'll trample it and leave dirty footprints and probably spill something poisonous."

Elena smiled. "I don't think that's how they mean it."

"I know. Only they're wrong."

She tried not to listen to the awful creaking and slurping sounds, the wet swish of fabric, the soft give of something organic and formerly human. And then a soft tinkling that inexplicably reminded her of the New Year tree ornaments and the long silvery strings of tinsel.

"What on earth is this?" Yakov said behind her.

Elena kneeled next to him. "I have no idea." Her voice held a quiet awe, and Galina turned.

The two of them looked at the dead man's face, his mouth open and his lower jaw jutting out at an unnatural angle. They stared at something in his mouth, and Galina looked, too.

A small object, the size of a sparrow's egg, bright metallic blue, lay under the swollen purple tongue as if that were a monstrous nest. Yakov reached out and touched it, and the blue sphere tinkled and sang. Galina drew a sharp breath through her clenched teeth, trying to ignore the ruined body around the shining blue gem.

Elena nudged Yakov aside, and plucked the object from its gruesome resting place. It rolled on her palm, still singing, sending icy sparks into the air that suddenly felt fresher, cooler. "I don't know what it is," Elena said, "but it certainly did not belong on the surface, just as this corpse does not belong here."

"What do you mean?" Yakov asked. He seemed to have noticed Elena for the first time and stared at her, wide-eyed, as if she was a greater miracle than the blue gem.

"Underground used to be more isolated than it is now," Elena said. "And I don't like that."

"Why not?" Yakov said. "Wouldn't it be great if people on the surface learned about this place, if they could visit here?"

"No," Galina said. "It wouldn't be great at all. It will become just like the surface if that happens."

Elena rolled her eyes. "Look at you two. You just got here and you already presume to decide for us. Now, can we go see Zemun?"

"Who's Zemun?" Yakov whispered in Galina's ear.

She moved away. "The Celestial Cow," she said. "Don't ask. That's all I know."

"I like cows," Yakov said. "But what's a celestial cow doing underground?"

"Like all of us, she's in exile," Elena said. She led them around the lake and through another labyrinth of twisty wooden streets. Galina surmised that there were no true boundaries to the city—it spread in rivulets between long stretches of woods and meadows and pulled in open plains, spreading with each new arrival. She did not want to think whether underground had a limit, or whether a day would come when the woods would have to go and the deep swamps would be drained to give way to more people. She did not want to consider what would happen to the rusalki and the forest spirits when there would be no more water or forests. She did not want to envision the underground world a darker, dustier copy of what lay above it. And yet, it was all she could think about.

8: The Corpse

THEY LEFT THE BODY IN THE CARE OF THE RUSALKI WHO ACTED fearful for a while, but soon giggled, reassured by Elena's whisperings, and played with it as with a gruesome oversized toy. Yakov wanted to object at first, but then decided that it made no difference, and watched the rusalki sink below the lake's surface, carrying their new amusement with them. After that, they left to find Zemun.

He regretted not wearing sturdier boots as the clay and mud of the meadow, wet from a recent flood, sucked on his shoes. The meadow, green with stolen sunlight, spread downward on a gentle slope. Small white and yellow flowers winked in the verdant grass, and among them the Celestial Cow grazed, languid. Yakov recognized her because she emitted a soft glow that lit the meadow with a wavering light that reminded him of the northern lights he had seen once, when he visited some distant cousins in Murmansk.

"What a pretty cow," Galina whispered behind him.

"Yes," Elena agreed. "I haven't seen much livestock back on the surface, but I like this one."

The cow lifted her head and studied them with an expression Yakov could only describe as 'wise'.

"Hi," Elena said. "We came for your advice. We found a dead man who came from the surface—"

"Was he dead when he arrived?" Zemun interrupted in a slow, melodious voice.

"Yes," Yakov said. "I'm Yakov, and that's Galina. We're looking for birds who used to be people. The dead man had something in his mouth."

Zemun nodded. "I will listen to your questions, but one at a time. What did you find in the dead man's mouth?"

"This." Elena opened her palm, and the blue egg pulsed, as if revived with her warmth.

Zemun sniffed at the gem, and even tested it gingerly with the surprisingly agile tip of her tongue.

"Do you know what it is?" Yakov asked. "Elena thinks it's magical, somehow."

"I don't really believe in magic," Zemun said, and sniffed at the jewel again. "But this is certainly . . . strange."

Yakov and Galina traded a look. Yakov wasn't sure what he expected from this cow, but he hoped for something more insightful.

"Can you help us?" Galina said. "If you don't know what it is, do you know who does?"

Zemun thought for a bit. "You know," she said. "I made the Milky Way."

"That's—nice," Yakov said, and looked to Galina for help.

"You don't believe me." Zemun looked mournful. "You think that stars just happen, that no one makes them."

"Not necessarily," Galina said. "But what about the people who turned into birds?"

"Tell me about that," Zemun said, still sulking.

Yakov did, and Galina butted in a few times, talking about

her sister. Yakov wished she would stop reminding him about that—he was acutely aware that he was not doing his job and missing work to boot; his mother was probably worried sick, and there was nothing he could do to help Galina.

His thoughts drifted to the young girl, Darya, and her missing mother. He wished he could send her a message to let her know that he was looking, that he was trying, and hadn't forgotten about her. It was like the sleep paralysis he used to get as a child—a feeling of utter helplessness and despair, and it felt like it was his fault.

Zemun chewed her cud, thinking. "I can help you," she said after a while. "I will help you find why all of this is happening."

"You mean you don't know?" Yakov tried to keep disappointment out of his voice. Nothing was ever easy, and he resented that his visit to a magical kingdom of fairytales was turning into a series of interviews. And corpse examinations. If one was a cop, this sort of thing would be unavoidable, he supposed. He just wanted a bit of a respite—and the ability to do something about it.

Zemun shook her head. "I suspect that the disturbances we're seeing originate on the surface. The surface world is changing, and so is this one."

"I don't get it," Galina said. "The surface always changes—the wars, the revolution, all the other shit that happened. Why now?"

Zemun looked up, into the grey haze that masked the absence of the sky. "Who knows? Maybe it is time for the worlds to merge, and maybe not. But my guess is that someone from here is working with the surfacers."

"Why?" Yakov said. "And working on what?"

"I would not know," Zemun said. "But Koschey the Deathless should be able to help you."

Yakov rolled his eyes. "Of course. Koschey the Deathless. I knew he would show up eventually. Do you want me to track down his death? I already know where it is; I watched a movie about him once."

"No," Zemun replied. "Just ask him. He knows about dark magic."

"I thought you didn't believe in magic," Yakov said.

Zemun measured him with her languid gaze. "What does my belief in it has to do with its existence?" she said.

"We better go," Galina said, and pulled Yakov's sleeve. "How do we find him?"

"Try the Pub," Zemun said. "Everyone shows up there sooner or later."

"Good idea," Elena said. "I'll come along too."

As much as Yakov tried to avoid any political involvement in his life, he had sat through his share of a variety of meetings and lectures on Marxist theory, which were just as boring and filled with the same dull rhetoric. When he was young enough to be a member of Komsomol, whose voluntary character was a bald-faced lie, he amused himself by carving obscenities into the edge of the large wooden table around which they all sat, under the watchful and blind gaze of Lenin and Marx gypsum busts. Their white eyes followed Yakov every time he lifted the green cloth covering the meeting table and carefully cut 'dick', 'fuck', and 'cunt' into the wood, the simple incantations warding against gypsum deities. He was thrilled with a mixture of joy and fearful anticipation, and cringed when he imagined the lightning bolts they could summon to strike him down. The profanities protected him.

Even here, underground, the word 'meeting' did not fill him with anything but a low-key ennui, even if it was a meeting summoned by the Celestial Cow. The Pub had a billiard table covered with green fabric, and its polished raised edges beckoned Yakov; he wished he had a penknife so he could carve his simple-minded charms into the exposed wood, the better to ward off boredom.

David bustled around, moving chairs and pushing together tables so that everyone could fit, including Zemun. Sovin helped, his old back and arms stiffening with the effort. He occasionally stopped to bark a cough and spit, but did not slow down. The patrons stood in clusters, whispering; Yakov wondered at first how the rumors managed to spread so fast, until he saw the group of rusalki. They had brought the corpse with them, water dripping in slow rivulets from its dark hair. Yakov had to look away from its gaping mouth and the dislocated lower jaw sticking out at a disturbing angle. The rusalki held the body up and moved its hands like a marionette's, laughing softly.

Yakov recognized some of the people and creatures present; others were new to him, and he tried to guess who they were. There was a man in a long military coat and hat with a large splayed star, the fashion he remembered from the movies about the Civil War; another one, narrow-eyed and sallow-faced looked like a character from a historical drama about the Golden Horde, and Yakov pegged him for a Tatar-Mongol circa 13th century or thereabouts. Others were dressed in less identifiable garb—checkered shirts and dark trousers that could belong anywhere in the twentieth century. The thought made him sad, that one could become so detached and lost in the stream of time.

Among the people, strange creatures mingled—besides easily identifiable vodyanoys and leshys, there were things that seemed the stuff of nightmares, or at least the fairytales he hadn't heard of. He was especially intrigued by a short stocky gentleman, flanked by two attendants brandishing iron pitchforks, with eyelids so long they brushed the ground. A large winged dog sat next to him on the floor, but seemed unaffiliated. Sovin's rats tried not to get underfoot but kept close to their benefactor, and glared a bit at the small creatures—some anthropomorphic, some not so much—who scurried about with pails of sawdust, covering up the dark spots left by water dripping off the corpse and the aquatic creatures, and Zemun's cowpats.

David touched his shoulder. "How are you making out?"

"Fine," Yakov said, and pointed at the long-lidded person. "Who's that fellow?"

"Viy," David answered. "What, you haven't read Gogol?"

"Sure I have. But I thought these were mythological creatures here, not literary."

"Viy is mythological," David said. "He's a general in Russian hell."

Galina walked up to them. "We get a special hell?"

"Not a Christian hell." David thought a bit, absentmindedly

wiping his hand on the stained apron. "A pagan hell . . . or underworld, if you will."

Galina nodded. "He's the only one who's *supposed* to be here, then."

Fyodor sauntered up, and an old man in a red coat followed him. "What's going on?" he slurred.

Yakov stepped back from the assault of alcohol on Fyodor's breath. "A meeting," he said. "We're just waiting for Koschey the Deathless."

Fyodor laughed and stopped, once he realized Yakov was not joking. He turned to his companion. "Know anything about him, Father Frost?"

The old man fluffed his white beard. "We're not friends, if that's what you're asking. But he knows a lot."

"There he is." David left the group and headed toward the entrance, to shake hands with a very tall and thin man dressed in a black suit.

"I expected him to be scarier," Galina whispered to Yakov.

He agreed inwardly; the villain of so many fairytales he read as a child, of so many movies that fascinated him on Saturday mornings, was always portrayed as not quite human, a deformed creature possessed of an unhealthy fascination with young women, and who invariably ended up defeated by those who could find his cleverly hidden-away death. He did not seem particularly malignant now, just stern.

"Order!" Zemun called, and shook her head from side to side; little stars swimming around her neck jangled like bells, and quiet followed on their wake.

Everyone settled at the giant table, set in the middle of the star-shaped pub, and for a few moments there was nothing but muffled coughs and shifting and scrabbling of the chair legs on the floor. House spirits started on a song somewhere in the walls, but stopped as soon as Zemun cleared her throat. Everyone remained silent except for the albino jackdaws, perched on the ceiling beams, who would not stop squawking.

The rusalki brought the corpse with them, arranging it carefully across several laps as they sat side by side. Yakov found a place between Fyodor and Elena, who rolled the blue gem from one palm to the other, the blue flashes of light playing across her high cheekbones. Koschey the Deathless, seated to her right, watched the stone too, and Yakov noticed how deep-set his eyes were. They twinkled with reflected light, somewhere deep in the dark eye sockets.

"Order!" Zemun bellowed again, and the shifting and the coughing stopped. At her signal, the rusalki rose to present the corpse.

"This," Zemun said, "has surfaced today in the Rusalki's Lake. It was just the day after these three newcomers arrived, following the birds from the surface who appear to pass freely between the surface and the underground. Moreover, there's reason to believe that these birds are people who recently underwent transformation. We are thus forced to conclude that there's magic on the surface, and the dead bodies are able to cross here."

Yakov smiled to himself, at the cow's ability to dispense with lengthy introductions and avoid any dialectics altogether. Based on his limited experience, he expected to hear about dialectics at every meeting. A buzz of excited conversation filled the room, and Viy's attendants used their pitchforks to lift his eyelids so he could view the dead body.

"Don't worry," Elena whispered to Yakov and Fyodor. "His gaze won't turn you into stone. It's just a rumor."

"Thanks," Fyodor whispered back. "I was worried about that."

"Does anyone know where this body came from?" Zemun said.

"No." Koschey's voice crackled like a dry twig. "But I can find out."

The collective groan swirled around the table.

"Not you, with your raising of the dead again," said a blue-skinned dripping vodyanoy, his large frog-like eyes bulging out of his scaly face.

"Why not?" Koschey replied. "At least now I have a dead body to raise. That'll shut your mouth . . . and aren't fish supposed to be silent anyway?"

Vodyanoy huffed, but offered no further argument.

"Has anyone else any objections?" Koschey stared at Zemun. "Maybe you, beefsteak?"

"Drop dead," Zemun murmured.

The rest of the demigods and spirits remained quiet, and Koschey turned to the people. "Any of you fleshbags have anything to say? In the old days, I swear, I would use your skins for upholstery instead of asking for your opinion, but I guess we have pluralism now."

"Do what you must," Elena said. "And don't get too excited—you might get apoplexy."

The rest of the humans tittered, and Yakov surmised that

the death of Koschey the Deathless was a favorite joke for many.

Koschey stood, especially tall and skeletally thin in the Zemun's aurora borealis lights and the blue glittering of the gem. He commanded attention, and Yakov wondered if Koschey indeed was capable of raising the dead man.

"Give me that, sweetheart," Koschey said to Elena and stretched out his hand, palm up.

She put the gem into it. "Do you know what it is?"

"It's a rather well-polished glass sphere," Koschey said. "What's more important is what's inside of it."

"And that would be?" Yakov said.

Koschey looked at him for the first time, and Yakov felt as if insects were crawling under the collar of his shirt. "And that, my succulent friend, would be this man's soul. You see, I know quite a bit about hiding away souls."

"I thought it was your death that was hidden away," Galina said.

"It's all the same, dear," Koschey answered. "Every soul contains the seed of its own destruction. Now, if I may proceed . . . "

Yakov could not shake the impression that he was watching a magic show, even as Koschey pressed the blue marble under the dead man's tongue and unwound the electrical tape around the corpse's wrists. He fixed his jaw, closing the stagnant mouth bristling with chipped and broken teeth, hiding the blackened tongue that sprang like a pistil of that obscene flower.

Koschey whispered some words into the corpse's ear, and patted his pockets. Looking annoyed, he left his ministering.

"Does anyone have two coins?" he said. "I didn't quite expect to perform a resurrection."

"Over here," Fyodor said. Everyone held their breath as he offered Koschey a faceless coin on a thin golden chain.

Koschey grasped the coin, and Fyodor pulled it out. He then once again passed the coin through the bony fist of Koschey.

Yakov watched the manipulation in confusion, until Koschey unclenched his fist and showed two glittering coins. He placed the coins onto the corpse's eyes, closing them. The bruised shadows spread under them, and Koschey resumed whispering incantations.

Yakov got bored and looked around the room. A part of him still expected to wake up in his room, with his mom hollering from the kitchen to come and get his breakfast; he felt guilty for thinking of her so little. He imagined her, like she always was, tight-lipped and slightly worried, always uneasy about something, when a loud jingling snapped him back to his present, in his grandfather's pub, at the table surrounded by people who should've been dead ages ago and things that shouldn't have existed at all. He looked at the table, uncomprehending at first, at the two polished coins spinning and dancing on its rough surface. Then he looked at the corpse, who opened its filmy milky eyes, rubbed his wrists, and shivered in his wet clothes. Then, he began to speak.

SERGEY NEVER THOUGHT THAT HE WOULD BECOME A THUG when he grew up—when he was growing up, thugs were not a viable career choice, and boys his age rarely dreamt beyond becoming cosmonauts or firemen; at least, once they realized that the positions of revolutionary heroes were filled long ago, and were no longer offered.

He had an obsessive love of cavalry, of Chapaev and Budyonny, and he read every book in the library dealing with the Civil War and the heroism of the Red Army. He was disappointed when he learned that cavalry was a thing of the past, and if he joined the army he would be more likely to see the golden, undulating grass of the steppes through the narrow slit of a tank than from horseback, the wind whistling by, the air saturated with the smell of dry grass and horse sweat. His love of war and horses left him alternately thinking of becoming a soldier and a veterinarian; when he graduated from high school, he applied to a veterinary institute. He failed the entrance exams, and was drafted into the army.

The army changed him—after a year of being hazed and another one doing the hazing, he decided that veterinary medicine was a passing fancy, and the life of a rural vet—a childish and embarrassing dream. He stayed in the army for the third year, not required by the draft, and started applying to military academies.

And then Things Changed, in a big way. Military spending was cut and he was sent home from his post guarding a nuclear silo. The rumor was that the nukes in there were earmarked for non-confrontational destruction, but Sergey did not really care. After privatization of everything started and co-op stores sprang overnight like shaky corrugated toadstools, something became obvious to Sergey: privilege that during his youth was reserved for the party members, that used to be won in battle before that, was now free for the taking for those with brains, business sense, and non-demanding scruples.

He knew that he had neither brains nor business sense; he only had a permissive conscience and good physical training. The co-op stores needed protection, only some didn't know it yet, and Sergey joined a group of sympathetic individuals who took it upon themselves to persuade business owners to pay for their protection from rival racketeers.

He never rose in the ranks, and he didn't concern himself with the whys or hows of it; he considered himself a simple businessman. When those who owed money did not pay, he experienced a sense of vague hurt and betrayal, and he felt righteous punishing the people who for some reason didn't think it was necessary to pay their debts. Some went so far as to deny the very need for protection—or a roof, as it was called. "You need a roof," Sergey would try to explain. "If you don't have protection, other gangs would do what they please to you, your company, and your money. What are you going to do then, huh? Go to the police?"

The subject then understood his folly and hung his head, and forked over whatever cash was required. Only the most obstreperous cases needed persuasive punishment.

Sergey worked with some real artists in his life—given an electric iron, a set of pliers, and a roll of electrical tape, they reduced the most cocky businessmen to sniveling, simpering piles of refuse. These crude instruments went out of favor, though, once thugs discovered hexes.

They were old wives' tales, Sergey thought initially. Potions, talismans, kabbalic symbols—they were all the same, incantations of curses and blessings; sacrifices to the unknown and too-ancient-for-names gods—silliness, he said. There were no mysterious energies, no obligingly aligned stars that would facilitate the outcome of a territorial dispute; no bunch of dried herbs would help his prehistoric car, a Volga, the sad legacy of some ex-communist functionary, start in the morning. Except they did.

He attributed it to coincidences at first, and while he didn't quite believe it, he didn't disbelieve it either. The watershed moment came when his associates conceived of the glass business.

One of them, Slava, a tall lanky guy who used to be in the same class as Sergey and who fixed him up with his current employment, took Sergey to a remote and largely unsupervised railroad branch—a single track picking its way through the few remaining apple orchards and patchy forests of Biryolevo, the wood of the railroad ties exhaling the smell of pitch and creosote in the summer heat, rare grass stems littering the stony ground in between them. The track was used to cart glass granules—small spheres of green, blue and clear glass, two centimeters in diameter—to a nearby glass factory. The granules were transported in open cars, moving with the speed of a vigorous jog, and wouldn't be difficult to get to.

"What do we need these granules for?" Sergey asked. "They're not worth shit."

"But not what you can do with them," said Slava. "Chechens will shit themselves when they hear that we have this . . . power. Did you know that glass can trap souls?" Slava was quickly becoming an expert in the occult.

"No," Sergey said. "Where the fuck do you find this info?"

"I have my sources," Slava said with a sly smile. "Are you in or not? Once they hear that we can not only kill them but have their souls for eternity, no one will ever mess with us. Ever." Slava spoke with relish, kicking the rail that sang in a low, resonant voice, and Sergey imagined that the sound of Slava's Adidas running shoe traveled far, to lands unknown, perhaps as far as Europe. "Chechens, they're afraid for their souls, they're Christians."

"Muslims," Sergey corrected. "Armenians and Georgians are Christians."

"Same difference," Slava said. "Whatever the fuck it is they believe, as long as they believe in heaven. We can deny it to them. How cool is that?"

A slow train rambled past, and Slava waited until it almost passed, then sprinted along and caught up to one of the open cars. He leapt and grabbed onto the edge. He didn't pull himself up but just reached inside and let go, landing in a squat on the tracks. He returned and showed Sergey a handful of green spheres. "This is cool." He offered one to Sergey, and held another one close to his eye, squinting up at the sun.

Sergey did the same. The small pockmarks and imperfections on the glass sphere's surface became enlarged, and he felt as if he were looking at the lunar surface, mysterious and luminously green, distorted by the slight curvature of the glass, smoldering with craters. He discovered that if he rotated the sphere in his fingers, the green world rotated with it, showing him its hidden mountains and deep fissures.

"Not a bad place for a soul to be, don't you think?" Slava said to him. "You game?"

And thus Sergey found himself in what they euphemistically called the glass business, and he accumulated a nice collection of souls as Slava and the rest expanded their territory. That is, until he found himself on the wrong end of the glass granule.

He grew increasingly curious about Slava's sources of arcane knowledge, and he asked questions. When the questions proved fruitless, he started to snoop. By then he could afford to ditch the Volga, rusted and heavy with class implications, and bought a Jeep—secondhand, but in better condition than anything he had owned to date. Slava, however, changed his Mercedes for a new one as soon as the ashtrays filled up, and Sergey suspected that his sources of income included other things besides racketeering and soul-trapping. He decided to track Slava's secret dealings.

He took a post at the entrance to Slava's apartment building, a well-appointed old house on Tverskaya; for that expedition, he borrowed an unassuming Zaporozhets (the make that in the city folklore was often compared to a pregnant ninth-grader, since both equaled family disgrace) from a friend, and kept vigil among the equally homely cars parked in the courtyard, with a good view of Slava's maroon Merc. He waited until well after midnight, when Slava emerged from his building, alone; Sergey's heart picked up its beat—the absence of the two meaty bodyguards that followed him everywhere lately indicated that Slava was about to do something secret.

Sergey waited for him to exit the yard and turned on his lights. He followed him through the slow crawling traffic, quite certain that the Zaporozhets was well below Slava's detection threshold. The traffic was dense, and Sergey worried a few times that he would lose his quarry. Once they merged onto the Sadovoe Koltso, the following became easier. Sergey headed south-east, toward Kolomenskoe.

The park was closed, but Slava easily scaled the iron fence. Sergey parked his car well away from Slava's, and followed over the fence. He followed the winding paths, stumbling in the dark and cursing under his breath, but never losing the sight of Slava's flashlight up ahead, between the trees.

The moon came out, and it was light enough to see some of the commemorative plaques. Sergey surmised that they were going to Peter the Great's shack—a tiny wooden house, transported plank by plank to Kolomenskoe, where it could be properly immortalized. And now, it seemed, it was the scene of some shady dealings.

Slava's flashlight disappeared inside the Peter the Great's shack, and Sergey tiptoed closer. There were voices inside—at first, Slava spoke, and a strange voice answered. Sergey felt cold sweat trickling down his spine, and the weight of silence around him. A small breeze stirred the leaves over his head and he was embarrassingly grateful for this sign that he was still in the park, in the human world, for the voice he had just heard certainly did not belong here.

He could not discern the words and was too spooked to look inside. He backed from the house silently, even more terrified to make a sound. He knew well what Slava was capable of, but the creature he conferred with seemed even more dangerous, unfathomable and otherworldly.

He made his escape and no longer followed Slava on his night expeditions. The change in his demeanor was noticed, and it was his turn to be questioned. He feigned personal preoccupations and even invented a knocked-up girlfriend who wouldn't get an abortion.

"All right," Slava told him, his eyes still dark with unease. "Just don't let it make you sloppy."

Sergey swore that it wouldn't; he felt relieved at not being found out.

The end came when Slava called him on his cell. "I need you to do something for me," he said. "Very hush-hush. There's a new hex in town, and I need you to find me a test subject. I don't care what or who it is, just get me a body. Just make sure it is alive."

Sergey drove through the streets of his neighborhood, to an open-air market where sloe-eyed Caucasian nationals sold roses and melons, tomatoes the size of a baby's head and bootlegged American thrillers. It was dusk, and the customers dispersed. Relations with the Caucasian gangs were strained as it was, so he decided to target one of the leaving customers. A middle-aged woman, her hands happily occupied by bulging plastic bags of southern produce, turned down a narrow side street, and Sergey followed. He pressed a gun against her ribs and persuaded her to follow him to the vehicle. He didn't worry about her being able to identify the Jeep—the subjects of Slava's experiments rarely got an opportunity to talk about their experiences afterward.

He called Slava back. "Got one," he said.

"Meet me at the central entrance," Slava said.

"I'll be there in half an hour."

He drove to Kolomenskoe, and parked next to the idling Merc. Slava waited inside, a cigarette smoldering in his narrow lips. "Good job," he told Sergey once he presented the woman, mute with fear and tear-stained. "Come along—I want you to see this."

Sergey and his captive followed. The tourists and the relaxing citizens had cleared out of the park by then, and the paths crossed by long shadows were especially mysterious. Slava kept quiet, and Sergey grew uneasy.

"What's that new thing for?" Sergey asked.

"Turning people into birds," Slava said. "Only it's not for us. It's a favor I'm doing."

"For those who gave all this magic to you?" Sergey asked.

Slava stopped and turned, his hands in the pockets of his maroon jacket. "Yes," he said. He took one hand out of the pocket and showed Sergey a blue glass sphere. "And this one is for you."

Several goons with tape and pliers stepped from behind the trees crowding the dark path.

Sergey struggled in their hands. "What did I do?" he asked Slava.

"I hate spies."

"I'm not a spy," Sergey said. "Why do you say that?"

"I never told you the central gates of what," Slava answered. "Stupid bitch."

9: *Oksana*

THERE WERE TOO MANY QUESTIONS THAT NEEDED ASKING, and yet Fyodor felt disinclined to ask them. He left it up to Galina and to Yakov; the latter continuously surprised Fyodor by his seemingly earnest caring about finding out what happened to the bird people. Ever since the resurrection, he had been locked in the back room of the Pub, interrogating the resurrected thug. Fyodor and Galina waited with the rest in the overcrowded main hall, drinking David's homemade beer, which Fyodor was growing quite fond of.

Galina and Elena were speaking in hushed tones, and he looked around for entertainment. Koschey, apparently satisfied with success of his feat, walked from table to table, smiling and nodding to the grudging praise. Fyodor smiled and thought that the underground felt cozy to him, as if he actually belonged here. He loved Koschey and Zemun, who leaned against a table where several rusalki and vodyanoys were sharing a pitcher of something steaming and delicious; he loved the Medieval Tatar-Mongol who argued animatedly with the Red Army soldier circa 1919 two tables over. He was used to the interstices of life, he fit comfortably into crannies which most people overlooked, and the underground was nothing but crannies and interstices. He was content to let Yakov and Galina chase after leads and interrogate dead thugs. He was quite happy to stay in the Pub.

His gaze traveled from one table to the next, snagging at patches of color and unusual faces, drinking it all in. He thought about the history they had learned in school, and felt a profound sense of gratitude that there was an underground, to supplement the stirring tales of conquests and orderly victories, of revolutions and heroes, of thwarted invasions; that there was that hidden side without which nothing made sense. All the while it had been there, and now Fyodor knew why the world used to feel so off-kilter, so careening, so missing something important. He wondered if everyone felt that way, that vague longing for something they believed lost a long time ago, but in reality just buried underground.

"What are you thinking about?" Galina asked.

He just shrugged, lacking the ability to verbalize the deep sense of calm and satisfaction at all the pieces finally tumbling into their proper place. "Just how cool this place is."

"Well, it won't be so pleasant much longer," Elena said. "Enjoy it while it lasts."

Fyodor sat up. "Why?"

"Weren't you listening to that—corpse?" Galina said irritably. "If the thugs know there's something here, don't you worry they'll come looking for more?"

"Not to mention that one of the old ones is helping them and turning people into birds," Elena said. "This is serious business. And still no trace of Berendey."

"Maybe he's just busy," Galina said.

Elena shook her head. "When Zemun calls a meeting, all the old ones come. Even Koschey made it, which frankly I found surprising."

"Do you think he's the one who's helping them?" Galina said.

Elena shrugged. "It would be in character, but I don't think we should be hasty in our conclusions."

Zemun sauntered over, her jaws moving in their indefatigable chewing. "Who has the most to gain? Answer me that, and you'll have found your culprit."

"Gain what and from what?" Galina irritably swatted a strand of hair that fell across her forehead. "We don't even know why whoever it is wanted people turned into birds."

"We can guess," Elena said, and Zemun nodded.

Fyodor resumed his survey of the Pub. He noticed a bright spot of green, red and blue out of the corner of his eye—the same swirl of intensity he dabbed on his canvas time and time again, remembering a jingling of bracelets on thin wrists and a flutter of black hair that swept over dark smoldering eyes. At the thought of her, his fingers itched to paint the forbidden, that which could not be understood or pinned down. He took another sip of his beer and turned carefully, expecting the vision to dissipate once it was in full view. It did not.

Fyodor shook his head to dispel the unbidden apparition; he told himself that it couldn't be her—she still looked the same as that day, years ago, on the bridge. She saw him too and frowned a bit, as if trying to locate his face in the gallery of her memories.

He smiled and she approached their table, petted Zemun's muzzle with a distracted hand, her eyes still on Fyodor's. "Excuse me," she said. "Do I know you from somewhere?"

He nodded. "I was rude to you and your bear. And I painted your picture."

The expression of her face did not change, but it was as if her soul suddenly drained out, leaving behind a perfect but lifeless and brittle replica of her face. "What are you doing here?" she said. "I thought I left you behind."

He nodded. "You did. I was looking for you, to tell you I was sorry. Have you been underground long?"

"Ever since I gave my luck away." She pointed at the gold chain around his neck.

"You can have it back if you want." He felt curious stares from Galina and Elena on him, and wished that the girl would just sit down.

She shook her head. "I can't. Once you give it away you can't get it back."

"I'm sorry," he said. "Why did you give it to me?"

She finally sat, wedging between him and Elena. She looked at him as if from a great distance of time and lived experience that separated them. "I just wanted someone to like me."

He laughed, surprised. "Like you? How could anyone not like you?"

"You didn't," she said, and gave a long sideway look at Galina.

"I was young and stupid."

She looked down at her hands, smiling a wan smile. "Then so was everyone else."

"What about your *tabor*?" he said.

"That's the thing," she said. "You always treated us like vermin and told us to stick with our own kind. We were never people to you, we were rats who should be grateful for your scraps and who are run out of town the moment you decide you're uncomfortable with our presence or you need someone to blame for a drought or an epidemic."

Fyodor wanted to argue, but he remembered his own fears and forbidden interest, the expression on his mother's face when she told him that gypsies would steal him. He nodded instead.

Sovin looked up from his table, where he was engrossed in a game of checkers with another old man, and waved. Oksana waved back, smiling. "Where are your rats?" she yelled over the din of the pub.

"Right here," Sovin answered, and several rats scurried from under the table and ran over to Oksana, climbing on her long skirt, racing to be first on her lap.

She petted them as if they were cats. "My friends," she told Fyodor.

"I can see that," he answered. "Do they do tricks?"

"Some," Oksana said. "I'll show you when there are more around—they work better in groups."

The rats settled, sniffing at Oksana and sometimes turning to Fyodor, testing his scent with their whiskers; they smelled Oksana's luck on him.

"You want to go for a walk?" he said, just to get away from the acute discomfort that intruded upon his idyll.

"Sure," she said. "Do you mind if the rats come too? They need exercise."

"Not a problem." He nodded to Galina. "I won't be long. Hope your cop friend finds something."

She nodded, without looking up, and Elena twined her arm around Galina's shoulders, whispering quick reassurances in her ear.

It was dark outside, and glowtrees dimmed, flashed and sparkled with seconds of brilliance, and dimmed again. White jackdaws and rooks slept in the branches, their heavy beaks tucked under their wings, and only occasionally a ruby eye opened to give the passing people and rats an indifferent look and closed again, filming over with leathery eyelids.

"Did you want to ask me something?" Oksana said.

He nodded. "I want to know how you got here—and you know, what it was like for you. On the surface."

Oksana knew the sense of misplacement before she could talk. As long as she could remember, she knew moving trains and changing landscapes, with the only constant of women sitting on their parcels, and children crying and playing under the wary eyes of their mothers.

She was lucky, she said, when her family received reparations from the Holocaust—an event she had a vague concept of, but because of it money was sent by some foreign humanitarian agency, and it was because both of her maternal grandparents had perished in a gas chamber. But the money was good, and they bought a house—a shack with no running water or indoor plumbing, but still a real house where they could stay in one place and Oksana could attend school. This experience only increased her confusion—other children asked her questions that had never occurred to her, and she struggled for answers.

She had to explain that she was a gypsy and that gypsies spoke a legitimate language, not any thieves' argot. She explained that her mother really could tell people's fortunes. That the movies about gypsies really weren't that accurate, and the songs that sold on shining black vinyl records, even though they were called "Gypsy Romances" were neither. And with every question the distance between her and her classmates grew. She started to hate her Ukrainian name, given to her because she was born in Kiev.

Then the money ran out, and they joined their old *tabor* again. Her mother ailed and told fortunes increasingly bizarre and dark; Oksana had to find a source of income more substantial than what walking the bear on a leash could provide. She started doing private parties at expensive restaurants, where she danced and played her guitar and sang the Gypsy romances. These songs were just like the real ones, with the point and the soul taken out of them—she could not understand why it was necessary to kill the germ of something alive and genuine in everything intended for mass consumption. It was the same with matryoshkas, the dumb soulless chunks of wood which enterprising artists sold everywhere; it was the same with sex.

They needed the money, but at first she balked when at the parties one or the another drunk businessman, red and sweating, his jacket unbuttoned and his tie long gone, asked her if she had lice and when she answered in the negative offered her a thin stack of large bills for something extra. Eventually, she could not afford to say no, and really, it wasn't that bad, just follow them to the bathroom or the backroom, close your eyes, chew your lip, and really, how was that different from what Fyodor was doing, selling her painted and repainted picture, her features just a smudge of dusky skin and black eyes and red lips, blurred by repetition of the movement, how was that different? How was that different from a cracked needle wearing a groove through old vinyl, going round and round and never arriving, how was that different from the birch stump spinning under the sharp incisor of the carver's knife until it acquired the pear shape of the stupid nesting doll?

The world spun them all around, in circles that bore an illusory similarity to spirals, until they were worn and stripped of all identifying features, like her coin, like a lollypop in a greedy child's mouth. She span in the dance, her skirt flying about her in a brightly desperate circle, she sang, she took it from behind, all accompanied by a dreadful feeling of being hurled into the gray void of an empty October sky.

She only felt balanced that day on the bridge, when on a whim she peered over the angular shoulder of the man with a notepad and saw the bridge and the church across reflected in paper just like the water reflected them—the same yet different, not defiled but honored. And right then, she wanted to see herself as he saw her, as others couldn't.

And when he painted her, she felt real. She felt less like an assemblage of exotic features but a primal creature of color and light, of primal planes and sharp angles. She was broken down and reconstructed on paper, not quite herself, but real, with the gravity her actual body lacked, free of binding spirals and the sandpaper fists of the world.

She gave him her luck and she showed him Misha, hoping

that Fyodor would recognize them for what they were, that he would realize that Misha was a soul at the last stages of being ground down to bare bone and splinters of broken teeth and claws. That he was what awaited her if she remained in this life. Instead Fyodor walked away, and nothing was ever right.

Oksana did not blame him, not directly; after all, no one owed anything to anyone else. She wasn't looking for a savior, just for someone who would understand. She was mad at herself for her failure to explain. Her singing acquired a cracked quality as her throat grew dry and something in her chest shattered. Her fingers slid limply off the strings of her guitar. Misha died in October.

They had moved from the train station then, and took residence in Tsaritsino—the park was under construction, large parts of it were closed off, and a gypsy *tabor* and a bear could hide there until winter, when they would head for the warmer climes or overwinter, cold and huddled but stubborn like crows. But now, they had a dead bear on their hands. Cremation seemed like the best option, and Oksana, grieving more than the rest, found something proper and almost poetic about it.

They built a funeral pyre from loose branches and a few small birches and lindens they assumed no one would miss, and the body of the bear, shrunken and desiccated, was rolled on top of it. It was night, and the leaves still clinging to the branches stood black against the indigo sky and the large pale moon.

The yellow flames licked the branches and crackled, drying the sap in a cloud of pungent black smoke, tainting the air with the taste of true autumn and bitterness. Their tongues twined around birch trunks, and the long curls of white bark whispered and lit easily like paper, every mark on their surface outlined in red for just a moment and then gone in a flash of pure orange flame. The flames reached for the dead bear's body, and the smell of leaves was supplanted by the stench of burning hair.

The rest dispersed then, satisfied that the flames burned hot and bright, and in the morning nothing would be left but a few ash-colored bones, easy to break apart into long sharp splinters and bury. Only Oksana remained, her eyes watering from the stench. She hugged her shoulders as the wave of heat slammed into her again and again, and greasy soot settled like fat black snowflakes on her hair, eyelashes, cheekbones, lips. The bear on top of the pyre seemed to come to life—his limbs contorted in the heat, as if he were waving to her to join him. She understood that the movement was the result of the contractions of drying muscles, before they turned to cinders. But she also understood that there was no point in waiting until she was as old and broken as Misha, her body heaved on a funeral pyre of her own. Or perhaps they would bury her, and the thought filled her with disgust—she did not relish darkness or the wet smell of earth, or the inevitable worms. She would rather go now, in a burst of flames like so many gypsy women of bygone days. It would be her only act of defiance—to confound fate by embracing it too early.

Oksana took a few deep gulps of breath, as if she were about to dive underwater, not into the roaring flames with the sizzling corpse of a dead bear inside. The flames surged upward, licking the pale moon with their red dog tongues, and curved inward, opening a dark glowing passage between them. Oksana closed her eyes and stepped through, buoyed by the blindingly hot gust of air from the pyre's heart; her feet left the ground and for a while she hovered, surrounded by gleaming walls of solid fire, her arms outstretched, flying like a bird, until it hurled her with the force of an ocean wave toward the dead bear, and she felt the two of them—burning, burning—hurled into the empty ocean of the dark October sky.

FYODOR REMAINED QUIET—WHAT COULD HE SAY? HE DIDN'T give any promises, he was blameless and yet guilt nestled somewhere close to the surface. He watched the rats streaming in a small dark rivulet around Oksana's walking small feet. There seemed to be more of them coming from the cracks in the pavement and out of houses, joining the glossy throng of brown fur. He looked up, at the white birds in the trees.

"All we see here are those albino things," he said to break the awkward silence. "I wonder where all the black ones went."

"There aren't any," Oksana said.

"I meant the ones that flew in from the surface. The ones we've followed."

She nodded. "I heard David and Sovin talk about that but I never saw any myself. That girl's sister is one of these birds, isn't she?"

"So I heard," Fyodor said. "But isn't it strange? These birds go here and disappear."

"It is strange," Oksana agreed and fell quiet.

He knew that she didn't want to talk about the birds or the

thug, of everyone's agitation. She was remembering a private pain, and at the moment it eclipsed everything else. Fyodor had no comfort to offer, and had he done so it wouldn't have mattered—she didn't want to be comforted.

"Do your rats have names?" he asked.

She nodded. "That one's Alex, and this is Sasha, and Sonya and Masha and Artyom."

"How can you tell them apart?"

"They are different," she said. "And they tell me their names. They try to tell me more but I don't understand."

"One of them was looking at the coin you gave me. I think it smelled you."

She gave a small rueful smile, briefly transformed into a naked skeletal grimace by the flaring of a glowtree. "They like me, and Sovin doesn't mind if they spend time with me. Want to see the tricks they can do?"

"Sure." Fyodor was eager for anything that would distract her from dark thoughts and self-pity. "There must be a hundred of them here."

Oksana whistled to the rats and they fell into formation—the blur of rat bodies acquired a shape as they parted like the Red Sea and formed neat rows, their eyes glittering red coals in the dusk.

Oksana whistled some more and the rats obeyed—they jumped on each other's backs, forming tall columns instead of rows. Fyodor admired their organization and architectural cleverness—each column had a base of several dozen rats, and grew slimmer as it grew taller, with only one rat crowing the taper of the column.

"Neat," Fyodor said.

She smiled. "Look at this." She whistled a low sad note that hung in the air a moment too long, trembling, and the rat columns twisted, falling toward each other. The rats formed chains, made of rats twining their tails back to back and holding hands face to face; the chains grew thicker, writhing, rising away from the ground, coalescing into shape—Fyodor recognized two stout legs and a bulky body, two long arms and a round head with a long snout. The creature stood before him, tottering a bit. And he laughed. "This is the weirdest thing I've ever seen," he said. "That's a bear made entirely of rats. Can it walk?"

Through a miracle of coordination, effort, and desire to please, the creature took one laborious, shuffling step forward, its arms swaying freely, giving a disturbing impression of broken bones.

Oksana tilted her head to her shoulder, looking the creature over critically. "What do you think?"

"It's impressive," Fyodor said. "I'm always amazed at how smart those things are—rats and crows. And they're just vermin, you know?"

"I know," she said, and stopped smiling. "Like gypsies—isn't it what you're going to say?"

"No," he said. "I know how people see you. But when I was little, my mom was telling me how gypsies would steal me."

"Sure," she said. "Blame it on your upbringing."

"I think I wanted to be stolen," he said. "And yes, I know you don't really steal children, but that's not the point. You complain that they treat you differently . . . "

"And *you* do."

"I just wanted something magical," he said. "I'm sorry. I didn't know that different is always bad."

"Of course. Admitting that different can be better is actually a confession of inferiority; who would agree to that?"

The bear made of rats took another stumbling step forward. Oksana judged that it was safe to resume walking, and the rat-bear stumbled behind.

The sleeping albino birds woke and suspiciously watched the bear glittering with a myriad of rat eyes and festooned with dangling naked tails. Some even joined along, hopping from tree to tree, exchanging quiet caws.

They turned back to the pub, the white birds still following.

"At least this bear is not going to die," Fyodor said. "You made yourself an immortal pet who'll never leave you."

She nodded, smiling, and walked faster, her skirt swishing around her ankles. Good, Fyodor thought. He had finally found the right thing to say.

10: Timur-Bey

GALINA COULD NOT SLEEP THAT NIGHT—IN SOVIN'S WARM house smelling of animals and the suffocating comfort of hay, it should've been easy to sleep. But every time she started to drift off she dreamt of Masha, sometimes human, sometimes a bird. Masha cried and reached for her with her jet-black wings and called in her sweet voice. "Where are you, Galka? Why aren't you coming for me?"

"I am," Galina told her. "I am looking for you."

"Don't leave me here," Masha pleaded. "Please don't leave me, don't forget me."

"I would never leave you."

"Find me beyond death, beyond the river."

Masha's eyes grew huge and wide and human in her bird face, and Galina woke with a start, Masha's high voice still ringing in her ears. She sat up on the inflatable mattress that was already sagging; must've been a leak. She was alone in the room—the years of privation and a habit of hard work prompted Sovin to build big when he got a chance, and his house sprawled, irregular, in a maze of small angled rooms. The naked beams of the walls, warm and worm-holed, felt rough and reassuring under her fingers.

She thought about what Yakov told her, and she felt uneasy. The darkness surrounding Sergey's associates' plans and their underground allies worried her. There was an expectation she learned in her childhood that the universe was essentially predictable, even if the life didn't always work out the way it was supposed to. She didn't expect to be diagnosed in high school and prevented from going to college; but things turned and she could find a job without any formal education, just a good working knowledge of English, French and German acquired through studying by herself, in the mental hospital, just to pass the time. Back then, foreign words and strange letters warded off the heavy breathing of stygian beasts that crouched around her bed. They were her talismans, those words, those varied shades covering the same meaning like masks. There was order in the world, even if it was occasionally disguised. It chased away the monsters.

She sat down on the floor, her back pressed against the door, and whispered her protective spells—she whispered the words for bread, earth, air in all four languages in turn. Water. Grass. World. The nightmares subsided, leaving only the sense of longing and confusion.

She knocked on Sovin's door—he didn't sleep during the nights out of old habit; she could see the weak light from the tallow candles seeping through the uneven crack under the door.

"Come in." He wore long underwear, and his thin old man's legs reminded her of a stork; a padded jacket over the stained shirt hung like a pair of atrophied gray wings.

"I dreamt of my sister," she said. "She told me to find her beyond the river—do you know what that means?"

"There is a river nearby," he said and sat on the padlocked

chest at the foot of his narrow pristinely made bed that reminded Galina of the hospital. "Have a seat, dear."

She sat on the edge of the bed, for lack of any other arrangements. "You live so sparely," she said.

He nodded. "The less you have, the less you lose."

"Or the more you lose the less you have," she answered.

"Could be. But the river . . . we don't cross it all that much—the vodyanoys and rusalki don't like people mucking it up. And getting across can be problematic. Berendey's forest is on the other shore."

"No one has yet seen him, right?"

He shook his head and hacked wetly. "Not that I know of. Zemun's worried, and Koschey is raring to go. Now everyone thinks that he's up to something, so he's eager to pin it on someone else."

"You don't think it's him?"

"I don't," Sovin said. "He's a chthonic figure, and they are always demonized without good reason. People just don't like anything associated with death and dirt. Do you even realize how different you and I are from everyone on the surface? Most people would rather die than live underground, without sun."

"I don't want to stay here forever. Just as long as I need to find my sister."

Sovin opened his mouth to say something but then thought better of it and just sighed.

"Thank you," Galina said. "I know it might take forever. I just don't want to think about it right now."

"This place sucks you in," Sovin said. "It's comfortable

here, and at first you want to see what else is here, you want to explore—and then you just settle and build a house and spend your days playing checkers."

"It won't happen to me."

"I suppose not." He chewed the air with his toothless mouth. "I suppose you do love your sister."

Galina nodded wordlessly. She'd forgiven Masha for marrying and having a baby; she just wanted her back now. "I'm so sorry," she whispered, forgetting about Sovin. "It's all my fault."

"Just be careful," Sovin said. "Look at David if you need reminders—he did love his wife and yet he never did anything to get her back. Now is a good time for you; everyone's talking doomsday and how the surface is going to overtake us; everyone's scared. Maybe you'll get someone to come with you across the river. And if you want my advice, go tomorrow, go while the pain's still fresh enough to egg you on. The day your heartache dulls, you'll be living here and drinking tea with her majesty Elena."

"You don't like her?"

"Not just her. It's the aristocracy I don't like."

"She seems nice."

"Oh, she is. But it's about the principle."

"How can you hate someone on principle alone?"

Sovin sighed and closed his eyes. "It is easier than you think."

Galina stood. "Thank you. I'll leave tomorrow. I guess you won't be coming with me?"

He shook his head, dejected. "I feel old. I don't want to

explore. You're welcome here anytime, but that's all I can do for you, sorry."

She returned to her room whispering *Je ne sais pas* and *Ich weiß nicht* to herself to guard from confusion. There was a river, then; did it mean that Masha's appearance in her dream was real? But she had been expecting a river all along, a dark twisting river smelling of dust, with a lone oarsman who would accept a copper coin in his palm, solid and crevassed as if carved from dark wood—and did it even matter? There were signposts, and she would be a fool not to follow them.

With that thought, enormous fatigue came, and she lay on her mostly deflated mattress; even before she closed her eyes, the dark waters rolled before her, and a small speck of light grew larger, as the boat moved closer toward her, guided by the uneven light of the lantern mounted on its prow.

The next morning, she asked Fyodor and Yakov if they wanted to go. Yakov nodded, dutiful. Fyodor thought a bit and shook his head.

"Zemun will go with us," Yakov said. "Yesterday, she was agitating that we need to do something. If you ask her, she'll have to go. Ask around, see who else is game."

"I think we need to bring that thug along, Sergey," Galina said. "He'll be able to recognize the voice he heard."

"It's not a bad idea," Yakov said. "Only he is a dangerous man, even if he was recently raised from the dead."

"Just take his soulstone," Fyodor said.

"Won't work. How will you talk to it? Through a medium?"

"Maybe put it into something else," Fyodor said. "A rat maybe."

"They can't talk either," Galina observed.

"Oh, fuck me." Fyodor slammed his palm on the table. "Just trying to help here."

"If you want to help, come along," Galina said.

Fyodor made a face. "I do what I can. I didn't have to lead you here, you know."

"Enough bickering," Sovin said. "Zemun and Koschey will figure something out."

They found everyone at the Pub. Galina wondered to herself if anyone ever went home, or if they sat behind the wooden tables, upright and silent in the darkness, all night long.

"I'm leaving to go across the river," Galina told Zemun. "I'll need someone to come along."

"We'll find someone," Zemun promised. "But we also thought that we need to mount an expedition to the surface."

Galina saw her point, but the thought made her unease flare up. If Sergey was telling the truth—and she had no reason to doubt his veracity—then who knew what his former friends were up to. A vision of the empty city came to her mind, deserted streets with garbage blown across the pavements, flocks of birds studding the power lines and turning the sky black; she imagined them watching from the roofs, looking through the windows of their former residences, longing for the lives they had been forced to abandon. She thought of her mother, an old grey crow, and Masha's baby—it would be just a hatchling, unable to fly on its own.

And what of her grandmother, locked in the hospital,

among the walls covered with cracking, piss-colored paint? What of the old woman alone, her wrinkles flowing around her eyes and mouth in a fluid pattern, sitting on a hospital bed, wondering dimly why no one comes to visit her anymore, not even her daughter—didn't she have a daughter? She remembers pigtails and cheap patterned dresses, she remembers mending white bobby socks, but the girls all blur together, daughter, granddaughters, nieces, grandnieces, extended family and friends; she could never remember Galina's name, and always tried a few others first.

Galina pitied the old woman in that abstract way one reserves for the old—a general pity for decrepitude and decline, recognition of one's inevitable fate in another. She pitied the old women who timidly waited by the benches where young people laughed and drank beer, until there was no one around so they could quickly snatch the empty bottles and turn them in at the recycling centers for pennies each, but they added up to enough for a bottle of milk and some cheap fish for the cat, they added to the destitute existence on government pensions that remained the same as the prices doubled, tripled, and quadrupled in a single day. She pitied the old men who pinned their medals to the threadbare jackets to hide holes on their lapels and who grew thinner by the day.

Most of all she pitied the chronically ill, confused, broken, incapable of taking care of themselves, stuffed into hospitals four or five to a room. She used to visit her grandmother in the beginning, when they still expected her to come home. As it became clear that she was there forever, Galina stopped, unable to face her guilt. Now, she wondered if the old people would turn into birds too, or if they would still sit in the hospital, forgotten, abandoned, wondering at first why there was no lunch, and then simply accepting it as they accepted all the unfathomable but ultimately cruel turns of life.

Yakov, Zemun, and Koschey conferred, with Sovin and David listening closely but not saying a word. Fyodor wandered around the Pub, looking for something—the gypsy girl he seemed so taken with yesterday, Galina assumed.

"Excuse me."

She turned to see the Medieval Tatar-Mongol warrior. She had to look down on him; not only was he quite short, but also his bandy legs detracted from his already unimpressive height. The hem of his long felt coat brushed the floor, almost concealing his soft-soled boots.

"Yes?" she said.

"My name is Timur-Bey. I heard about your sister," he said. "I am sorry. Is there anything I can do to help?"

"You can come with me," Galina said. "But why? Everyone here seems to want to stay, not go traipsing through Berendey's woods."

His expressionless narrow eyes looked up into hers. Galina realized that the man in front of her was very, very old—five hundred years? Six? "Redemption," he said. "I have yet to atone for my crimes."

"You mean the Golden Horde?"

He shrugged. "We did what we had to. But there are cruelties I've done without compulsion."

Galina smiled. "My name's Galina," she said. "I do appreciate your help, whatever it is you think you've done wrong."

He gave a curt nod, tossing the long sleek braid of black hair shot through with a few silver threads over his shoulder. Galina thought that he looked just like the Tatar champion on the famous painting depicting the battle at Kulikovo Field—only the copper helm and armor were missing. She imagined the small man armed, battling the Russian champion, a giant monk named Peresvet. The image was almost comical, and she shook her head. It was a long time ago; still, her own slightly slanted eyes and cheekbones sweeping up like wings were the heritage of the Golden Horde's occupation. The marks that Masha had avoided somehow, with her button nose and wide gray eyes. Masha, she reminded herself. She mustn't be distracted; she mustn't try and learn everyone's story, see how they all fitted together; it didn't matter how history had abused or forgotten these people. They won no wars, they showed no valor; the winners didn't spare them a second thought, and neither should she. Masha was her only concern, her sister was her only obligation.

Soon it was time to go. Galina, Yakov, Zemun, Timur-Bey and Koschey were to go to the river, which, so Zemun asserted, was less than a day away. David packed them a parcel with bread, beer and some dry fruit. "Sorry," he said. "Didn't have any fresh ones—without Berendey around, there's no one here to bring sunlight to my garden."

"Don't worry about it," Galina said. "But have you seen Elena?"

He nodded. "She left this morning. Said she wanted to talk to the rusalki and the vodyanoys about something. Don't worry, I'll tell you when she gets back, and maybe she'll send you a message with one of her watery friends. Look for them when you get to the river—it's crawling with all sorts of water spirits, and they sure do talk."

"Thank you," Galina said.

Yakov took the parcel from David. "We'll be back soon," he said.

David nodded. "Just be careful there, grandson." He got the word out with some effort, as if he was still getting used to it.

"Of course," Yakov said. "It's not like anything can go wrong there, right?"

David shrugged. "It's not a safe place," he said. "There's no such thing as a safe place. Like there's no such thing as a good czar, no matter how much people want to believe it."

"What are we going to do about Sergey?" Galina asked Zemun.

"We took care of him last night," she said. "He's coming with us, but Koschey made him harmless." Her large soulful eyes flicked to Koschey, and he dug in the pockets of his jacket and extracted a large albino rook; its wings were clipped, and its eyes flashed with indignation. "Fuck you," it screeched.

"Now, now," Koschey said. "I told you it was temporary. And honestly, dear boy, you should be happy you got resurrected instead of rotting in that river, with eels slithering in your eye sockets. So you'll be a bird for a bit; enjoy the new perspective it affords you, hm?"

"Did you put the soulstone into that bird?" Galina said.

Koschey nodded. "I promised I would free his soul from its glass confines eventually, but for now I prefer him—portable."

"Don't piss me off," the rook Sergey threatened.

"Or what?" Koschey's bony finger wagged in front of the bird's beak.

The rook made an unsuccessful attempt at pecking it. "I have friends," it said.

Koschey chuckled—an unpleasant sound with the consistency of scratching fingernails. "No, you don't. They killed you, remember? Your only hope now is to behave and help us, and if you do well, you might yet live again as a person." Koschey stuffed the agitated bird back into his pocket.

"Everyone ready?" Zemun said. "Let's go then."

Zemun led the way, and Galina thought it difficult to take their expedition seriously, as long as they were led by a large gleaming-white cow, whose udders swayed in rhythm with her energetic step. She also considered whether the talking intelligent animals needed to wear clothes—Zemun appeared naked to her, somehow.

Yakov and Koschey followed, and Galina and Timur-Bey brought up the rear. It felt like a school trip, and Galina had to restrain herself from trying to hold hands with Timur-Bey; despite his diminutive stature, he appeared quite formidable. Besides, Galina thought, he had never been herded with a group of other children to a museum or an exhibition of the country's agricultural prowess. It was frustrating, thinking of that man and realizing that they had never shared an experience; was it possible to be so remote in time and circumstance that there was simply no overlap?

"I don't like the grass here," Timur-Bey said. "It's so white and wet. You know what grass should be like? Golden and dry, and it should whisper in the wind, run in waves, part before a running horse like a beaded curtain. It should smell of sun and wormwood and wild thyme. Have you ever seen the steppes?"

"Not really," Galina said. "Only in the Crimea; I went there when I was little. But I remember the smell of wild thyme—on hot days, it was so strong it made my head swim."

"It does that," Timur-Bey agreed. "I lived most of my life there."

"When were you—living?" Galina cringed, but could think of no tactful way to ask this question.

"Under Uzbeg-Khan," he said. "He started his reign in 1312, when I was a child."

She nodded. "Forgive me for asking this, but did you find that the people here, underground, were all right with you? They didn't hold a grudge?"

He gave a short laugh. "Not against Uzbeg-Khan they didn't. He was allies with Muscovy, didn't you know that? Muscovites and Tatars fought against Tver together."

Galina decided to change the subject—she did not want to exhibit her ignorance of the finer points of history, as well as suspecting that the history in question was rather unsavory. It shouldn't make any difference to me, she thought; and yet the thought of her city allying with the invaders for whatever purpose bothered her, even it happened over six hundred years ago. "What brought you here then?" she said. "Were you at Muscovy?"

He nodded. "I fled there, after the rebellion against Uzbeg-Khan was suppressed. He changed the religion of our ancestors to Islam, which I and a few other generals could not abide. How could we abandon the voices of the spirits, how could we betray the living steppe that whispered to us?"

Timur-Bey had three wives, but he loved the steppe better than any of them. He came out of his ger every morning and smiled at the golden waves that stretched from the camp to the horizon. He remained in the remote outpost even though his position among the Khan's foremost military advisors often required travel to Sarai Batu; he could not bear being away for long. He participated in enough military expeditions as it was. He was there to suppress the uprising of the Tver princes; he was there when the treaty with Muscovy was signed.

Uzbeg-Khan had done much to unite the warring tribes; the only trouble was, he wanted to abandon the religion Timur-Bey knew in his heart was true—not out of fervor or divine inspiration, but because the grass and the sky and his horse, a sturdy bay pony, spoke to him in many voices. He never set his dirty foot into a clean stream, afraid of offending the water spirits.

For several years he struggled with the new faith, but in the end he decided to leave.

"The trouble is," he told Galina, "is that it was not easy to leave the Golden Horde. It was so big—how do you leave the world?" He smiled but his eyes remained sad. "The Muscovites were our allies, and they were a dependency, not a real part of us. So I went there."

"How long did you last?"

He shrugged. "Not long."

"I'm sorry."

"But can you blame the sheep if the wolf who stole their young in the night, who demanded the very fleece off their backs, if that wolf came among them and said, 'I have changed, I now want to live among you as a brother'? Can you blame the sheep when the wolf said, 'I will not eat your food or worship your God, but I want you to accept me'? Can you blame the sheep?"

"I can't," Galina said. "Although I do not like the sheep comparison."

He bowed his head. "I sought not to offend. But you're right; judging by some of my friends, the metaphor is deficient. There were as many wolves among your own people, and the sheep were ready to riot."

"Who do you mean?"

"There is a man who used to be an Oprichnik," Timur-Bey said.

Galina hugged her shoulders, fighting the chill this word—so old, almost meaningless now—brought with it. She thought of the Ivan the Terrible's army, the brooms and the dog heads with red tongues and milky dead eyes tied to their saddles. When they studied them in history class, she had screaming nightmares where they chased after her, the maws of the dead dogs slavering.

Timur-Bey watched her from under heavy eyelids. "It's a terrible thing," he said. "The evil doesn't die, no matter how much you atone for it. The old evil is always fresh—four hundred years? Six? What does it matter?"

"People should be able to forget," she answered. "Things that happened so long ago—it's meaningless. Where would we be if we forever hated those who did something wrong? Russians would still hate Tatars, Jews would hate Russians—"

"You mean they don't now?" Timur-Bey interrupted. "And you're still bothered to think about Oprichniks."

She nodded. "I'm just surprised," she said. "I wouldn't think to find one here. I mean, why did they let him in?"

"Why did they let you in, whoever they may be?" Timur-Bey shook his head, his braid swishing across his back, back and forth. "Virtue has nothing to do with it. Only those who are damaged enough can find this place; I wish I could tell you that suffering makes people better."

"I know it doesn't," Galina said. "It's just . . . "

"You wish it did."

"It would make sense, wouldn't it? Otherwise, there's no meaning."

"But there is a chance of redemption," Timur-Bey said. "And that's all one can ask for, isn't it?"

11: The Boatman

Yakov had never seen a river like this. Black as soot, with a quiet matte surface, rippling slightly as if tremendous pressure had been building underneath. Thin wisps of fog floated over the dead river, moving with a will of their own, twisting like ribbons and then unwinding; they dipped closer to the surface and drifted up, coalesced into a massive formidable cloud and broke apart again in an endless hypnotic dance, and Yakov could not decide whether he was more disturbed by the apparent life of the fog or its mindless stereopathy.

The bank was devoid of any vegetation; not even the glowtrees dared to colonize the barren black basalt of the embankment, natural or artificial, Yakov wasn't sure. Even the pale grass recoiled from the black, slow water and the living mist roiling above it.

"How do we cross?" Yakov asked Zemun.

The cow looked at the river thoughtfully. "We wait for the boatman."

Yakov glanced at Galina over his shoulder. "Did you hear that?"

She nodded. "I told you there was a Styx down here somewhere. We should've taken Fyodor and his coin with us."

"How long until the boatman shows up?" Yakov said.

Koschey shrugged. "Whenever he damn well pleases. Takes his time, that boatman."

"David said Elena might send us a message," Galina said. "With some rusalka or vodyanoy."

"And this will further our search how?" Koschey said.

"It won't hinder it either," Zemun said.

Yakov watched the fog, hoping that a boat would appear out of it, gliding across the sooty surface, steered by a tall man on the stern, a long pole in his withered hands—he shook his head to dispel the vision. "Why did you think there would be a river?" he whispered to Galina. "How did you know?"

She shrugged. "There's always a river in the underworld. Or at least a bridge."

Yakov left her to talk to the Tatar-Mongol, and sat down on the bank, half-annoyed, half-relieved that he was left alone for a bit longer.

Yakov wasn't always like this, defeated in advance, dutiful out of habit. He once was a rose-cheeked youth fresh out of school who had wanted to be a policeman since he was a little kid, even though he didn't remember that the original inspiration and desire for the grey and light-blue uniform came from a rhymed illustrated children's book about a very tall policeman who had the ability to rescue cats from tall trees without any need for ladders or cherry-pickers.

He also was once a lover and a husband, an optimist; he looked to the future with his wife Tamara, a girl as pink and light-haired as he was, who worked at a textile factory and shared a small apartment with her alcoholic father and long-suffering mother, of whom Yakov only remembered that she had the most spectacular dark circles around her eyes that he had ever had the misfortune to observe.

They courted and married, and moved in with Yakov's mother, whom Tamara seemed to like more than her own, even if they did argue occasionally about insignificant things; Yakov had the feeling that both had a slight embarrassment about getting along so well, and engaged in perfunctory conflict (usually soup-related) superstitiously, to ward off the demons of serious fights.

Yakov did not like to think of that time; he both resented his wide-eyed idiocy and regretted losing it. He hated himself for changing, yet could not see how he could've avoided it. He still remembered Tamara's face, but only because his mother refused to take their wedding picture off the wall where it hung next to an icon of St Georgiy. He could never understand why his mother was so partial to the patron saint of this city, dragon or no dragon. Yakov was especially unimpressed because the dragon on the icon was puny, the size of a large dog, and wingless. His eyes usually lingered on the dragon, reluctant to move to the left and look at the glowing pink face of Tamara surrounded by the cloud of white veil. He always looked eventually.

It was easier to think about that time now, on the solid basalt shores of the dead river, under the watchful thoughtful gaze of the celestial cow who claimed to have made the Milky Way; it was easier to believe in the magical cow than in his own capacity for happiness. Koschey the Deathless sat on the bank, cross-legged, teasing the soul of a criminal trapped in the portly smooth body of a white rook. Galina and the Tatar-

Mongol argued about the nature of memory, and whether it was possible to forgive a trespass without having to forget it.

The water by the riverbank bubbled up, and a small scale-covered vodyanoy surfaced and swam ashore with an awkward breaststroke. Its seaweed hair fanned out in the water like a halo, and its webbed hands, green and speckled with large triangular scales, splashed the pitch-black water. It clambered up on the bank, and its large bug eyes searched their faces.

"Did Elena send you?" Galina said.

The little vodyanoy nodded shyly, and dug through the festoons of algae decorating its body to produce a crumpled and wet note covered in black swirls of river water, but otherwise undamaged. Galina thanked him and unrolled the note.

"What does it say?" Zemun asked and attempted to fit her large head under Galina's elbow to take a better look.

"That she is considering sending Fyodor, Viy, and Oksana to the surface. She also says to be careful."

"Oh, great idea," Koschey said. "I'll bet you fleshbags didn't even think of that."

"You're not as invulnerable as you think," the rook Sergey said. "I know where your death is."

"So do I," Yakov said.

The rook gave him a haughty look. "Did you ever watch 'Visiting the Fairytales'?"

"Yeah," Yakov admitted. "Every Saturday morning . . . or was it Sunday?"

"Sunday," Sergey said. "We had school Saturday. Didn't know cops fancied that sort of thing."

"I was ten," Yakov said, but found himself smiling. "I think they mostly showed movies from the forties and fifties."

"Those fairytales were disguised Communist propaganda," the rook said.

Yakov stopped smiling. "I don't think so."

"You're so naïve," the rook said. "They brainwashed you, and you don't even know. This is why you're a cop."

Yakov just shrugged. He didn't like it when people he had just met somehow developed the illusion of knowing him better than he did.

"Where's that boatman?" he said to Zemun.

Instead of another vague answer enticing him to patience and waiting just a bit more, Zemun pointed silently with her hoof. Through the fog that for a change remained stationary like a curtain, Yakov saw a shadow and heard weak slurping sounds.

The little vodyanoy shrieked and dove into the river, disappearing like a stone.

"What got into him?" Galina asked, and a vertical wrinkle settled between her dark eyebrows.

"He's worried that the boatman will collect from him," Koschey said. "Stupid thing. The boatman doesn't care about spirits and gods and those who've already paid. He only takes from fleshbags, and this one," Koschey pointed at the rook perching sullenly on his shoulder, "this one is already dead. I guess that leaves you two."

Yakov and Galina traded an uncomfortable look. "What is it that he takes?" Yakov said. "And why didn't anyone tell us?"

"You'll find out soon enough," Koschey answered and

smirked. "Maybe that'll teach you to blab about where people might want to keep their death."

"I traveled across the river once," Timur-Bey said. "He takes memories, nothing else."

Yakov wanted to know more—what sort of memories and why—but the narrow boat made of grey wood touched the bank. The old man looked over them, at the meadows and forests they left behind. "Come aboard," he said in the indifferent sing-song voice of a merchant, "come aboard, one memory per party, buys a round-trip."

"What memories do you take?" Galina said.

"The precious ones, the ones you'll miss and wonder day and night what it is you have forgotten," the boatman said. "You're paying?"

"I am," Yakov said. "I don't think I'll miss any of mine."

The boatman's deeply set eyes looked at him out of his creased leathery face. Thin wisps of white hair blew in the wind and mingled with the fog, indistinguishable from it.

Yakov felt an uncomfortable presence inside, as though the boatman's bony hand reached into him and sifted through the contents of his soul panning for gold nuggets.

"This will do," he finally said. Yakov felt a twinge when something in him tore loose. "You want to think it one last time?"

Yakov shook his head. "Just take it," he said, and closed his eyes.

THE BOATMAN'S VISION TEEMED WITH SO MANY MEMORIES, SO many visions, but this new one was a welcome addition. It had a complex bouquet—a hint of habitual misery provided a weakly bitter background to red-hot rage and feeling of helplessness that buckled the boatman's knees and made him want to forget his immediate task. The pole dug into the silty bottom, pushed away, heaved up in a familiar movement that let him concentrate on savoring his new acquisition. Good choice, he thought, good choice. Not exactly original but nonetheless exciting. Intense. Sadness so profound, his dead heart felt crimson and heavy, like a Persian rose dripping with honey and dew.

Divorce, a slow melancholy regret, swirled milky-white, obscuring the pulsing black hole in the center of the memory. The boatman marveled that there were no names here, nothing was alluded to directly—just oblique hints and sideway glances that people used to hide the pain from themselves, to swathe it in many gauzy layers of circumstance and irrelevant detail. Shivering with anticipation, the boatman pulled them back, like bandages from a wound, cringing at the inevitable febrile blooming of a gangrenous flower.

And there it was. Swaddling cloth, blue blanket with yellow ducklings and red-and-green watermelons, a swirl of downy white hair, going clockwise around the summit of a tiny skull. Wonder, the same in every adult, at how small the fingers and toes were, how diminutive the nails like small pink shells one finds on the sandy beaches of the Baltic. How small and how human and how alive—the mind refused to believe it. And accepting it (him) as your own seemed beyond the realm of possibility.

The boatman marveled briefly at Yakov's skill at self-deception—this memory had been buried so deep under heaps of irrelevant debris that the boatman almost overlooked it. He never tired of the novelty, of these strange nuggets of pain and joy he extracted so carefully, so lovingly from the souls that came to the banks of his river; he could not understand why they tried so desperately to hide them.

He rolled the image of the baby, of its squeezed-shut eyes and balled-up fists, in his mind, like a child turning a piece of hard candy on his tongue, savoring its unique scent and texture. And then the infant disappeared, just like that, leaving in its place a balled-up blanket with red-and-green watermelons and yellow ducklings, and the boatman could not understand where it went. He rifled through the memory, turning bits and images over like wilting petals, looking, searching for answers but finding only one veil after another, one discarded wrapper after the next, and only ash, ash in between.

He finally looked outside of himself, at the people crouching at the bottom of the boat. Yakov, the light-haired man who footed the bill a few minutes ago, sat with his head cradled in his arms, and the woman sat next to him, patting his shoulder in a weak gesture of support. "Come on," she kept repeating. "It can't be that bad. Can it?"

The man just shook his head and looked up with tormented eyes.

"I'm sorry," the woman said. "Can I do anything?"

"No," he said.

The boatman had collected his fee; he knew he had no right to ask for more. But his curiosity had gotten the best of him. He let the pole trail in the black water behind the stern. "What happened to the child?" he asked Yakov.

"What child?" he whispered.

"Don't play with me," the boatman said. "You know what I've taken." The memories he extracted were not gone; they just lost the emotional meaning, but the facts, their empty exoskeletons, remained.

"I don't have to tell you anything," Yakov said, petulant. "Leave me alone."

The boatman returned to the contemplation of his new memory. It was unlike any other, so small and yet so distorted and twisted. He ran through its labyrinth, untwisting every snag and dead end, every turn and hidden corner. He was good at it—he had been feeding on their memories ever since they first started coming here, and he could not remember what he used to do before then; the memories taken from others had subsumed his own.

He thought of the American dancer, her memories swathed in unfamiliar language; he only recognized the images of her surrounded by several children (her own? Someone else's?) trembling in the snowy night, by the black pier in some strange port, where the dark sea water was fringed with ice, and floes rubbed against each other with a slow, grating sound. He remembered the stage and the tense faces of the audience, and the red drapes, swirling in her field of vision as she swirled, arms outstretched, for eternity. She remembered the face of a yellow-haired man, once handsome but now wrecked by hard drink and late nights, and the same face later a smoldering ruin shattered by a pistol shot. These images stood as signifiers of mystery, unexplained but precious all the same.

The boatman wondered if it was a sickness, this compulsion

for the taste of other people's memories. He wondered if he could take something else as his payment, perhaps food or money, or if he should just take them across for free. He did not enjoy inflicting pain; in fact, he used to believe that he was helping them, taking away the emotional torment and intensity of unfulfilled desires. He used to think that he was doing good.

No matter how much their memories tormented them, they suffered even more when these memories were removed—like wounds left by splinters, they festered and grew inflamed, and one had to wonder if they were better off with all their splinters and warts. They became a part of them, developed from foreign bodies into integral parts of the souls. He could never understand that, but he could not stop either, compelled into removing and absorbing every painful nugget, so it could become a part of him, so he could feel real just for a little while longer.

THE BOAT TOUCHED THE OPPOSITE BANK, AS DESERTED AND stony and black as the one they had just left—it felt like ages ago to Yakov, though he knew that only a few minutes had passed. He climbed onto the bank on awkward wooden legs, and stretched. Galina stood by him, silent but exuding sympathy and guilt. "It's all right," he told her. "It's not your fault."

Zemun clambered out of the boat, her hooves sliding on the wet rocks of the embankment. Koschey and Timur-Bey followed, both avoiding stepping into the black water.

Ahead of them there was a forest—Berendey's forest,

and Yakov immediately guessed that this was where Father Frost spent his days. The trees and branches were covered in snow, festooned with icicles, gleaming with rime. Berendey's Forest had real trees for a change—Yakov recognized white and black-speckled trunks of birches, the slender branches of willows, the tall high-strung groups of quaking aspens. There were sturdy oaks and grey-barked ashes, red maples that swept upward with the grace of dancing girls, dense green paws of spruces, the haughty grandeur of pines . . . he didn't realize how much he had missed them.

"It's winter here," Galina whispered. "Do you think it's winter on the surface?"

"Don't be silly, we've been here just three days," Yakov answered.

"What if time passes differently here?"

"Then there isn't much we can do about it, is there?" he said with rising irritation.

"I guess not," she said, and fell back, next to Zemun.

They entered the forest, and despite Yakov's current upset he felt like a kid who had stumbled into a real fairytale. Despite the frozen trees, the air was only slightly cooler than elsewhere underground, and the ghost of the sun shone above, lighting the hoarfrost on every surface with a prismatic glitter of blues, reds and yellows. The delicate tracery of the frost formed flowers and fantastic animals and they wound like magical canvas around every trunk.

Carefully tended paths meandered between the trees, and Yakov realized with a sting of embarrassment that he was looking for woodland creatures that usually hung out in

Berendey's Forest, at least according to the movies. He noticed a white hare darting away among the trees and the heavy horned head of a moose peering between the spruce branches.

"Can I borrow your rook for a sec?" Yakov asked Koschey.

"Knock yourself out," Koschey answered, and extracted the rook Sergey from his pocket. "Just don't let him get away."

"Where do you think I'm gonna go?" Sergey said, and fluffed his feathers. "God, it's cold here."

"It's not bad," Yakov said, and carefully placed Sergey on his shoulder. "Does it look like you would expect?"

The rook blinked in the bright light and looked around with his red eyes. "It looks like a movie set."

"Except that it's real."

"Or so you think."

Yakov briefly considered stuffing the rook into his pocket, but decided to give him another chance. "Do you remember how to find Berendey?"

"Find him? I've only seen him in the movies. There's a scene change, a cutaway, and then he appears. I guess we wait for a cutaway."

Yakov just shook his head.

"He's right, actually," Zemun said behind him. "Berendey knows what happens in his forest, and if there are any trespassers he won't be long."

They continued walking along the paths because it was pleasant, and the forest was so pretty it seemed a shame to leave it unexplored while one had a chance.

"How old are you?" Yakov asked Sergey.

"Twenty-five," he answered. "You?"

"Thirty. I was just thinking . . . what was your favorite ice-cream when you were a kid?"

The rook squawked a laugh. "Remember the one in wafer cones, with a crème rose on top?"

"That was my favorite too. Remember those little chocolate-covered cheesecakes they used to have? I could live on that stuff."

"Me too," Sergey agreed. "Funny how good the food was when we were kids. Now everything tastes like shit. I wonder if it's because it's all imported and comes from a can, or if it's just how memory works?"

Yakov shrugged. "A bit of both, I suppose. And not all the food is shit. Imported chicken is pretty good."

Sergey made a contemptuous noise deep in his bird throat. "Humanitarian help? They call them Bush's legs."

"So I heard."

"Those chickens are fucking monsters. What do they feed them in America?"

"I don't know," Yakov said. Still, he felt closer to Sergey, another shared experience, as meaningless as it was, somehow making them alike. He did not like the feeling—Sergey was a criminal and a lost soul, wedged temporarily into the body of a fat white bird. He was nothing like Yakov, and not a person Yakov wanted to be friends with.

Yakov looked ahead; the crystal light and the magical forest were growing habitual, and he wondered why Berendey hadn't apprehended them yet; then he remembered the rumors of his disappearance, and his mood darkened. He started to think that they could spend an eternity wandering through this forest, and doubted if they would be able to find their way back.

"Look!" Galina said behind him, and Sergey flapped his wings in excitement.

A dark cloud coalesced over the trees, and the sounds of cawing and hooting filled the air. Black birds, brown birds, gray birds. Yakov had never seen that many birds together—they obscured the sky as far as the eye could see. "Where did they come from?" Yakov said.

"I don't know," Koschey said, "but I'm more concerned with what they're doing."

The birds, despite their immense numbers, seemed to home in on a particular spot, just ahead, where they circled restlessly and cried.

They rushed through the wood, trees growing sparse as they approached a clearing.

"It's like a picture book," Galina said. Yakov agreed inwardly; the house in the clearing, a trim cabin built of even reddish logs, with a thatched roof and a chimney from which curly white smoke rose, wouldn't be out of place in a fairytale, as a peaceful dwelling of a virtuous woodcutter or some other benign but slightly misanthropic character. The roof and the porch and the banister running along three steps leading to the front door were grey and black with sitting birds.

Sergey stiffened on Yakov's shoulder.

"Relax," Yakov murmured. "They don't know who you are. They might not even be the same birds."

"Of course they are," Galina said. She pushed him aside and ran up the steps. "Masha?" she asked every jackdaw in sight.

They looked back with their shiny, black eyes, their heads with a little tuft of feathers tilted to their shoulders, but none answered the call.

Zemun and Koschey approached the closed door, and Koschey tugged on the handle. "Locked," he said.

"Maybe he isn't here," Zemun said.

Timur-Bey shook his head. "Dear Celestial Cow," he said. "We cannot leave without seeing if Berendey is inside. I do not know about your kinds of gods, but the spirits of my ancestors tell me that gods are mortal. We have to see, and if you permit I'll be glad to kick the door in."

"Let's knock again," Yakov said. "Maybe he didn't hear us the first time." He didn't mention the thought that started bothering him the moment he'd seen the birds: what if Berendey was the entity Sergey overheard conspiring with Slava? He certainly seemed to be one of the very few underground inhabitants who visited the surface frequently to steal sunlight; he had the opportunity, and Yakov's experience taught him that opportunity often outweighed any motive.

Timur-Bey smirked. "I know what you people say. 'An uninvited guest is worse than a Tatar', right?"

"It's just a saying." Galina gave a sheepish smile.

This smile irritated Yakov—it reminded him of his ex-wife, of her constant desire to pacify and dampen any disagreement, smooth out the wrinkles on the surface no matter what resentment brewed inside. He turned to face Timur-Bey. "Yeah. Would you prefer we said that an uninvited visitor is better than a Tatar?"

To his surprise, Timur-Bey laughed, showing small uneven

and very white teeth. "I see your point, although I still doubt the compulsion of such comparisons. Go ahead, knock."

Yakov did, and for a few minutes all of them—people, birds, the cow—listened for any sound inside the house. There was none; Yakov thought that he heard a faint buzzing, but there was no way of deciding where it originated, and whether it was just an artifact of the ear straining to hear something—anything at all.

After a while, Yakov nodded to Timur-Bey. "On three."

He counted to three, and his and Timur-Bey's shoulders made a shuddering impact with the sturdy door. It gave on the second try—the wood by the jamb splintered and the door fell halfway in, hanging by the still-locked deadbolt.

Inside, the house smelled of wood shavings and pine resin, of sun and hay. The birds poured in through the open door, as if compelled by some invisible force.

"Hello?" Yakov called through the roomy entrance hall and into a darkened corridor.

There was no answer, and he motioned for everyone to remain where they were. He had never carried a gun in his life, but now he wished he had one on him, as he moved through the corridor, his left shoulder brushing against the wall, and kicked open the door on his left. It was a kitchen, judging from the well-polished copper pots, and he wondered briefly why spirits and demigods even needed a kitchen. The recently swept floors smelled of fresh pine, and the pot-bellied woodstove stood clean, not a speck of ash in its roomy interior; neatly split fire logs were stacked in a corner, just waiting for someone to start the fire with the long curls of dry birch bark piled by the stove.

The birds that now filled the hallway and the corridor avoided the kitchen and instead mobbed the door at the end of the corridor; they flapped their wings and threw themselves against the locked door and fell to the floor, only to take wing again. Wave after a black wave crashed against the door, and Yakov had to push his way through them, wings beating against his face. Sergey's claws dug into his shoulder, as if he were afraid that the insanity of the birds around them would take possession of his bird body and fling him against the locked door in a mindless attack.

Yakov pushed through the squawking and the fluttering, soft downy feathers of an owl's wing brushing against his cheek in an almost tender gesture. It was a barn owl, and he remembered the girl Darya in the long-ago, her small and dusky apartment with the railroad just outside her window . . . the same railroad, he realized, that passed by his house, the same railroad that conveyed the glass granules—soul-stones—to the glass factory. He shook his head—he was stalling, reluctant to open the door, fearful of what might be inside.

He put his shoulder to the wood, and the feeble lock gave on the first try. It was a bedroom, filled with soft light filtered through the closed curtains; the bed, decorated with a surprising mound of decorative pillows, was covered with a white feather duvet, and a shiny, brassy chamber pot peeked from under it. St Nikolay and St Georgiy (and his ubiquitous lizard) peered from the icons on the wall with wizened dark eyes. And on the floor, parallel to the bed, a dead body lay stretched out as if in sleep. Dark blood pooled around it, dripping across the broad chest dressed in a mossy-green caftan from a wound over the dead man's heart; a bayonet protruded from it, and although he was no expert, Yakov recognized that the bayonet was old.

"This is a Napoleonic war weapon," Sergey said from his shoulder helpfully. "You might want to get it before these birds swarm him."

Yakov nodded. The birds, granted access, flitted inside in an almost comically solemn procession. They settled on the floor, on the dead man's wrinkled, kind face, on his white beard that fanned across the chest and turned red in places; they lit on his green cap and his red calloused hands lying palms up on the floor, on the pointy toes of his boots and along his legs.

There wasn't much left to do, and Yakov called to the rest of his companions. When they stood in a respectful semicircle by the body of the dead demigod, Yakov yanked the bayonet out.

Koschey sighed. "I warned him," he said. "I told him that one's much better off with one's death hidden away. I really can't recommend it highly enough."

"Shove it," Zemun said with a force unusual for her. "Show some respect—there weren't that many of us left, and now we are one fewer."

12: Pogrom

Fyodor spent the whole day with Oksana, the gypsy girl as he still referred to her in his mind. No matter how he tried to explain how terrified he was of the gypsies and how it wasn't his fault, she refused to show any sign of sympathy. It was as if she didn't realize how much effort it took for him to even talk to her.

This predicament occupied most of his attention—and Oksana, no matter how much she scoffed, still sought his company, as if expecting something from him, and her retinue of rats tagged along as they went for another long walk. They returned at suppertime, to discover that there was another assembly in progress.

Fyodor felt bitter—after so many years, there finally was a place where he belonged, where he felt happy, where he didn't have to claw a living out of the fissures of life, even though even here the ghosts of his past in the shape of Oksana haunted him. The surface world managed to intrude, forcing its preoccupations on Fyodor, never letting him be.

He slid behind a table next to Sovin. "What's happening?"

Sovin moved on the long bench to give him and Oksana a place to sit. They wedged close together, and Sovin whispered to them, "Berendey's dead."

"Are they back?"

Sovin shook his head. "They sent a note with a vodyanoy—one of Elena's pals, I reckon. They said they wanted to follow some 'lead'. I guess your friend the cop wrote that one."

"He ain't no friend of mine," Fyodor said. "I like the cops as little as you do."

Sovin smirked. "That's always been a problem, see? Can't like the thugs, can't like the law. Just the other day I was talking to some folks, and you know what? No matter what period you look at, the cops and the secret police and the thugs all worked together; sometimes you couldn't even tell them apart."

"Nowadays cops aren't that bad," Fyodor said. "Sure, they take bribes . . . but they're nowhere near the KGB's level of evil."

"Level of evil," Sovin repeated. "I like that. And you're right, I suppose. That Yakov seems like a decent guy, and David's grandson to boot. He means well; the trouble is, he tries to work with a fucked-up system."

Zemun was not there to run the meeting, and Elena took over that role. Fyodor envied her confidence, the way she could just stand and speak in front of dozens of people and creatures and god-knows-what-elses. "This is a more dire situation than any of us had anticipated." Her clear voice carried through the smoky air, reaching every table in every tucked-away corner of the pub. Even the little domovois who usually bustled around with drinks and buckets of sawdust stopped in their tracks, listening with grave expressions on their small bearded faces.

"The vodyanoys tell me that they found other things from the surface world in the river—weapons, knives, handguns. They tell me that there are more soulstones in it everyday, and they tell me that the rusalki don't go to the surface anymore, even when the moon is full and they should dance on the embankment. And now we hear that Berendey is dead."

A whisper traveled over the crowd, like a gust of wind stirring the grass and falling silent again. Fyodor waited for her to tell them what they should do—go deeper underground, retreat and run to environs unknown and unexplored?

"It is clear what we must do," Elena said. "We must take the fight to the surface; it wouldn't be the first time and I assure you that it won't be the last—at least if we are successful."

"What does she mean, not the first time?" Fyodor whispered. "I thought it was the whole point, to stay as far away from the surface as possible."

"That is true," Sovin said. "As long as I had been here, it was the case. The old ones do meddle, but they're usually subtle. But I heard about times when the interference was more direct, and even people got involved."

Fyodor settled, his head resting on his folded arms, ready to listen to another story.

"What are you looking at me for?" Sovin grumbled. "Ask them." He pointed at the table almost hidden from Fyodor behind a corner. He could only see the dark jacket of a man and the feet of a little girl in laced-up boots that generously showed her toes in a wide yawn. "Who are they?" Fyodor asked Oksana.

"Jews," Oksana said. "Come on, I'll introduce you. I usually sit with them."

"Why?" Fyodor stood and followed her.

"Because," she said. "When you have no country, no one thinks you have a right to be your own people. Like if you have no land you should have no language either, like it's your fault. Jews and gypsies, and no one else is like them."

The people at the table—a family it seemed, the men dressed in long severe jackets, the children in well-worn hand-me-downs, the women in grey and black—looked at him with dark eyes, and smiled as if uncertain of his intentions. "This is Fyodor," Oksana said. "Probably the only man alive who doesn't know what a pogrom is."

"Have you heard of the Protocols of the Elders of Zion?" the man with a long beard and a kindly scattering of wrinkles around his eyes asked him.

"I heard something about them," he said. "Weren't they a fake?"

The man sighed. "Has it ever stopped anyone?" he said.

THEY USED TO LIVE IN THE PALE OF SETTLEMENT—THE PALE for short, in the town of Vitebsk. Hershel's family lived in that *shtetl* for generations, ever since the Pale was established. They were merchants and butchers, clerks and occasionally soldiers. They had large families, and were pious when the circumstances allowed—as a young man, Hershel studied Torah, and eventually got admitted to the University in Kiev. He came back to Vitebsk as soon as he graduated, a trained doctor, able to do good work for his community. He married Rosa soon after. It was 1876; his first son was born in 1877.

In 1881, things had changed. Hershel found it rather pointless to speculate as to hows and whys, but Alexander the Third, the successor of Alexander the Second the liberator and all-around good czar, just had it in for the Jews. Moreover, for reasons unknown, everyone seemed to blame the Jews for Alexander the Second's assassination. It did not surprise Hershel—he had lived long enough to know that if there was trouble, sooner or later the culprit would be found, and the culprit would usually be of Semitic origin.

The secret police, Okhranka, was never openly involved; but when the Jewish stores were ransacked all over Vitebsk, Hershel did not wait for the Black Hundreds to work their way to the private homes and bodily violence. He decided to move to Moscow, hoping that there, among millions, they would be hidden from misfortune. They could've converted or emigrated to the promised shores of America, but, much like Sovin, Hershel did not believe in emigration—can't run from yourself, he told his wife when she brought up the possibility, and can't run from your fate.

"Isn't moving to Moscow running?" she asked skeptically, and stroked the hair of the youngest of their daughters, who clung to her mother's long skirt.

"No," Hershel said. "Russia is our home—we're moving to a different room, but not leaving the house."

Rosa muttered something derogatory about the quality of the home, and suggested that when a house collapsed it was only wise to step outside. Hershel pretended not to hear. America was too far, and he was not convinced that the distant land would be really worth months on the boat. He looked around his clean, small dining room, its freshly whitewashed walls, and hated saying goodbye to it. He hated leaving behind the talkative neighbors who had grown quiet and subdued lately, and he felt guilty for his privilege—as a doctor, he was allowed to leave the

Pale. The world to the east was unknown and terrifying, but so were the steep hills of Vitebsk and its narrow, twisty streets.

Moscow greeted them with cold and severe frozen stone. They settled by the river, in a dank and small house. They missed their clean and dry house in Vitebsk, where despite the overall poverty Hershel had achieved respect; here, they had to build it all anew. There were few Jews in their new neighborhood, and Hershel ministered to them and—on occasion—their cows and horses.

The youngest of his six children was born in the fall of 1890. The cleansing of Moscow Jews started in 1891.

Their neighbor's house was burned, and Stars of David were painted up and down the street in ash. They complained to the gendarmes, but the disinterest of the authorities was palpable. They were advised to convert.

"Perhaps we should," Hershel told Rosa.

She heaved a sigh and adjusted the baby in her arms, patting her back. "And what good will that do?"

"We'll have new papers," Hershel said.

"Oh, my dear naïve husband," Rosa replied. "Don't you know that they don't ask a Jew for his papers before they cave his face in? And you need to look in the mirror if you think you look like anything but a Jew."

America was starting to look much more attractive, especially when half of the Jewish population of Moscow were evicted, most of them in chains.

There was nothing special about Hershel's family, he supposed, and thus it did not seem fair that they were the ones who were saved. He remembered that day clearly—Passover, cold spring, snow still thick on the ground, but the smell of wet earth grew stronger with every day, telling that the spring, the true warmth and flowers and sticky first leaves, the pollen in the air and the fluff of shedding from tall poplars, the smell of sweet linden blooms, were not far off. It was the time when one dreamt of crocuses blooming under the snow, of seeds swelling in the dark earth, ready to burst forth with the fresh energy of new life, of renewal; it was also traditionally the time when the word 'Christ-killer' was heard more frequently than Hershel liked.

"I am a useful Jew," he told Rosa. "Nothing bad will happen to us."

She sighed and said nothing, which was in itself an unusual event—Rosa rarely wanted for words. Hershel supposed that the sight of so many of their people in chains, the rumors of so many deaths ignored by the police took even her voice away; or perhaps it was the shame of remaining untouched by the misery, of being 'useful'. She never called Hershel a traitor, but he suspected that she thought it, and perhaps more often than she would admit.

"What would you have me do?" he pleaded. "And what of the children?"

She shook her head, still silent and inconsolable, and left him alone in the dank dining room that still held the smells of the previous day's Seder, its low ceiling oppressive and dark. Light from the lone tallow candle flickered and exhaled thin streams of soot, adding to the deposits darkening the already hopeless dwelling.

That night, as Hershel learned later, the inhabitants of the underground grew restless, stirred up by the clouds of despair on the surface and their slow seeping underground. Hershel explained that this was how it usually went—the prevailing mood of one place reached the other, but the emanations and their effects were usually weak enough to be masked by the native emotion and mood. It was only at the times of great tragedy that they grew disturbing enough to spur the underground dwellers into action.

"I don't get it," Fyodor interrupted Hershel. "I mean, no offense, but what was so special about that time? There were plenty of other tragedies."

"I don't know," Hershel said. "We all have our reasons and guesses, but do they matter? Sure, there were other times. But I guess that time everyone had enough."

Hershel's house stood close enough to the river for him to be concerned about the spring floods, and in the spring the ice-bound river was clearly visible between the naked trees; he always worried about the children—especially his fearless and headstrong firstborn Daniil—playing on green and uncertain spring ice, where black freezing water could show itself through a crack like a slow smile at any moment. Hershel always kept an eye on the river, especially at night, fearful of the children's disobedience and of the incomprehensible ways of the world.

They came through cracks opening in the ice, they sprang among the trees. Hershel watched, terrified and yet not surprised, convinced that the grotesque creatures coming from every surface cranny, from every fresh snow patch, from every fork in the tree branches, had something to do with the exodus of his people. He was not wrong—he realized it when a large vaguely human head protruded through the only glass pane of the dining room window, without breaking it but instead seemingly originating within it, and demanded to know where the Jews were.

Hershel found himself at a loss for a proper answer; instead he just whispered, "Who are you? What do you want?"

The head chewed with its slack-lipped mouth. "I'm a friend," it promised. "My name is Pan. We came to take you, to help you."

"Most have left," Hershel said. "They took them to the Pale in chains; there is no one but the useful Jews left." He was surprised at how much contempt colored his words.

"And these 'useful Jews'"—the head repeated the words without grasping their meaning—"they want to stay here? Despite all the cries and complaints we heard all the way underground?"

"I don't want to stay," Hershel said. "But where would we go? There's suffering everywhere, and too much of it to boot. What am I supposed to do?"

"Find those who want to leave," the antlered head advised. "We will come back tomorrow, and we will take you somewhere where your suffering will be lessened." The head whistled and disappeared back into the murky glass, and with it the rest of the apparitions were gone, as if they had never existed.

This description sounded suspiciously death-like to Hershel, but he didn't think he had a choice. Finally, a solution that would mollify Rosa; he called her and the children, and only then realized that unless they had been looking through the windows in the last ten minutes, they would have trouble believing his story.

Instead, he told them to knock on the doors of their neighbors and ask them if they wanted to leave. He didn't say where or why, only that whatever it was it had to be better than staying here, waiting for them to outlive their usefulness. Waiting to be killed or converted, waiting for Konstantin Pobedonostsev to give another one of his speeches, talking about Russia as the heiress of Constantinople and Byzantium, and Moscow—the third Rome. Waiting for him once again to remind everyone who killed Christ and who would never be forgiven for it. Hershel assumed that whoever the horned creature was, it was not friends with Christ; at that point, it seemed good enough for him.

But not for anyone else. It was his punishment, he supposed, for his former cowardice and minor but common betrayals. Everyone said that they were fine where they were, and some threatened to sic the Okhranka on him. Everyone liked to think that the worst was over, and that they were either important or inconspicuous enough to survive. Hershel smiled sadly at their self-deception and felt embarrassed by his conceit—he was not so different from them after all.

In the end, only Hershel's family wanted to go to the underground. There was a lesson in this, he supposed—a sad lesson of the sad state of the land, where the only escape possible was underground, and the only ones who cared about his life were the pagan deities he didn't even believe in.

Fyodor nodded, mute; he sat next to Oksana who snuggled against Hershel's and Rosa's youngest daughter, an eternal infant still in swaddling clothes. The girl babbled happily, and Oksana laughed. "Isn't she the cutest?" she asked Fyodor.

He shrugged, not willing to debate the issue; he felt indifferent toward children, especially the ones who didn't talk yet. Instead, he listened to the voices rising all around him. Distracted by Hershel's story, he had missed something important, and now he strained to catch up. It seemed that Elena insisted that a foray to the surface was the best thing they could do, and the only question was who would lead this expedition. Definitely not Pan, Elena said. Pan, long-antlered and sad-eyed, sulked in a corner, his goat legs and human arms crossed in defiance.

It's nothing personal, Viy explained. Last time it was too chaotic, too disorganized. You just don't chase all your minions to the surface and make a colorful appearance that practically assures that you'll be mistaken for a devil or a hallucination. They could've saved more if they'd only sent someone more human-looking.

"Like you," Pan said from his corner, to the general titter of laughter that fell silent as soon as Viy's attendants moved in with their pitchforks to lift his terrible eyelids.

"Viy does have a point," Elena agreed, "especially considering that this is a mission of reconnaissance. We should send people. How about you, Fyodor?"

Fyodor did not expect that. "Me? Why?"

"Because," Oksana said. "You came from the surface recently. And so did I."

"You can take my rats if you wish," Sovin said. "I would come too, but—"

"It's all right," Oksana interrupted. "Really, you don't have to make excuses. You can just not go."

"Can I do the same?" Fyodor asked.

"No," Oksana said. "You haven't paid yet."

One had to pay for everything; Fyodor knew as much. What he didn't realize was that his suffering was trivial, that he was judged and found lacking. His little dull torments were deemed irrelevant, affectations of an essentially wealthy soul, deprived of abuse and true sorrow. He thought it strange to feel so guilty and undeserving, while his entire life was nothing but bleakness and slow descent to the lowest energy state imaginable. And what did he get for it? He was about to be thrust back into the seething gutter he had escaped, only a gypsy girl and a pack of rats for company and support.

"It's not so bad," Oksana said and patted his hand carefully; suddenly, she was the strong and reassuring one, the one in control. "I'm sure it'll be all right."

"How do we get back to the surface?" Fyodor said.

"I don't know," Oksana said, and looked expectantly at Elena.

Elena shrugged and looked at Pan.

Pan scoffed into his beer. "You don't want my help, you find someone you want."

"I can get you there," Father Frost said. Even though he sat quite a long way away, by the bar, his voice boomed, and the top of his red hat was easy to spot. "As long as you don't mind an early winter."

Fyodor thought of the bums and beggars, of the long

fluorescent tunnels of underground crossings and subway transfers. "Not too cold," he pleaded.

"Not too cold," Father Frost agreed. "But there will be snow."

It was night, and the moon was appropriately full. They walked out of the frozen forest—garlands and flowers and wondrous trees of pure ice, only to look back and see that the forest was just a layer of rime on a storefront window. Fyodor tilted his face upward, watching large wet snowflakes sift through low clouds, backlit with silvery moonlight.

"I missed this," Oksana said, and shivered, her hands deep in the pockets of her worn jacket with bristling fake fur on the collar and patches on the elbows. "I really did."

"Me too, I suppose," Fyodor said. He wondered briefly if his failure to be moved by the beauty of the snow and an unusually quiet night—only now he realized that the usual roar of traffic and an occasional drunken shout were silenced by the thick blanket of falling snow. He suspected that this inability to feel things like this was some sort of an inborn defect, and he wished he could do something about it, that he could learn to feel anything but the persistent fear of gypsies and the world as a whole.

The rats surrounded them like a dark puddle—they expanded and collapsed again, pressing close to each other and lifting their pink feet in turn, to keep them off the snow.

"We better get going," Oksana said. "They're cold."

"Where are we going?" Fyodor asked.

"Where can we hide with a pack of rats? The *tabor*, I suppose."

Fyodor blew on his fingers. "Do you even know where they are?"

She shook her head. "It doesn't matter. We can go to any train station, see if there are gypsies there." She looked up, at the skyline. "Kievskiy would be the closest. Let's see who we can find. Or we can try a park, if you prefer."

Fyodor followed her down the snow-covered street. The low wind raised brief vortices of snow; they reared up and fell again, weighted by the heavy thick flakes. Bad skiing weather, Fyodor thought, the snow is too heavy and wet. It would get stuck to the skis in great heavy clumps.

The rats pressed closer to Oksana's feet, trying to find cover under her skirt and the heavy hem of the coat. Some grew bold enough to jump on Fyodor's shoes and squeeze up, under his trouser legs, their fur surprisingly warm and soft against the skin. With a sigh, he scooped up a few and put them in his pockets. Others saw it as an invitation and climbed on his shoulders and under the thick quilted jacket he had borrowed from Sovin, too long in the sleeves and narrow in the chest.

"They like you," Oksana said, smiling. The white snow settled on her black hair, crusting it with a thick translucent crown as it melted and froze again.

What about you? he wanted to ask, but could never make his tongue turn to utter these words. It was better to wonder silently, than to be assured once and forever that his inability to feel rendered him unlikable; he never tried to ponder the paradox of his indifference and his intense desire to be liked by someone, even a gypsy—especially a gypsy.

13: Bird Gamayun

Galina dreamt of Masha again. In her mind, she still saw a jackdaw, huge and swollen with disease, but with her human arms, full and smooth just like Galina remembered. "Sister, sister," Masha cried. "Why won't you help me?"

"I'm coming for you!" Galina yelled, and woke with the sound of her voice still ringing in her ears, her throat hoarse.

She sat up and looked at the frozen forest outside of Berendey's house window. They had decided to spend the night here, but any delay grated on Galina, like a hard shoe against tender skin. Every day felt like a nightmare where she was wading through molasses even though every fiber of her soul screamed for her to run like the wind.

She had spent all night going from one bird to the next, all of them still perching around Berendey's dead body which Yakov had covered with a sheet. Galina looked at every jackdaw, calling her sister's name, but none of them answered; they just watched her with shining black eyes.

"It's no use," Koschey said. "Get some sleep; the morning is wiser than the night."

She couldn't help but smile at the familiar words—in every fairytale it was true, and the hero woke up to find the impossible task done. Maybe she would wake up too, and find herself back at home, with Masha pregnant and safe and sound; even waking in the hospital bed didn't seem too terrible. To save her sister, she would welcome such an outcome. She loved her enough to trade her own sanity for Masha's safe return.

The morning came, and she was still in the forest underground, cramped from sleeping on the floor of Berendey's kitchen. God, she whispered, I swear to you, if you let Masha be safe, I won't mind spending my whole life in the hospital and I swear I will never complain.

"Which god are you talking to?" Zemun asked from the corner where she had slept standing up.

Galina shrugged. "It's stupid, I suppose. Is there a god who could make it come true?"

Zemun shook her heavy horned head. "I don't know, dear. We're underground, and we can't go anywhere else. Our time has passed, and I know nothing of the new gods."

"God," Galina corrected.

Zemun nodded. "God. I don't know his power, I don't know who he is. Back in my days, we could do things. I made the Milky Way—did I tell you this?"

"Yes." Galina thought for a bit. "Why do you think Masha wasn't with the birds here?"

"I don't know that either," Zemun said and heaved a sigh. Galina could tell she wanted to discuss the Milky Way. "We used to have many birds here—the Firebird, Gamayun, Alkonost, Sirin . . . "

"Where did they all go?"

"Flew away, maybe," Zemun said. "Or died. Or maybe they're still around somewhere."

"There was something I wanted to ask you." Galina hesitated

a bit, unsure of Zemun would be upset by her question. "I was wondering about the gods—the major ones, like Yarilo and Belobog and Svarog—what happened to them?"

"You are correct," Zemun said. "They were the real gods. And they were too proud and too important to be exiled. This place is for those of us who don't mind being small, who can live without being noticed. Those who are not ashamed to hide. But even we fade away eventually—you can't be small forever without disappearing."

Galina nodded that she understood. They heard movement in the other parts of the house, and she guessed that Yakov and Timur-Bey were up. Koschey didn't sleep at all, or so he claimed—he stayed up all night, guarding. He wouldn't say why or from whom.

They set out before long. Galina was relieved when Koschey and Zemun decided not to retrace their steps, but to go further into the woods, to look for whoever had done the deed—he still had to be on this side, since the boatman swore that he had taken no one across in quite some time. And Galina held onto the hope that they would see more of the dark-colored birds, and somewhere, among them, she would find her sister.

"Tell me about those birds you mentioned," she asked Zemun as they picked their way through the melting snow. The first snow anemones peeked through the melting transparent crust, their white petals and yellow centers looking at the world shyly. They seemed artificial under the snow, and Galina stopped to uncover the blooming flowers and thin, delicate leaves.

Zemun waited for her, chewing patiently. "I suppose I

could," she said when they resumed their walk. "It'll help pass the time. Alkonost and Sirin, yes, sisters—and the Firebird—you probably know about her yourself. But it is Gamayun I think about most."

Galina noticed that Yakov picked up his pace, straining to catch Zemun's story, and the albino rook on his shoulder listened too. Galina smiled despite her somber mood—they were all like children, eager for a good story.

"It all happened a long time ago," Zemun started. "When heaven and earth had meaning, when only the dead lived underground."

THE BIRD GAMAYUN WAS RELATED TO ALKONOST AND SIRIN IN some vague fashion—even the most casual observer would've noticed that all three of them were not entirely birds; they had the faces and breasts of women, severe but beautiful. And when their lips opened, they sang in women's voices, deep and rich and bittersweet.

Alkonost, resplendent in her white feathers, sang of joy to mortal people, and when they heard her voice, all their cares and troubles lifted off their shoulders, and the old felt young, the sad rejoiced, and the tired became refreshed. Alkonost made her home in the Garden of Iriy, in the branches of the tree that grew with its roots planted in heaven, and its branches stretching toward the earth. There, she sang to the gods, and lightened their hearts burdened with the worries inherent in running the world.

Sirin of the dusky-gray feathers and long sweeping wings sang for the saints and gods and holy men only—if any mortals heard her, they were so entranced by the beauty of her voice and serene face, they followed her to their death; some lost consciousness and never regained it, forever lost in the wonder of their visions. Many said that she lived in Navi, the kingdom of the dead and the lost. Others maintained that she lived next to her sister Alkonost, in the branches of the heavenly upside-down oak. Every night, they sang down the setting sun in a duet so sweet that even the gods became quiet and contemplative. The songs of joy and sorrow mingled together, and as the giant flaming sphere of the sun settled for the night's rest, the heavenly oak itself froze motionless, not a single leaf daring to flutter on its branches.

But Gamayun, her feathers black as pitch, her face white and mournful, did not sing, nor did she make her home in Iriy. Damned with the gift of prophecy, the bird Gamayun flew from one end of the world to the other, screaming her visions of doom to anyone who would listen. The black hair on her woman's head streamed in the wind, and her graceful wings beat the air with heavy strokes; her clawed feet clutched at empty air in a futile attempt to gain hold of something, like a drowning man who grasped at the churning water around him, his hopes of feeling anything solid in his fingers growing more distant and yet more desperate with every second. Such was Gamayun, her voice loud, harsh and piercing, as she cleaved the skies in her flight.

Gamayun never rested in the branches of the celestial oak, she never sang the sun down with Alkonost, and people feared her more than they feared Sirin. While Sirin promised a certain death, she also promised pleasure and sweet visions, a quiet contented slide into unconsciousness. Gamayun's voice only portended disasters, with no hope or consolation, with no solutions to prevent the foretold doom. She was worse than the One-Eyed Likho, worse than the blind Zlyden who attached themselves to people and caused misery and poverty—at least, one could get rid of Likho by luring it into a barrel, or sweep Zlyden out of one's home, but there was no hiding from Gamayun's prophecies. Even the gods avoided her once she started promising the end of their time and a bleak long decline underground. Such was Gamayun's fate.

The prophet bird could not stop, driven by the fire deep in her heart; her wings never stopped cutting through the air, and her voice, hoarse and terrible, never ceased shouting the prophecies born within the bird. Her eyes became mad and black, with dark circles surrounding them. And when her tortured predictions came true, Gamayun found herself underground.

Alkonost and Sirin missed the sun, and grew silent and ill. They did not sing anymore, and only ruffled their dull feathers high in the branches of a glowtree. But Gamayun could not stop prophesying, even though her voice was so strained that it became little more than a coarse whisper. She hissed and sputtered, and whispered fiercely of the terrible things happening on the surface, and the things that were only going to happen.

Gamayun spoke of fire and ash, she promised a burning like none in times past, she promised that the proud city above them would be consumed in a conflagration greater than any before it; she promised blood and destruction like never seen, and she promised that the Moscow above their deep grave would be turned into a flower of fire, beautiful and horrid; she promised its raging febrile bloom and the seeds of black ash.

The gods and others did not mean to ignore Gamayun, but her prophecies were simply too unbearable to be acknowledged. Still, the underground denizens turned a troubled gaze upward and sighed every time they imagined the sound of hooves and the crackling of fire.

Father Frost raged and promised early and cruel winters, and the leshys ventured to the surface woods, to lead away and confuse the invading armies. And Gamayun was the one who screamed and hissed and promised fire, and she was the one who disappeared on the day Moscow burned and smoldered, and Napoleon took the city, then not much more than a handful of cinders.

"And now there's a Napoleonic bayonet and birds," Galina said to Zemun. "Do you think there's a connection?"

Koschey sneered at her from his considerable height. "Did you think of it all by yourself? Or do you really think that stating the obvious is somehow helpful?"

"We didn't know about Gamayun," Yakov said. "If it was so obvious to you, why didn't you mention it?"

"Because it's not obvious," Zemun said. "I haven't thought of this in a while."

Galina turned to Yakov; even though she doubted his overall competence, he was her main hope in finding Masha. "What do you think?" she said.

He opened his mouth but Sergey the rook interrupted.

"You all jump to conclusions too quickly," he said. "Napoleonic bayonets? You can buy them; so many people collect antique weapons nowadays. Why do you think that everything has something to do with your private obsession?"

Galina swallowed and fell silent. Sergey was right, she thought; she had seen everything as a sign, as a personal message that would lead her to her sister. She was no different from the people she'd seen in the hospital, the ones who received secret communications on TV and saw every minor event as a coded message meant for them alone. She remembered a woman who always sat by the TV every Saturday, waiting for the announcement of winning lottery numbers. She never bought any tickets as far as anyone knew; but she wrote the numbers down anyway, and deciphered them, her brow furrowed and her lips moving in tortured concentration. Galina was just like her, and once again she looked at Zemun and Koschey, wondering whether they were really there.

Yakov touched her hand, his fingers rough and leathery. "Don't listen to him," he said. "What does he know?"

"I watched the same TV show as you," Sergey the rook said. "And they always try to make you think that you understand how it works, and you rely on it, and it always backfires when you need it to work the most."

"Will you three just stop that?" Zemun said, her usual docility broken. "Stop trying to guess; it's not a game. There are no rules. It's about our lives too, and they are as important as yours."

Koschey nodded. "You people always think it's all about you. Like we're here just to entertain you. You haven't thought that Berendey was my friend, have you?"

"You didn't seem too upset," Sergey squawked.

"Most of us are dead," Koschey said. "At some point, histrionic displays just run out. It doesn't mean that one isn't mourning."

Galina looked up at the rust-colored leaves—winter had ended, either due to Berendey's passing or Father Frost's absence—and fall foliage spread yellow and orange as far as the eye could see. Squirrels, their tails as bright orange as the leaves of oaks and ashes, ran up and down the trunks, stopping only to screech and chitter their disapproval at the travelers passing by.

There was a rustling in the branches of the tree they were passing under. Galina looked up, only to meet the gaze of a pair of incredibly large and yellow eyes slit by vertical pupils. A tiger, she thought. While she didn't expect to meet one in this climate zone, she was underground, where stranger things were common. Still, she wasn't sure if the thing in the tree was dangerous, and she remained standing.

"What's the holdup?" Yakov said once he realized Galina wasn't following.

She pointed wordlessly, and Zemun looked up and laughed.

"That's Bayun," she said. "Come down, cat, and tell us what you've seen."

The Cat Bayun descended from the tree in two graceful leaps. He turned out to be considerably smaller than a tiger, but much larger than a housecat—as big as a collie, Galina decided. He arched his striped back and yawned, his claws digging at the ground, as if plucking invisible guitar strings.

His gaze never left Galina's, and his lip hitched up, exposing long sharp mother-of-pearl canines. "I haven't seen nothing," he said in a husky, almost adolescent voice. "What are you looking for?"

Galina had heard about Bayun before, but she could not remember whether he was supposed to be good or evil. While Zemun explained the situation to him she tried to figure out whether she should be afraid of the strange talking cat—he seemed menacing. "Excuse me," she whispered to Yakov. "Do you know anything about Bayun?"

"Not much," he answered. "I think when he sings he can put you to sleep, and he is supposed to live in Thrice-Ninth Kingdom."

"He's also related to Scandinavian myth," Koschey said. "His children are the two cats that pull Freya's chariot; at least, according to some sources."

"I hadn't realized Russian fairytales were related to other religions," Yakov said.

Koschey laughed. "You're kidding, right? Most of Russia's pagan gods were borrowed from elsewhere—Scandinavia, Phoenicia, Greece, Egypt . . . you name it. There's very little original folklore here."

Galina thought it strange that mythological creatures were capable of discussing their own origins. But then again, why wouldn't they be? "Is it true that he can put people to sleep?" she asked Koschey.

He nodded, and picked up a robust, rust-colored leaf off the ground, twirled it between two fingers. "It is not just the sleeping," he said, and smiled a wan smile. "It's the dreaming you should be interested in. He can make your dreams . . . worthwhile, to say the least."

KOSCHEY WAS RIGHT. GALINA'S DREAMS WERE UNUSUALLY powerful and vivid, and as she dreamt she really believed that she was back home, in their small apartment, with grandmother in the kitchen doing something to the cabbage to make it smell. Their mother was at work, and Galina was getting ready to go to the night classes she'd been taking during her rare periods of lucidity. Masha was still in school then—she sat in the living room, oblivious to the blaring of the TV, her elbows propped on the windowsill, the open book in between them.

Galina felt guilty then, because she was a bad big sister—absent, distant, frail and unsure of what was real and what wasn't. She wanted so desperately to be there for Masha—so young, so pink, so brimming with health and hope. She wanted so badly to connect. "Homework?" Galina said.

Masha looked up from the book, her gaze momentarily snagging on something outside before turning to meet Galina's. "No, just reading."

"What?" she persisted, admiring the round contour of her sister's cheek. How old was she, anyway? Eleven, twelve? Something like that.

Masha consulted the cover. "Hamlet," she said. "Do you know that one?"

Galina smiled. "Yes. How're you liking it?"

Masha made a thoughtful face. "They all speak in verse . . . but I do like it. Especially the part about forty thousand brothers . . . that's a lot of brothers, isn't it?"

Galina nodded. She understood the quiet awe in Masha's voice—none of the kids they knew had large families, and a girl was lucky to have a big brother. It was a generally accepted truth that brothers were better than sisters—they could be strong and protective, and they were the closest thing to a father for a girl who didn't have one. Big sisters were generally useless, because they moved out and had children, and couldn't protect one.

"You wish you had a brother, don't you?" Galina said.

Masha looked guilty for a moment, but then smiled. "I would like a boy to live with us. Wouldn't you?"

"Not really," Galina said. "You're lucky you don't remember Dad."

Masha looked furtively toward the kitchen, but their grandmother remained there, ensconced in the sizzling of the vegetable oil, the clanging of the oven door and the smells of cabbage and fried onions. "Grandma is making pies," Masha said. "Tell me about our father."

There wasn't anything new to tell, but this conversation had the comfort of familiarity about it. "He was a jerk," Galina said.

"And a drunk," Masha said with conviction.

"Not so much a drunk," Galina said. "The neighbors said that Mom was crazy to let him go. Where else would you find a sober man, they said. But he just . . . he wasn't anything. I don't think he ever said a word to me. And Grandma hated him."

Masha nodded, smiling. "I guess it's good that there aren't any boys here then."

"If you say so."

"You'll be late for your school," Masha said. "Why do you go to school at night?"

"It's evening college for those who work," Galina said. "Like me. I can be late a little."

Masha gave her a penetrating look, modeled so perfectly off their mother's that Galina had to laugh. "You really have to be taking this more seriously," Masha said. "If you keep on like this, you'll never have an education, and I'll probably be married before you."

"Of course you will." Galina laughed still. "You're the one who wants boys in the house."

Masha shrugged. "Galka," she said thoughtfully. "Would you rather be deaf or blind?"

Galina weighed her options. "Deaf, I suppose. What about you?"

"Blind," Masha said. "This way, Mom will have no choice but let me get a dog."

"You have it planned out, I see," Galina said. She looked at her watch and sighed. "I have to get going, I suppose. Don't go blind just yet; maybe we can talk Mom into getting you a puppy."

Masha beamed. "Thanks, Galka. You know what I really want? I mean, besides the puppy?"

Galina looked out of the window, and saw her bus pass by. There would be another one; she sat down on the couch and kicked off her shoes. "What do you really want?"

Masha stared at the passing bus. "I want to be someone else."

"Who?"

Masha shrugged. "I don't know. Not me."

Then there was guilt again; Galina couldn't stop feeling that it was her fault also. Who would want to be a girl with a crazy sister and no brothers or a father? Who would want to be a girl with such a severe mother and silently disapproving grandmother, who constantly cooked fried potatoes, pies, borsch that tasted of frustration and suppressed anger? Who would want to be a girl in a house filled with damaged women, and no hope of ever becoming something else herself?

"I'm sorry," Galina said. "You know, things can change. It doesn't have to be this way forever."

Masha nodded. "Go," she said. "I love you, as much as forty thousand brothers."

Then the scene changed—they were in a darkened room, with sooted wooden walls. Masha was older now, but her eyes still watched Galina with a hopeful expectation. "You'll help me, won't you?"

"I've been doing nothing else," Galina said. "I'm here looking for you, with a stupid cow and Koschey the Deathless, while Mom is home with your baby."

Masha looked confused for a second. "A baby?"

Galina nodded. "But we'll talk about that later . . . in person. Now just tell me where you are."

"I'm in a castle," she said. "Although it doesn't look like a castle, but they tell me Peter the Great used to live here."

"Who are *they*?" Galina tried to keep her voice steady.

Masha shrugged. "I don't know. There are several of them, or maybe just one and he wears a different face every day."

"What do they want with you?"

"I don't know. They keep us here and send us, always send us to look and tell them what we saw. They have so many birds, and we see every corner of above and below. They take the images from our eyes and the memories from our heads, sounds from our ears and voices from our tongues . . . please come find me before we're all deaf and mute and blind."

"WHO HAS MANY FACES AND A CASTLE?" GALINA ASKED Zemun as soon as she woke up under Bayun's tree. Look at this, she thought; I'm talking in goddamn riddles. And I'm asking advice from a talking cow. And I talk to birds and cats. It's a good thing my schizophrenia is in remission.

"Hmmmm," Zemun said. "Dvoedushnik, maybe. But who knows what other creatures lurk in this forest?"

"What do you mean?" Yakov interrupted. "I thought you all knew each other."

"Do you know every person in Moscow, or even in your neighborhood?" Timur-Bey countered. "When this place was formed, some chose to build a city. Others stayed in the forest. Didn't anyone tell you it's not safe here?"

"David did," Yakov admitted. "He didn't say why."

"There's also something you might want to know," Galina told Yakov. "Remember the house of Peter the Great in Kolomenskoe that Sergey mentioned? I dreamt that it was here, in this forest."

Sergey the rook hopped onto Galina's shoulder and peered into her face. "You mean to say that this forest is actually Kolomenskoe?"

"I don't think so," Galina said. "But maybe there's a connection."

"Perhaps," Koschey said. "I'm ashamed to say that I don't know anything here that belonged to any czars."

"I do," Timur-Bey said. "And incidentally, that's not the same as the house in Kolomenskoe."

"How do you know that?" Zemun said.

"Because," Timur-Bey said, "the one here ended up underground after its above version was burned by Napoleon."

Galina and Yakov traded looks. If one didn't think too hard about it, it almost made sense—Kolomenskoe and Peter the Great and the birds—but the moment one looked at the pieces directly they fell apart again, like bits of mosaic that formed a picture if looked at from a distance but a meaningless jumble up close.

Yakov apparently felt the same way—he shook his head and sighed. "Think we're getting closer?" he asked Galina.

She nodded. "I don't care about the puzzles," she said. "I just want my sister back; you can have the rest."

Yakov produced an uncertain smile. "That sounds like a bargain," he said.

14: Napoleon

The world used to make sense; Yakov remembered that much. And yet, here, underground, he couldn't avoid the thought that the apparent sense and order was just a result of his wistful optimism. It also occurred to him that the closer he found himself to evil, the harder it was to maintain the illusion of a sensible universe.

He resented the vague and abstract quality of evil—it was always in the plural, be it thugs or communists or Chechen terrorists. It was never a person with a face and a possibility of affixing blame, at least not after some time passed; only then could evil be identified and labeled as such, but who could believe something after so much time had passed? And after living underground and hearing the denizens' stories he started to doubt that historians on the surface ever got the real meaning of anything.

Now, he felt lost among dreams and speculations, in a dark forest so big that the initially sprawling and overwhelming underground city became but a speck lost in a mosaic of trees—some frozen and leafless, others just starting to sprout their first sticky leaves: a patchwork of seasons and—Yakov suspected—times. And somewhere deep within the forest there was a palace of the czar who had abandoned Moscow for St Petersburg. And within this palace there were birds who used to be people but were now subjugated to some unknown but menacing enemies—numerous, faceless, like any other evil.

Timur-Bey led them, following landmarks only he could see; he sometimes stopped to look closely at a tree trunk or a patch of grass, or to rub the delicate skeleton of a fallen leaf between his small dry palms.

"What is he doing?" Yakov whispered to Galina. "What is he looking for?"

"I don't think he's looking for anything," Galina whispered back. "I think he's praying."

"Praying? Who's here to pray to?" He heaved a sigh and fell silent, suddenly overtaken by the thought that here, underground, there was no one to hear his prayers. He was never particularly religious, despite his mother's efforts to make him go to church and to consider his soul. Still, there was a certainty that if he ever had the fancy to pray there would be someone to listen; at least his mother assured him that it was so. Here, there was instead the bleak knowledge that all the gods that had any power were dead, and he was instead at the mercy of strange creatures with unclear motives. It was no wonder then that he looked to Galina for support.

But she seemed preoccupied. Ever since the dreams of her sister started, she grew more distant and anxious by the day, as if a part of her strained ahead, leaving behind the rest that couldn't keep up. "It's like a bad dream," she told Yakov. "You know the ones when you're trying to run but can't or only move very slowly?"

He nodded. "I think everyone has those."

"It's strange, isn't it," Galina said. "It's not like anyone ever had an actual experience of running in molasses. I wonder where this dream comes from."

"Walking through mud," Yakov said. "The place I used to live, there was so much mud, especially after the rains started. There was construction everywhere."

"Sounds like my neighborhood," Galina said. "There used to be an apple orchard, and now it's just dirt and railroad."

"I remember," Yakov said. "I'm just two streets down from you, by the supermarket and the liquor store."

"And the glass factory," Galina said. "The one Sergey talked about. Isn't it strange, how we lived so close and yet never knew what was going on there, with thugs and magic?"

"I suppose. But isn't it even stranger that there's a whole damn world under our feet, and nobody knows about it?"

"Yeah," Galina said, her forehead furrowing in the habitual pattern of narrow lines that were getting permanently entrenched in her smooth skin. "But someone has to know. The KGB probably does—how can they not?"

Yakov shrugged; he did not share Galina's conviction although he had encountered this particular belief many times—perfectly reasonable people often believed that the KGB was all-knowing, and ascribed to them a superhuman competence. It made it easier to swallow that way, he supposed; if the evil was all-knowing and all-powerful, one could not be too hard on oneself for being a victim. And there was comfort in this belief in the omnipotence of the KGB—not always pleasant, perhaps, but better than the alternative; who wanted to live in fear of a mere shadow?

Yakov sighed. "Maybe not. This place . . . even if someone

knew about it, who would believe it? I'm here, and even I expect to wake up at any moment. It's so weird that I don't even know how to act most of the time . . . I met my dead grandfather, for crying out loud. I don't get it how you can be like this."

"Like what?" Galina looked toward the ground under her walking feet.

"Like all this . . . like it's real. You're taking it seriously."

"I have to," she said. "My sister is here. And you . . . after I saw what the boatman did to you, I think you're taking it pretty seriously too."

"I don't want to talk about that." Yakov picked up his pace. He looked at the trees, long beards of Icelandic moss undulating in the wind, the dark needles of black spruces casting a deep shadow over the narrow path, and felt deeply unsettled, just like he did under the unblinking gaze of the boatman when the icy fingers of his mind probed and sifted through Yakov's memories. And just on the edges of them, a sound stirred—a thin piercing cry, tearing the night silence apart like a sharp needle, and then falling silent. The night seemed so much quieter and colder now than before that cry started, and the hole left by the removed memory ached, like the phantom limb of a mutilated soldier.

Timur-Bey seemed to be nearing the goal—he stopped less, and forged ahead down the path overgrown with brambles and lamb's ear. Zemun followed closely behind, trampling down the vegetation with her hooves to make the way passable for the rest, although Yakov suspected that Koschey was far too inured to such minor obstacles to pay attention, and that Zemun's effort was for Yakov's and Galina's benefit.

The forest around them changed again, as it did many times

on this journey. The trees changed from spruces to birches, and light played across their golden heart-shaped leaves. The path also widened, as if it had been recently traveled. The air opened up around them, and Yakov realized how suffocated he felt under the closed canopy of the spruces. Birches were so much nicer, so much more pastoral—they reminded him of the ubiquitous sentimentally patriotic paintings, always with birches and blue skies, always about the transcendent quality of the Russian forests and other natural habitats. But right now, he was glad to see them.

The clearings gaped at them from the right and left, soft succulent meadows of long rich grass, sharp sedges fringing the wet meadow margins where a brook gurgled in its gentle idiot tongue.

"Wait," Timur-Bey whispered, and kneeled to examine footprints in the soft ground.

Yakov was not an experienced tracker, but even he could see that the meadow was thoroughly trampled.

"These are bare feet," Timur-Bey pointed. "And these—not quite bare, but quite close. It looks like their boots are falling apart."

Sergey flapped his wings and hopped awkwardly to the ground. He half-hopped, half-ran to Timur-Bey's side, peering at a deep oval depression filled with murky swamp water. "This is the butt of a rifle," he said.

"Or a musket," Timur-Bey agreed. "Didn't they use to say that the bullet is stupid and the bayonet is wise?"

"Maybe a musket," Sergey said. "My point is, we should probably be quiet and not attract attention."

"Maybe they're friendly," Zemun said.

"They have guns," Koschey said. "Not that it bothers me, but you fleshbags should probably keep it under advisement. Bare-footed men with large guns are rarely in a good enough mood to chat before shooting."

"I don't like this," Galina said.

The rook squawked with laughter. "The large gun part or the men part?"

"Oh, leave her alone," Yakov said.

"I'm just saying," Sergey said. "You don't like men much, do you?"

Galina shifted her shoulders uncomfortably and slouched. "No. What's your point?"

"Enough," Yakov interrupted. "This is really not a good time." It was true, of course; at the same time, Yakov did not particularly relish the subject. He knew Galina; she had grown up the same way he had—without a father, among women hardened by bitter life experience. She had no reason to feel any differently than she did, and yet he felt guilty the moment that 'no' left her lips. Like it was his fault somehow—but then again, he had left his wife. Or perhaps it was she who had left him; he couldn't remember anymore, not through the cobwebs of lies and rationalizations and retellings of the same story over and over to himself, until the details took on the shape of his words, and the words themselves became the truth and the substance, their underlying memory forever lost, like the wax mold of a death mask.

They moved along the road, under the sparse cover of the trees. The shadows of thin branches and leaves weaved in patterns of light and dark, breaking up and concealing the shapes of people and the cow that moved below them. The meadows disappeared, supplanted by patches of rough scrub—bushes and goldenrods, willow herbs growing through the charred remains of some long-forgotten buildings.

The trees receded, and they stood between the overgrown ruins and a tall palisade, made of thick and long logs fitted together side by side, their sharpened ends threatening to pierce the distant sky. They could not see what was hidden behind the fence, only a curlicue of smoke rising from behind it, and a strong smell of burnt wood tainting the air so strongly Yakov tasted it on the back of his throat.

"Something's burning," Galina said.

Timur-Bey shook his head. "It's not burning; it had burnt, many years ago, but it still smolders. Like they do." He pointed with a nod.

There were five men there, standing and sitting under the shadow of the fence, dressed in rags; their feet were wrapped in remnants of rough sailcloth, and muskets rested on their shoulders. But Yakov looked into their faces—red as if boiled, their beards and eyebrows singed or burned off, their eyes the blind white of a cooked egg. Their nails, trimmed with mourning black, bubbled as if melting off their fingertips. Their rags were covered in soot, but Yakov guessed them for military uniforms, even though it was impossible to see the insignia; he guessed that they were from the early nineteenth century, but could not determine their allegiance. At least, until they spoke.

"Hey, Petro," one of them called. "What time is it?"

"Who cares what time it is?" Petro replied and spat philosophically. "Does time even have meaning anymore?"

One of the others nodded and sat down, resting the musket across his knees. "And for what sins are we being punished so?" he said. "What sins have I committed, dear Lord in heaven, to guard the fence of a burned building for all eternity? What sins, what sins are so great to merit such a punishment? Dear Lord, forgive me my trespasses, lowly sinner that I am, and deliver me from this torment."

"Shut up about your sins, Corporal," the one named Petro said with a stifled laugh. "Who's to say sins have anything to do with this fence? And who's to say whose sins are greater?"

A general murmur of agreement emitted from the rest of the soldiers.

"I suffer so," the Corporal said.

Collective groans of annoyance were his answer, and Yakov decided that for the past hundred and eighty years the Corporal's suffering had been getting on his comrades' nerves.

Yakov and the rest had all agreed that a direct approach would be the most foolish one; instead, they decided to rely on an old-fashioned deception—rather, Zemun and Koschey decided on it, while Galina and Yakov rolled their eyes at each other and shook their heads in disbelief. Timur-Bey and Sergey remained neutral on the matter.

"Seriously," Yakov said to Zemun. "Trojan horses have been done before."

"It's not the same," Zemun said. "There's no one inside me." She sounded hurt, and Yakov didn't argue further.

They watched Zemun as she approached the gates, her

jaws moving rhythmically, and her eyes as empty as those of a regular cow. The soldiers at the gate turned to watch her with their blind white eyes.

"What's that?" the Corporal asked.

"Looks like a cow, Corporal," Petro said, and stroked his bare face thoughtfully, as if he expected to find a beard. "A beauty of a cow, too."

The rest muttered that it was a nice enough cow, yes sir, sure was.

"I haven't had have any milk in ages," Petro said. "Or cheese, for that matter."

The corporal stopped lamenting the cruelty of his fate, and smiled. Zemun let herself be led inside, and Yakov heaved a sigh. He only hoped that the plan wouldn't backfire too badly.

When night fell, the gate in the tall fence swung open, lit from the inside by the ghostly blue light of the celestial cow, and Zemun herself motioned for them to come in. Inside the gate there was a yard of tightly tamped dirt; every pockmark and trough stood out in stark relief, like craters on the moon's surface, illuminated by pools of light. There were stars strewn about, and their blue and white rays pierced the darkness like spotlights.

"What happened here?" Yakov asked, pointing at the globes of pure light littering the bare yard.

"They tried to milk me," Zemun answered, and looked sullen. "But I don't think they suspect anything."

Galina exhaled an unconvincing laugh. "Of course not. Why would they?"

Yakov looked past the scattered stars and forgot about the

danger and everything else, gaping at the wooden palace that towered over them. The facets cut into its smooth light walls reminded him of the palaces in the Kremlin, and the gilded onion domes topping seven slender towers appeared more beautiful than any buildings he had ever seen. "What is this?" he whispered.

"That," Timur-Bey said, "used to be one of the oldest buildings of the Kremlin."

"It's all stone now," Galina said.

"It used to be all wood," Timur-Bey said, his almond-shaped eyes dark and stark in the grounded starlight. "I remember it; the Tatars burned a few of those palaces . . . and they kept burning throughout history. Your people rebuilt them in stone, but some of the old buildings made it here. This one . . . I hear that Napoleon burned it . . . Moscow burned for many days then."

Moscow burned for many days then. Historians argue about who started the fires. Some said it was the Russians, intent on depriving the invaders of food and shelter. They burned the houses and the food stores, the shops and the warehouses; they did not care that the privation would affect them too. Others said that the Napoleonic troops burned the Kremlin on purpose and everything else by accident, due to the windy weather and too many unattended cooking fires in their encampments. Yakov didn't know who it was, and it didn't seem important to him, but he did wonder how the soldiers they had seen—Petro and the corporal and the rest—ended up here. He could imagine it now—burned and injured, suffocating from smoke, their mouths tasting of ash, they stumbled through fire and sparks, wincing at the crashing of the great beams of the palace burning around them. They must've seen the doorway, distorted by heat and smoke, and rushed through. He thought they were soldiers, probably used to fighting and routing and shooting and stabbing, but not this, not being caught in a burning building, gilded with molten flames. He imagined a despair great enough, a fear powerful enough to pick up the ghost of the stately building that roared and collapsed in a tornado of fire and howling smoke, and to bring it with them underground . . . even though Yakov suspected that they were not as much underground as on the other side, in some unseen lining of the known world.

ZEMUN HAD DONE A BIT OF RECONNAISSANCE—SHE KNEW the sheds and the piles of firewood in the yard, the small barracks where the soldiers with burned hair and boiled white eyes sat in dreamless sleep all night long. She still did not know who was inside, since the palace's gates were locked tight. They decided to wait until morning, hiding in one of the sheds filled with half-rotten logs and rusted axes.

Galina kept looking up, searching for something in the molded ceiling beams.

Yakov guessed that she was looking for birds. "They're not there," he whispered.

She nodded, still looking up, as if expecting them to materialize out of the surrounding stale air. Yakov looked too, squinting up into the cupped ceiling, where shadows grew dense in the corners, reaching for the thickly hewn supports and twining around them in an elaborate chiaroscuro. If he squinted and tilted his head, the shadows shifted and something glinted between his eyelashes, impossible to see directly but shifting to the corners of his vision and dancing and taunting, they twinkled like the stars that fell out of Zemun's udders, like large slow drops of magical milk.

Galina watched them too; she asked, "Did you have a kaleidoscope when you were a kid?"

"Of course," Yakov said. "Show me a kid who didn't."

Sergey the rook squawked in the affirmative on Yakov's shoulder, and Yakov felt sudden and acute pity for this man, a criminal imprisoned in a bird's body, at yet another similarity, another reminder that he used to be a child too, and that he and Yakov shared many experiences, few things being unique in the mass-manufactured Soviet childhood.

"Did you ever break yours open?" Yakov asked Galina.

She smiled, finally looking away from the ceiling and meeting his eyes. "Of course. Every kid does—how can you not want to see all those treasures inside?"

Yakov smiled at the memory. There was nothing of interest inside that cardboard tube, slightly dented at the end where the plastic caps fitted, one of them with an eyepiece. There were several small mirrors inside that tube, and nothing but a button, a glass bead and several triangular pieces of colored paper. "That was messed up," he said. "I cried for hours afterwards."

Galina nodded. "It's funny how everyone goes through this kaleidoscope thing. You think the adults do it on purpose?"

"Why?"

"To teach the kids something . . . I don't know."

Sergey huffed. "Teach what? The illusory nature of the world?"

Galina shrugged. "Maybe. Or the futility of beauty, or something depressing like that. I still don't understand adults, even though I am one myself."

"No you're not," Sergey said. "You don't have kids. Neither do I, so don't feel bad. See, I figured it all out guarding the nuclear silo—I always felt like a kid, you know, just playing a game or something, like I just pretended to be a soldier with a stick for a gun. And there was a lot of time to think. So I figured it all out. You're either a parent or you're a kid. As long as you don't have kids of your own and become a parent, you're a kid. So, Yakov, what are you?"

Yakov couldn't decide which one he was—neither a child nor a parent felt right. "I don't know," he said. "But that day when I broke that kaleidoscope, I swore that my kids would never have one of those things. Damn depressing, and a horrible toy to give to anyone. I wouldn't be one of those asshole parents that teach kids nothing but how much everything sucks and that the world is messed up."

"It is messed up," Galina said. "In case you haven't noticed, we're underground. With a talking cow and Koschey the Deathless, about to ask a bunch of soldiers circa 1812 why on earth did they kill a beloved fairytale character with a bayonet. Also, my sister is missing."

"I'm sorry about that," Yakov said. "That part is indeed messed up. But everything else . . . it's not too bad. Is it?"

"No," Galina said. "It's not. I always dreamt of a secret

place like that . . . I just wish I found it under better circumstances."

"You can't get here under better circumstances," Timur-Bey said from the darkness in the corner of the shed. "Haven't you been paying attention?"

"Perhaps we should sleep a bit," Sergey said, and hid his head under his wing.

"I don't feel like it," Yakov said.

Galina snuggled against Zemun's flank. "Neither do I."

Zemun smiled. She seemed content now, peaceful. "Why sleep when you can talk?" she said. "Just keep it down. There are enemies afoot."

Yakov moved closer to Galina. "Sorry if it's too personal," he said. "But you mentioned—that you were hospitalized before?"

Galina let his half-question hang, unanswered, for a few seconds as she frowned as if gathering her thoughts. "Schizophrenia," she said, finally.

Yakov was surprised. She didn't seem crazy, at least most of the time. "You look normal to me," he finally mumbled, and cringed. Now she would think that he doubted her veracity.

"Thanks," she said instead. "It comes and goes. They call it sluggish schizophrenia—ever heard of it?"

He did. It was a fake diagnosis for political malcontents, as far as he remembered. A convenient way of oppression that did not require prisons. He looked at Galina with pity—she seemed like such a small woman, so hurt and broken up about her sister, so driven with the desperate resolve of the one who had very little of value in life and would fight for the last thing that was left for her.

He didn't know how to tell her, and whether he should tell her at all—that the disease they diagnosed her with did not really exist, that it was a fabrication. He wondered if it would do any good to tell a person who believed herself crippled that she was not—would it fix her, or would it become a crushing burden? He tried to imagine what it would be like, to reconsider his concept of self, to find that he was not what he thought he was—would it be liberating or devastating? "Yes," he finally said. "I heard of it. You seem to be dealing with it well."

Galina smiled, grateful. "My mom," she said. "She was the one who thought there was something wrong with me when I was just little. Funny how she foresaw it—I started having hallucinations after she said I had to go to a hospital."

"Uncanny," Yakov muttered. "Do you think it's possible that being in the hospital was maybe not the best thing for you?"

She stopped smiling. "Of course I thought about it. What, do you think I'm stupid? But it doesn't really matter now, does it?"

"I guess not," Yakov said. "Sorry I brought it up."

"It's all right," Galina said. "But I'm tired now. Mind if I sleep a little?"

"Go ahead," Yakov said.

Galina rested her head on Zemun's flank and closed her eyes with a sigh. Yakov remained sitting, listening to the crying of an imaginary baby somewhere in his mind, on the very edge of hearing, so that even he couldn't say whether it was a memory or just a ringing of the frayed nerves. He waited for morning.

15: Kolomenskoe

There were many parks in Moscow—the ones in the old city, the white city, were there for recreation and entertainment, some complete with Ferris wheels and lemonade stands, the kiosks that sold everything under the sun, including gin-and-tonic in a can. The ones in the outskirts, Tsaritsino and Kolomenskoe, were different. These felt like real places that existed regardless of people's presence. The churches in Kolomenskoe and the palace in Tsaritsino were real as well—perhaps damaged by age and neglect, perhaps speckled with bird droppings and the twinkling fragments of broken bottles; but in their old age they remained stately, dreaming, it seemed to Fyodor, of the days that slipped by them, the days that decorated their facades with weathered brick and stubborn splotches of lichen as they went away forever, leaving the buildings in their wake like the skeletons of distant shipwrecks.

He looked at the reflection in the river—they were in Kolomenskoe now, and the river here was lively enough to resist the stiff embrace of ice that started to form along the shores. But in the center the water remained black and clear, as if purified by the early frosts of oil and other contamination. The snow fell, touching the clear black mirror without a ripple, dissolving quietly in the white apparition of the reflected church.

They had scaled the fence to get there. Oksana snapped a few slender birch branches and started a small fire. It melted a small crater in the snow, and they sat next to it, watching the river and the snow. Fyodor's hands warmed over the flames, but his back felt numb from the cold. He moved closer to the flames.

"Careful," Oksana said. "You'll set yourself on fire."

"Better fire than hypothermia," Fyodor said. "I saw that guy once, in the hospital. His temperature dropped so low, the only way to warm him up was to put tubes in his chest and pour warm water through them. I was one bed over, and I remember the water sloshing in and out of his chest. Weird sound, that. Nothing quite like it. It slurped."

"Sounds awful," Oksana said. "I saw people freeze to death too. The key is to stay awake and keep the fire going. There're no ambulances here, and they won't find us until the morning."

"If then. No one comes here in winter."

"It's still fall."

"Same difference. Who would go for a walk in such weather?"

"I hope that Sergey's friends would."

"Perhaps." He tossed another branch into the flames. "Where's your *tabor*?"

She jerked her shoulders, irritable. "I don't know. Maybe they moved on, to Ukraine or somewhere south."

"Why don't you look for them?" Fyodor asked. "Because of me?"

"You're an outsider," she admitted. "Most Roma don't like outsiders. But with me, I think you'd be all right."

"Why don't you look for them then?"

"Maybe in the morning." She sighed. "It's difficult. I spent so much time among Russians, I feel like an outsider myself most of the time. The trouble is, you can't live in two worlds—you always pick one, even if you don't mean to."

"I think I know what you're saying," Fyodor said. "Most of the time you don't even know that you've already chosen." He fell quiet, thinking of the summer of his eighteenth year when he failed the exams and never went home. There had been nothing keeping him from going, except that he just didn't. Couldn't. "You never know until it's too late to do anything about it."

Oksana slouched more, digging her hands deeper under her bent knees. The rats pressed closer around her, in a protective circle of warmth. "It's like when you're a kid, and then one day you realize you're ashamed of your parents, and you don't even know how it happened. Everyone gets embarrassed of their parents at some point, I think. I just didn't know one could be embarrassed of an entire people."

"I know how you feel," Fyodor said. "I think."

Oksana shrugged. "Everyone does to some extent, I suppose. Doesn't make it any easier."

"No," Fyodor agreed, and looked at the sky that was growing gray over the river. Morning was coming, and he turned to look behind him, at the palimpsest of a path, almost invisible under the thick snow swaddling the ground in its soft embrace. There were crosses of bird prints between the white silent trees, becoming slowly visible as the daylight grew with every minute, imperceptibly at first but quickly gaining strength. The fire burned out, leaving a black scorched circle that stared at them like an empty eye socket from the gently sloping face of the riverbank.

"I suppose we better go check out the cabin," Fyodor said.

They found it with ease—there were snow-covered signs everywhere, which detailed directions and historical irrelevancies in two languages. Really, Fyodor thought, who cared where the cabin was transported from, log-by-log? What did it matter if Peter the Great decided to move the capital to St Petersburg? Was there any significance to the fact that Peter was the first czar to be crowned with a crown made in Western style, indistinguishable from those of European monarchs, and scorned the Helm of Monomakh? He remembered that helm, displayed in one of the Kremlin's museums. It looked like a regular hat, save for the abundance of jewels and the cross that topped it. The museum guide explained that Monomakh's Helm symbolized the transition of the seat of power from Byzantium to Russia, and that since Byzantium was heir to the Roman Empire, this is why Russia was considered the third Rome. He spoke about the legacies of early Christianity, of the terrible and ancient heritage. Fyodor understood with a vague animal instinct why Peter the Great—the ticcy, twitchy, narrow-chested giant—would want to avoid this legacy, already replicated ad infinitum in the shapes of church roofs and fur hats everywhere.

It wasn't about control of the sea, Fyodor though as the virgin snow crunched and gave under his freezing feet, toes curled inside his oversized army boots. It wasn't about Peter's training in Europe or infatuation with the West. It was all about escape—escape from this blasted city with its terrible history buried deep underground, with its oppressive Byzantine past. Peter could not bear this place, suspended between worlds, and he chose a new alliance and built a new city, European and clean, where the streets ran in a grid instead of meandering drunkenly up and down the seven hills of Moscow. So Peter fled, Fyodor thought, fled in self-preservation, into the cold and sterile embrace of the Baltic. Who could blame him?

They saw the cabin from between barren trees frosted with sparkling ice, icicles festooning the branches like candy. Fyodor could taste the familiar crystalline pure flavor of them, unforgettable since childhood.

"You think anyone is in there?" Oksana whispered.

Fyodor examined the snow on the path leading to the cabin's door. "Nothing from this side, at least."

"That's good," Oksana said. "Sergey said that other guy used to go there at night."

The door creaked on its hinges and opened under Fyodor's push. There was a smell of neglect—a sour stench of spilled beer and a whiff of stale air. The cabin—a small room with a soiled floor, strewn with beer bottles and rags—was empty.

Fyodor breathed with a mix of relief and disappointment. "No one here," he said, and waited for Oksana to come in, stomping her feet and clapping her hands. Her long hair had frozen in a fringe of icicles, and he fought the temptation to break one off and suck it, like a child would.

"We should've come here at night," she said.

"Should've," Fyodor agreed, "only you were too scared last night, remember?"

Oksana shot him a nasty look. "I was not scared. It just didn't seem like a good idea, to rush into something dangerous in the middle of the night. Now, we at least know where everything is, and we can hide here and wait."

Fyodor shook his head. "Why don't we go and find that Slava character?"

"Where would you find him?"

"Sergey said, he liked to hang out by the Tsaritsino marketplace. Let's go there, check it out. I'm not staying in this cabin all day. At the very least, we can find some food there. We'll leave a few rats to keep watch for us, yeah?"

"I haven't any money," Oksana said.

"Neither do I. We'll just have to improvise."

"If you're expecting me to steal, you're out of luck."

Fyodor laughed, the sound reverberating off the old walls. "No," he said. "Of course not. I'll do the honors."

THEY TOOK THE SUBWAY—JUST THREE STOPS. UNEXPECTEDLY the turnstile at the entrance of the station took the changeless coins Fyodor offered it, and for the first time in god knows how long he rode the subway lawfully—at least somewhat. It was past the rush hour, and they found seats, even though they did not have long to travel. Fyodor always found thinking on the train easy and pleasant, with the dark tunnel enclosing the rushing train securely, like a glove, and the lights on the walls of the tunnel whooshing by with comforting regularity. He let his mind drift then, images and thoughts traveling through his mind—he imagined himself rushing like the train, and his thoughts were just brief stationary flashes of light he was passing by, given an illusion of movement by his own unstoppable momentum.

He watched the faces of the people sitting across from him—old ladies, mostly, now that everyone else was at work; old ladies with eyes lost in nests of wrinkles, and thick woolen kerchiefs swathed around their heads; their darkened hands were folded on their laps or clutched grocery bags. There were also bums who smelled of urine and alcohol, and Fyodor thought that it had been almost twelve hours since he had his last drink. His hands felt itchy and restless, humming with some fool energy that would soon turn into shakes.

"I need a drink," he whispered to Oksana.

She eyed him with mild disgust. "It can wait."

"No." He held up one hand, palm down, the trembling of his fingers now buzzing, subsonic, visible. "It really can't."

Oksana sighed, and looked away. "We'll get you something at the market," she said. "Just don't fall apart on me, all right?"

He nodded and stared at the two teenagers sitting by the door at the end of the car. The rest depressed him too much.

Oksana's disapproval didn't bother him—he was used to tisking and looks that mixed disgust with pity; he was even bored with the regret and self-loathing that were common to the point of cliché with every drinker he knew. He just wanted to get his drink and get on with the task at hand. It wasn't so bad, really; how many people needed to take their medication every day? How many couldn't get out of bed without their pills and unguents? Alcohol was his medication and unguent, and he saw nothing shameful in that.

The train pulled into the station, and he followed Oksana onto the platform. As he watched the train leave, he wondered briefly what would happen if he threw himself at the glistening windows once again—would he be transported back underground, or would he shatter the glass and plummet along with the waterfall of hard sharp shards onto the tracks that already hummed with the arrival of the next train? Would the two minutes between the trains be enough to scramble up the tall cement walls that separated them from the platform, or would he be too dazed to do anything but stand on the tracks, staring into the approaching lights and roar and brimstone of the next train?

Oksana tugged his sleeve. "Let's go," she said. "No point in waiting."

"There's always a point in waiting," he said, remembering all the times when he waited, vaguely, for something or someone to transport him, to steal him away. But the gypsies were not coming for him, and he followed her to the exit, slouching more with every step, his mind growing feverish in the absence of medication.

They ascended the stairs to the surface within a dense crowd—the market did a brisk business. Despite his shaking hands, Fyodor scoped the crowd. It was cold enough for people to wear bulky coats, and even a clumsy pickpocket could expect a measure of success. As they shuffled up the stairs, side by side, pressed together, waddling like penguins, he let his fingers slip into an old woman's pocket, warm and cavernous. There was no wallet, but his fingers closed on a piece of paper. A single note, barely enough for a drink, but it was all he wanted. He stuffed it into his pocket and slowed his step to fall behind in case his victim discovered the injury inflicted on her.

Oksana shook her head but said nothing, even as he stopped at a kiosk at the underground crossing and bought a gin-and-tonic in a can. He drank it on the spot, feeling the tremor leave his fingers almost instantaneously. He tossed the empty can in the direction of the several stray dogs sleeping peacefully by the kiosk.

“It’s cute,” Oksana said. “I always see these strays in the subway crossings, and people always step around them so carefully. Even when their legs are outstretched no one ever steps on them.”

“I just wish the vendors wouldn’t feed them,” Fyodor said. “Look how fat they are. And if they keep feeding the lazy curs they’ll never leave.”

“And where would you like them to go?” Oksana wanted to know.

He shrugged, indifferent. “Should we go to the market?”

The rats shifted under his coat, eager to get on with it. Fyodor thought that he would’ve preferred some more substantial reinforcement than the rats—a gun, perhaps, would be welcome when dealing with career criminals.

They ascended the steps. The market entrance—an open gate made of hollow aluminum bars—was to their left, and through it they saw the snow on the ground kneaded by the multitude of feet into dirty slush, the makeshift counters which displayed a scattering of awkward co-op-produced clothing and shoes, lost amidst a sea of knockoff T-shirts, duffel bags, and jeans, with words like ‘Nike’ and ‘Jordache’ in careless stitching, more of a gesture than any genuine attempt at deception.

Oksana walked along the counters, her gaze occasionally lingering on a handbag or a blouse; Fyodor worried that she would be distracted by the abundance of shiny objects around her, but she held all right. Fyodor's gaze searched the crowd, looking for the obligatory maroon jackets and gold chains. He had never met Slava but he knew the type.

The crowd was predominantly female and elderly, and Fyodor was growing disappointed, until the smell of lamb and cilantro attracted his attention. Like most heavy drinkers, he was not particularly interested in food, but the kebob shack from which the smells emanated seemed like a good place for the racketeers to congregate.

Oksana apparently thought the same—she sniffed the air and swallowed hard.

"Maybe they're in there," Fyodor said. "Let's check it out."

"I'm hungry," Oksana said.

He should've felt guilty at that. Instead, he cased the market for the shoppers absorbed in examining the wares and the seams on the garments, liable as they were to fall apart at the slightest provocation. He walked past them, his hands now steady, dipping casually into pockets and purses, until a sweaty crumpled wad of bills lay in his hand. "All set," he told Oksana. "Come on, we'll get you something to eat. And for your rats, too."

The rats responded with enthusiastic shuffling under his coat, pressing to get closer to the sleeve openings.

Fyodor and Oksana entered the shack, indistinguishable

from any other establishment of this sort. A sweaty individual in a wifebeater manned the counter, and the dense smells of onions and lamb mingled with the more delicate fragrance of cilantro and chives. The plastic tables stood empty, except for the one at the corner, where tobacco smell and low male voices hung thick. Out of the corner of his eye Fyodor noticed a swath of maroon and a flash of yellow, and stepped to the counter to order. They took their plastic plates filled with kebobs—chunks of greasy charred meat and a pitiful scattering of herbs for garnish—to the table by the door, where they could watch the thugs unobtrusively. Fyodor was tempted to get a shot of vodka, but decided against it. For once, he judged sobriety preferable. Besides, it was expensive nowadays. Gorbachev's quaint attempts to ennoble the national character by discouraging drinking were getting on Fyodor's nerves, and even though the push for alcohol-free weddings (which, Fyodor supposed, would eventually lead to immaculate conceptions) was largely over, prices never fell to their pre-Gorbachev levels.

Apparently, the thugs at the other table felt the same way. They were involved in an animated discussion about using a pressure cooker to make moonshine. "It's perfect," one of them said. Judging by his sloping shoulders and mangled ears, he was a retired boxer. "In a small apartment, yeah? You can use sugar, or grain, or potatoes, and then just distill it with the pressure cooker. I have a fermenting jar, fits behind the sofa in the kitchen, it's maybe thirty liters. Takes like an hour to put it through the pressure cooker to distill. Good stuff, barely smells or anything, and no hangover."

"My neighbor distills twice," said the one Fyodor surmised

was Slava. "He's a chemist, so he has all this equipment—Bunsen burners, and what not. And those twisty glass tubes."

"With the cooker you don't have to distill twice," the ex-boxer said. "It comes clean the first time. Or you could just make wine—saves the trouble."

"Grapes are expensive, though," another thug said.

The ex-boxer waved his hand dismissively. "Use raisins," he said. "I don't get why they're cheaper than grapes, but there you go. More sugar per kilo, too."

Fyodor studied the man he assumed was Slava—younger than his companions and slim in a way that suggested erratic eating habits rather than a vigorous exercise regimen, he looked like the brains of the concern rather than its muscle.

Slava seemed distracted—he often glanced at his heavy metal watch that clanged with a quiet satisfaction of wealth, and rubbed his face, flashing several large rings every time he raised his hand. Fyodor noticed a slight trembling of his thin fingers, pale as the cuff of his cream-colored shirt. The cuff slid back, exposing what Fyodor took for a tattoo—a dark triangle surrounding three circles—and Slava pulled it up hastily. He looked up and Fyodor barely had time to look away. The afterimage lingered, and he whispered to Oksana, "Did you see that tattoo?"

"It's not a tattoo," she whispered back through a mouthful of meat and cilantro. "It's a burn."

"How do you know?"

She shrugged, chewing with great energy. "Looks . . . like . . . it." She didn't eat her bread, but instead stuffed bits of it up her sleeves, where they disappeared with alacrity. The rats were hungry too. She passed Fyodor a slice, and he offered it to the rats that settled like a warm, breathing shroud around his middle, concealed by the coat but giving him a paunchy appearance.

The thugs ate in silence now, hurried along by the impatient glances and sighs of their leader.

Oksana whispered into her sleeve, and one of the smaller rats plopped to the floor, apparently climbing out of her boot.

Fyodor looked around, worried, but no one but him had noticed the brown streak of fur crossing the linoleum floor decorated with puddles of melted snow and dirt, and darting under the thug's table. Fyodor held his breath as the little rat, following Oksana's instructions, climbed up the chair leg and slid into the seat next to Slava. He seemed too preoccupied to notice the pink twitching nose and two small, strangely human hands examining the contents of his pocket. The rat had to duck as he opened his jacket and extracted a wallet from the inner pocket.

The thugs paid and exited, still talking about the relative advantages of sugar over raisins. Fyodor and Oksana waited for the door to slam closed, before paying for their meal. The rat had darted back, its head held high and something glistening in its mouth.

Oksana bent down to collect the reconnaissance rat onto her palm. She plucked the small round object from its mouth, and gave it to Fyodor.

A small sphere of green lunar glass rolled in his palm, warm and a bit wet. He thought he felt it pulsing with a suppressed breath and heaving of life, and he shuddered trying to imagine what it would be like, having one's soul encased in a tiny glass cocoon like a fly in amber.

They returned to Kolomenskoe. The traffic must've been bad—the thugs barely overtook them. Fyodor saw them from across the street of the park's central entrance, exiting the maroon Merc that matched their jackets, and stretching their legs.

"There's just no point in driving in Moscow," Fyodor said.

"It's not about speed," Oksana said. "It's about being able to afford not to take the subway."

At this moment, Fyodor acutely missed the good old Soviet days, when everyone was poor enough for the subway, except a few apparatchiks with government-issued black shiny Volgas. He remembered his stepfather being keenly suspicious of everyone who had a car, assuming that it was ill-gotten, through bribery or theft; he was usually right, Fyodor thought, as much as he disliked agreeing with his stepfather.

He despised him a little too, for being such a working drudge, for wasting his life in gloomy joyless labor at one factory or another, never actively hating his job but not liking it either—as if there wasn't enough life left in him, oppressed by the routine and boredom, to summon even a shred of enthusiasm for either. As unenviable as Fyodor's life was, he comforted himself by saying that at least it wasn't as bleak as his stepfather's. He had no notion of where his actual father might be, but hoped for the sake of the man he had never met that it was not dreary.

"We need to find out whose soul this is," Oksana said.

"How do we do that?"

She nodded at the pack of jackdaws industriously pecking at the snow.

"Do you think it'd work?" Fyodor said.

"It worked with Sergey and that rook," she said. "We can try it."

"How do we catch one?"

Oksana glanced around to make sure there was no one watching them; Fyodor thought that to the passersby they were invisible, too ordinary to draw attention. When she was content that there was no one paying them any mind, she shook several rats out of her sleeves, and pointed them toward the birds.

Fyodor was skeptical at first, but the rats were faster and more organized than he expected. They broke into two groups, outflanking one of the birds and cutting it off from the rest of the flock. Just as the bird noticed that it was surrounded and raised its wings, ready to fly, the rats pounced all at once, like a pride of tiny, well-coordinated lions. The bird squawked once and was overwhelmed, buried under the shifting mass of fur and agile tails.

"Don't you eat it," Oksana called to the rats in a scolding voice. The snow crunched under her boots as she approached the fallen bird, still pinned under its attackers. She picked it up, ruffled but unharmed, and stuck the glass granule into the wide-open beak quivering in distress.

The bird swallowed hard, working the round foreign object into its crop. Then the bird spoke.

His name was Vladimir, and he used to be a businessman—the real kind, not one of those thugs and racketeers who only called themselves businessmen but had never done an honest day's work. Vladimir was among the brave few who were the first to open co-ops; his manufactured carpets and pseudo-Persian rugs, and business was good. His story was sad in its familiarity: at first, there were several gangs extorting and threatening, and he did what everyone else had to do—he chose the lesser of the many evils that beset him to rob him blind. Even 'lesser' was a relative term. He couldn't quite distinguish between them, coming and going, robbing and threatening, brandishing electric irons and pliers, their favored instruments of persuasion and extraction of assets, confessions and on occasion teeth. They even looked the same: back in the day before maroon jackets, they all wore their hair short, their torsos clad in leather jackets. For comfort and freedom of movement they wore track pants, just like back in the days when their favorite occupation was forcible shearing of hippies. Vladimir wished that they had remained on the fringe and never even entered the consciousness of the budding entrepreneurs, but there they were, fully in view and menacing from every corner.

He went with Slava because he had the appearance of a member of the intelligentsia, with his thin fingers and tired but kind eyes, with his habit of nodding thoughtfully along with the pleadings of his extortees. He was a reader too, given to quoting from John Stuart Mill and Jonathan Swift; he was fond of Thomas Mann and Remarque. Vladimir chose him as his protection—his roof, in the vernacular with which had become disconcertingly familiar—because if he had to be subordinate to someone, he wanted that someone to be an educated man. Just a small vanity, he thought.

But there was danger in being under protection of a man who liked to consider whether personal experience was the limit for one's imagination, and whether it was possible to invent a truly alien creature, for example, not just an amalgam of familiar beasts. There was danger in being subject to someone who wondered whether the dragon on the city's crest was related to the Komodo dragon it so closely resembled, and if so, when St Georgiy had a chance to travel to Komodo. The man with imagination could notice the magic that was seeping into the world, cast for him to notice, like round shining lures.

"You know about magic?" Oksana said.

The jackdaw flapped its wings. "Of course I do; I did from the time he first started thinking about it. He borrowed some books from me—books on Kabbala. My grandmother was a Jewish mystic of some sort. The books were old though; valuable. I knew nothing about that crap, just had no interest in it at all."

"But now you do," Fyodor said. He glanced around, making sure that no one eavesdropped on his conversation with the bird. "Tell me, why do they come here?"

"That I don't know," Vladimir said. "But if you want to follow them, now's the time." He pointed his wing at the three men who finished their stretching, smoking and leisurely conversation, and headed down the freshly plowed path.

"We know where they're going," Oksana said. "What did Kabbala have to do with it?"

"From what I understand," Vladimir said, "he wanted to learn magic. Kabbala seemed like a good place to start; he even got some symbols branded into him. It didn't give him any abilities, but he said that it was like a sign for the forces from the other side to find him."

"What forces?" Fyodor asked, feeling the fine hairs on his neck prickle.

"You know," the jackdaw said. It didn't actually shrug, but Fyodor imagined that it did. "The usual—Satan or whoever, I guess."

"All right," Oksana said, and tugged on Fyodor's sleeve. "Let's go check out the cabin."

"Thanks for putting me into a bird," Vladimir said, "but . . . would it be possible to maybe make me human again?"

"We don't know any magic," Oksana said. "I suppose if were to put your soulstone into a person . . . "

"I doubt it," Fyodor said, and started down the path after the thugs who had by then disappeared from view. "We do know someone who might be able to help you, though. If you help us, we'll talk to him on your behalf."

"That would be acceptable," the jackdaw said. "Very satisfactory, in fact." The jackdaw settled on Fyodor's shoulder. "Is there anything else I can help you with? And where are we going, by the way?"

"Peter the Great's cabin," Oksana said. "Meanwhile, do you know anything about people turning into birds?"

"Of course," Vladimir said matter-of-factly. "Everyone who pays attention knows. The cops were looking for all the people who went missing. Where I live, Biryulevo, one of our cops disappeared too. The rest of them lost their heads over it, interrogated every Chechen and Georgian and illegal they could get their hands on. They started asking business people, too—who disappeared, why, that sort of thing. No one wants to cross the racketeers, but people know. They see the gang strutting by, and the next thing you know your mate is flapping his wings . . . I was sort of hoping for that fate when they came for me. Always wanted to fly, ever since I was a kid."

"Who didn't?" Fyodor muttered.

Who didn't indeed. Even now, quite free if the delusions of childhood, he occasionally dreamt about flying. He never rose far above the ground nowadays, hovering just above the nodding stems of autumn grass. He always flew over the grass fields in his dreams, a cartoon yellow from one horizon to the other, nodding, whispering. If he closed his eyes, he could hear the rustling of one stem against the next, he could feel their stiff bristles trailing against his bare toes and fingers.

He snapped back to the crunching of snow when they heard the voices coming from the cabin. The sun was setting already, long tree shadows stretching long and blue, undulating across snow drifts and hollows. Still it was too light to approach the cabin; they stopped, and a moment later the voices inside stopped too.

"Did you hear anything?" said one of the men inside.

"Spies," answered a rustling, despicable voice; it felt like the scratching of a nail across a windowpane. "Go get them."

There was nowhere to run, and Fyodor turned to Oksana for support.

She faltered and then whistled; the rats poured from her and Fyodor's sleeves, came running from the cabin. There were so many of them—Fyodor thought that the wild rats joined them too, subject to Oksana's peculiar charm. Rat on rat, column on column.

Three maroon jackets stood in the cabin's doorway, their eyes troubled. Guns glinted in their hands, but they didn't shoot, as transfixed by the rats' performance—tail twisting with tail, hands holding hands—as Fyodor. They didn't shoot even when a bear made of rats stood to its full height, raised its arms, and stepped toward the cabin.

16: One-Eyed Likho

The soldiers went about their business outside—Galina heard their footsteps, accompanied by the cheerful clinks of their spurs against the cobbles of the yard.

Timur-Bey shook his head in disapproval. "Tearing up their horses' sides, that's not good. Horse is a clever animal. It's like spurring your child."

"I don't know about that," Yakov replied. "Be quiet—I'm trying to hear what's going on."

The voices that reached them were muffled, the words indistinguishable. And then there were other sounds—scratching and awful quiet slurping, and whispers like icy needles. Galina bit down on the knuckle of her index finger, trying to keep herself from screaming and running in blind terror.

The terrible sounds—she didn't dare to imagine their source, but she knew without verbalizing it that the calamity outside was not human—drew closer. It was as if someone was licking the door of the barn with a scratchy yet wet gigantic tongue. Stories, stories forgotten out of fear when she was still a child, flooded her memory, as fresh as years ago. The witch that licked through oven doors made of seven layers of cast iron. Creatures with tongues hanging down to their withered breasts, their claws finding the eyes of their children-victims with the unflinching accuracy of fate. Words like needles, eyes like coals.

The snuffling by the door. A giant wet nose pressed against the treacherous boards, sniffing out the human flesh inside. Hot fetid breath reached her face through the gaps between the wooden planks, bathing it in a stench of rotten onions. She bit harder in order not to gag.

Even Zemun seemed scared—her massive body pressed into Galina, seeking comfort and almost toppling her. She pushed back, and the warmth and the milky smell of the cowhide momentarily comforted her. She wondered what was inside Zemun—was it real flesh or just stars? If one were to poke a hole in her white hide, would the blinding light spill out, burning everything in its proximity to hot astral cinders?

And then, just like that, something burst through the boards, like a blast from a sawed-off shotgun. Galina saw spread claws and a giant eye, burning like the stormy anxious sun, and she felt a knock on her chest, an impact throwing her to the ground. Yakov and Timur-Bey grabbed at the intruder, and Zemun's hooves beat the air as she reared up. Her horns tilted and threw the attacker against the wall. He landed with a dull thump and Galina sat up, her breath ragged and wheezing.

The creature was smaller than she had originally thought—it was human-sized, but with sharp talons and tufts of feathers on wrists covered with puckered livid skin. Its lipless mouth twisted, baring large yellow teeth square like the grid of a chessboard. Its single eye blazed from the middle of its forehead, and Galina realized who had just laid hands on her.

Zemun spoke first. "One-Eyed Likho," she said. "I thought we were rid of you two."

Galina heard the stories about Likho and its companion, Zlyden. She knew these two parasitic entities, the embodiments of bad fortune, that attached themselves to their victim until the victim lost everything and was eventually killed by the sheer constellation of bad luck.

Likho breathed heavily. "Stupid cow," it said in a rasping voice. "You think putting me into a barrel and throwing me into a river would get rid of me? There's always some poor fool who will open it. People can't stand closed barrels and chests and boxes—haven't you learned that?"

"Those soldiers let you out then," Koschey said. "Stupid mortals."

"Yes, they did," Likho gloated. "And we stuck to them, stuck to them like tar to fur. We followed them home, only they were dead and dumb, stuck on the wrong side of the river, never to find their kin, never to find your stupid little town. Too dead to know what bad luck is."

"Why are you staying with them then?" Timur-Bey asked. "And why the birds?"

Likho gave a small, demented titter. "Too curious and yet too blind. Blind like Berendey—stupid old man, thought he could lure us back into a barrel. But we changed his luck, changed his luck. And your luck will change too, you two—insane girl, lazy cop. You'll have it so bad you'll think you had it good before."

The soldiers crowded the doorway, muskets at the ready.

Zemun lowed and shook her head at them. "You don't have to do what Likho and Zlyden tell you to."

"Yes, we do," said the Corporal. "They promised us life, they promised us that we will walk the earth again, escape this tepid hell and live again. They promised us eyes and wings of birds that fly, that see . . . ."

As his voice trailed off and his musket lowered, its bayonet leveling at Yakov's chest, he stepped forward. The embrasure left where the door used to be let in the scant light, and Galina's gaze followed the upward sweep of the palace wall outside. The roof was too high above to see it, but she could imagine it, crusted over with the black mass of poor displaced birds. "Masha!" she screamed.

The soldiers stepped closer but stopped, unsure whether they should do anything—after all, she was not fighting them, but calling. "Masha, Masha!"

A thunderous clapping of wings and cawing answered her, the birds startled by her screams. She could picture them, circling, crying out—and then they came, pouring in a feathered stream, black as pitch, through the doorway.

The birds seemed confused as they attacked the soldiers, then turned on Galina and her friends. Zemun chased the flapping birds away with flicks of her tail, unimpressed by their sharp beaks and shiny eyes. Yakov just covered his head with his folded arms, but looked up into the cloud of birds, as did Galina, both of them searching for the impossible recognition—every jackdaw looked the same as any other, every crow was the same too. Maybe Masha was among them, maybe not. And she suspected that Yakov was hoping to see his pet crow Carl, and perhaps ask his forgiveness.

She peeked between the fingers protecting her eyes, and

saw that the soldiers chased the birds away with their muskets, even knocking some out of the air with the stocks. There were feathers fluttering through the air. One of them, shiny-black, spun past her face like a miniature helicopter rotor.

"Please," Galina whispered to the spinning feather, even as rough hands and wooden musket stocks pushed her through the doorway, "please don't let me die before finding you. Please don't let them kill me before I talk to you again." She whispered to the feather until it hit the ground, like it was a falling star.

"OF COURSE THEY'RE NOT GOING TO KILL US," YAKOV SAID. "Weren't you listening? Why would they kill us if they can just drain our luck? Use your brain, for once."

Galina bit her lip and didn't answer. Ever since they had been ushered into the palace, all the while fending off frenzied, screeching birds, Yakov had seemed unsettled. His usual apathetic demeanor was replaced with irritability and occasional vicious malice.

The room they currently occupied was a bona fide dungeon—underground, with a crisscrossing of thick beams, a heavy bolted door and a stern tiny window in the door, guarded by iron bars. There was plenty of straw to sleep on and a dim light in which Yakov's face seemed haunted and angry. Perhaps it's just the beard, Galina thought, giving him that hungry, desperate countenance. But his angry words still rang in her ears, and she retreated to a corner, wishing nothing better than to bury herself in the straw and disappear.

Yakov paced the room. "I can't believe it," he said. "This

place . . . they plunder everything you believe, then they take your memories, and now our luck. What kind of place is this?"

"Elena said it wasn't supposed to be a utopia," Galina said.

Yakov shook his head and continued pacing. "Where did they take Zemun and the rest?"

"I don't know," Galina said.

"Well, think!"

She dug herself into the straw and hugged her knees to her chest. She would've killed for a bath about now, and for an opportunity to be alone just for a little while. With Yakov acting like that, she couldn't concentrate on anything. She felt irrelevant and small, just like she did when a teacher quizzed her in front of the class and she couldn't get any answers right, and the more she scrambled the more she messed up. She felt like crying. "I don't know," she repeated. "Stop talking to me like this."

He stopped and spun around. "Like what?"

"Like this," she repeated. "You keep acting like it's my fault."

"And it's not?"

She shook her head in disbelief. "You're the cop here."

"And I was doing my job. I was doing it well, thanks, and then you showed up and dragged me to meet your crazy friend who nevertheless was smart enough to stay out of this little adventure, and then we all are here. How do you know your sister is here? How do you know this kerfuffle has anything to do with us?"

"The birds . . . " she started.

"Yes, yes, I know. The birds are everywhere. And how does it help?"

"They are their eyes," she said. "They see everything. Maybe if we could find a way to learn what the birds know . . . "

"And how do we do that?"

Galina sat up, straightening. "Do you have any food left?"

"No. Well, just a bit of that awful fruitcake David made." A brief smile lit his bearded face when he thought of his grandfather, and Galina felt a pang of guilt at denying him this reunion.

"This will do," she said. She took the sticky slice covered in lint and grime from Yakov's calloused fingers. Her father used to have hands like that, she remembered. Hard and tough as leather, and she had thought that all men had hands like that. She remembered her surprise when she shook hands with one of her mother's coworkers, and discovered that his hands were soft, feminine. In fact, she soon learned that very few people had hands like her father; that was one of the very few things she remembered about him still.

She kneeled by the grate in the door and crumbled the fruitcake on the floor, cooing gently. If she craned her neck, she could see the length of the corridor outside and at the end of it the small embrasure of a window too small for a person but large enough for a bird. "Come on," she cooed. "Come, little birds, I have a nice cake for you."

A bird perched on the sill of the tiny window, its black feathers slicked and its head cocked, the black shining bead of an eye trained on the bits of fruitcake strewn on the floor.

"It's no use," Yakov said. "It's not going to come."

"And how do you know that?" Galina asked without turning.

"We have no luck," Yakov said. "Don't you get it? When Likho and Zlyden are both around, we have no chance. Any time anything can go wrong, it will."

Galina didn't answer and crouched lower. Her fingers grew numb from crumbling the cake; it crumbled and crumbled and turned to fine dust.

They used to feed pigeons, she and Masha; Masha was only little then, and for some reason she wanted nothing better than a pet pigeon. Galina smiled, remembering the wooden crate they found by the back door of the neighborhood liquor store, and how it smelled of fresh wood shavings and sour spilled beer; how they found a stick and borrowed a ball of yarn from one of the morose old ladies who liked to knit sitting on the bench by the entrance of their apartment building. Of how they propped the crate up with a stick wrapped in bright cerulean yarn and crumbled day-old bread under it. How they waited, breathless and giggly, for the pigeons to crowd under the crate, as if impatient to be caught.

Galina wished to feel like she felt that day—a bit flustered and apologetic, ready with excuses for any grownup who would question their purpose in trapping the pigeons, but happy with anticipation, happy that her little sister looked at her with such admiration, was so impressed that Galina, generally useless and awkward, was in possession of such arcana as building pigeon traps. Usually Masha, only five at a time, treated Galina with the kindness and sensitivity extended by adults to ailing children. Galina was not ungrateful—on the contrary she was convinced that Masha was the only person under the sun generous enough to love the unlovable—but she cherished the rare glimpses of memories where she was competent.

She frowned when she remembered the pigeon they managed to trap in the frantic scattering of other birds and the heavy thud of the crate, how the bird flapped against the wooden slats of its prison, almost lifting the crate off the ground. The crate hopped on the pungent heated asphalt if the yard as if possessed, and they laughed guiltily, and hurried to examine their prisoner. It was an average enough pigeon, gray under most circumstances but blooming with greens and purples, like an oil slick on a puddle, when the sun rays struck its feathers at the proper angle. Masha seemed pleased and stroked the bird. "Its heart is beating so hard," she said. "I can feel it jumping on my fingers."

It was then that Galina noticed that the bird was not quite right—its feet, clawed and leathery and reptilian, seemed bigger than they were supposed to be, a swollen purple in color.

Masha noticed too, and gasped. "Look," she said, and pointed at a dirty bit of thin string dangling from one of the pigeon's feet, and cried. Galina tried not to cry too when she realized that someone—probably the boys who terrorized the local stray cats and spent most of their time playing in the concrete pipes of the nearby construction site—had trapped this bird before, bound it with string and flown it like a kite. The string was tied too tight and cut off the circulation in the bird's feet—this is why it was so easy to trap the second time.

Galina wiped Masha's tears and led her home, the poor bird still nestled in her hands, not fighting its capture anymore.

The bird with the swollen feet lying passively in the five-year-old's open palms stood clear in her mind, as perfect an image of defeat as she could wish for. They tried to remove the string, but the swelling was too great—the scaly skin bunched over it, and the pigeon trembled every time they touched its injured feet. Soon, it couldn't stand, and they took the bus to the vet clinic. The pigeon died on the bus and they saw no point in getting off but traveled to the final stop and waited for the bus to turn around and take them back home. They buried the pigeon in the remaining orchard patch, and never tried to trap another one again.

The bird on the sill hopped onto the floor of the corridor, hesitant, studying Galina and the crumbled fruitcake with one eye, then the other.

"Just be still," Galina whispered to Yakov. "Please, I beg you, be still."

He didn't answer but stopped his pacing. Galina couldn't see his face, but she imagined he watched the bird's reluctant progress and frequent backtracking with the same intensity as she.

The bird pecked at the crumbs tentatively, glancing sideways at Galina's hand resting on the floor palm up.

"It's all right," Galina whispered. "Go ahead, eat."

The bird did, its neck bobbing with each peck. Its crop swelled with fruitcake, and the bird appeared thoroughly absorbed in its dinner. Galina moved her hand, centimeter by centimeter, until it almost touched the bird's foot. The bird stopped pecking and studied the hand that again came to rest on the floor.

Galina chewed her lips, feeling the dry skin peel under her teeth, giving way to tender flesh and pungent wet blood. "Don't move," she whispered, "be still."

The bird hesitated, and Galina lunged. She hit her head on the metal bars of the door—she had forgotten they were there, and the impact made her cringe with pain. Her hand grasped at the bird and brushed against the wing just as the startled bird took flight, avoiding capture without much effort. It disappeared through the embrasure of the window at the end of the hallway, and still Galina grasped at empty air, her overextended arm aching in its socket, creaking at the elbow. She felt a hand on her shoulder.

"It's gone," Yakov said. "Don't feel bad—you almost got it."

"Almost is never good enough," she whispered. That's what her mother used to say anyway.

"What would you have done with that bird?" Yakov said. "Think about it—if Likho can talk to the birds, it doesn't mean you can do the same."

"We have to try," she said. "What, you want to rot here?"

Yakov opened his mouth to answer but a flapping of wings interrupted them. A fat white rook squeezed through the window and half-fell, half-fluttered to the floor. In short hops it approached the cell.

"Finally," it said. "It took me forever to find you."

"Sergey!" Galina picked the bird up and cradled it, resisting the urge to give it a kiss. "How'd you find us? Why did they let you go?"

"I played dumb," the rook said, and even its high-pitched bird voice couldn't hide its self-satisfaction. "They didn't think

I was important enough to chase—they were talking to Zemun and Koschey."

"What about Timur-Bey?" Galina asked.

"Him? I don't know. He's human, so they probably put him somewhere to get to his luck, if he has any left after all these years underground." Sergey chuckled, pleased with his wit. "So I went to look for you, but you'll never believe what else I found."

SERGEY COULDN'T FLY, SINCE HIS CLIPPED WINGS WERE USEFUL enough to buffer a fall but too short and ragged to support real flight. He hopped and fluttered his way out of the barn and into the first-story window of the palace; there, he traveled from one room to the next. He found many birds and a few more soldiers, some of them French. All of them paid him no mind and he soon discovered why—albino birds perched on windowsills, mingling with black-feathered newcomers, and pecked at the fruit in the tree branches outside. Sergey still found it strange to think of himself as a bird, but he had to admit that in this case it was handy, a perfect disguise. He hopped across the hardwood floors and hand-woven runners striped in red, yellow and blue; he flitted awkwardly up onto the sills and out to the balconies, hopped up the winding staircases, lost direction in the endless corridors and galleries of empty rooms inhabited only by dust bunnies. He stopped caring after a while if he came into the same room as before, and wasn't particularly sure if he was moving up or down.

He didn't remember how he arrived at the entrance of one of the seven towers; he only knew that he had to crane his neck to see the next turn of the wide staircase that swept up and to the left, its steps stacked at a slight angle so that it took them a whole floor to turn all the way around. He hopped upwards, thinking that only a really tall tower would have a staircase with such slow turns. He spiraled upwards, occasionally zoning out and thinking that he was still guarding a silo, still in his human form, and that his corporal had sent him to fetch something from the storage facility. Then he came to and saw that the sun was setting, and then it rose again—funny things happened to time on that staircase.

It was then that he heard the singing. The voice sounded small and ragged, and stopped often to gulp air in large noisy swallows, and resumed again, trembling, weak and uncertain. At first, he imagined a child, a sick child perhaps, a little boy with asthma who passed the time in his sickbed by pretending to be in a church choir. Then another voice joined the first, and a feeble duet echoed in the stairwell. The third attempted to sing but coughed, wailed and dissolved into sobs before falling quiet again.

Sergey hurried up the stairs. The voices didn't sound like Likho or its soldiers, and he decided that there were prisoners. They didn't sound like Zemun or Koschey, or even Galina for that matter, but he hurried, hoping to find out who it was that sang so piteously.

At the top of the staircase there was a single door with a narrow slot at the bottom. Sergey squeezed through the opening with some effort; his biggest worry was to encounter a cat or to be forcibly ejected by the inhabitants, but he did not expect to feel such fierce pity and anger.

At first, he thought that he was looking at three naked women chained to the wall; whatever small sordid joy might've stirred in his heart at the sight of female bondage had evaporated as soon as he saw the long bloodied bruises on the wrists of narrow fingerless hands, the drooping narrow breasts and the bird's feet so swollen that puckered flesh half-concealed the manacles. The faces that reminded him of Byzantine saints and angels—with large dark eyes that took up half of these narrow faces, the fine-boned Eastern cheeks that tapered into small sharp chins, and small but perfect lips half-opened in suffering.

Then he noticed that their naked bodies were shapeless sacks, reminiscent of plucked chickens, and he realized with a start that they were the bodies of birds—picked clean of feathers, with just a few downy tufts and jutting feather shafts remaining in place.

"Who are you?" he whispered to the bird-women.

One by one they lifted their faces, their eyes half-hidden under heavy dark eyelids, and whispered in turn, "Alkonost," "Sirin," "Gamayun."

17: Alkonost, Sirin, Gamayun

Yakov interrupted. "What happened next?"

Sergey ruffled his feathers. "I would've told you already if you hadn't interrupted me. So just listen, yeah?"

Yakov nodded and kept quiet.

Sergey continued with the tale—how he froze to the floor by the door, unable to turn away or rush forward to help, paralyzed by a mix of terror, revulsion, and pity. How he also grew acutely aware of his own small and fat bird body, and imagined what his wings would look like naked—handless sticks covered in blue puckering skin—how he shuddered.

The dark Byzantine eyes watched him from the wall, drawing him in, and he was unable to look away at the rest of the room, just their eyes and bloody manacles holding the unspeakable, unimaginable abominations.

"Why are you here?" he croaked finally. "What are they doing to you? Why . . . " He wanted to ask why they were naked, but thought better of it. "What happened to your feathers?"

"They took them," Sirin said in a halting but sweet voice, and her lips trembled. "They took them to make into charms, to give to evil men."

"They grow back," Alkonost added, "but they take them again."

"You will die twice," Gamayun hissed, her eyes burning with insuppressible madness.

"Can I do anything to help?" Sergey whispered. Sadness filled him as no feeling had ever done; he thought that it was the first time in his life that he truly felt something. He wanted nothing more than to help them.

"Take my last feather." Alkonost shifted awkwardly, turning to expose her flank, naked but for a single small white feather. "It's a charm."

"What does it do?"

"I don't know." Alkonost bit her lip and almost cried. There was nothing majestic about her now.

"Take mine too," Sirin said, and twisted, moving her heavy body to the side, exposing the dusty-gray feather in the hollow under her wing. "It's a spell."

"Take them all!" Gamayun struggled against her bonds wildly, drawing blood from her ankles and wrists. "Take my curse, take my hate, take everything we got, but stop this degradation." When she ceased struggling and hung helpless and exhausted against her manacles, her head on her chest, Sergey saw the black smudge of a feather in the nape of her neck.

He collected the three feathers, and stopped in the doorway. It seemed impossible to leave them like this. "I'll come back for you," he said. "I promise."

The three bird-women said nothing; Alkonost started with her song again, a childish lullaby Sergey had heard too many years ago to remember the words of, but the melody stirred his heart with an unfamiliar longing for the happy time without responsibility, for the time when he could be tucked under the thick quilted blanket and no worry could touch him there. He swallowed the bile rising in his throat and squeezed through the slit in the door. He felt lighter somehow, emptier.

He moved his wings, trying to explain. "It's like this, see," he said. "Nothing will ever be the same again. It's like my life broke in half. Do you know what I mean?"

Yakov nodded. He did. He knew the distinct before and after, he felt the rift that cleaved his life in two separate and irreconcilable parts, where he felt that one had nothing to do with the other; he was a different man now, and he felt like throwing himself on the cold floor of his prison and weeping and striking his fists against the boards when he thought that this rift, this separator, this memory had been pried out of his soul by the bony spirit fingers of the boatman.

"Where are the feathers?" Galina asked.

Sergey smirked and lifted his wings. There, among his own dirty-white feathers, there was a brilliantly white one, a gray one, and a black one, their shafts entangled securely in his down.

Yakov picked them out, his stubby fingers particularly ungraceful, and studied the feathers. "What do we do with them?"

"A charm, a spell and a curse," Galina said.

Yakov sighed and closed his fist. "What does it even mean? Everyone here speaks in stupid riddles, like if throwing words together would somehow give them meaning. Well, it doesn't; it's all gibberish to me. So don't you start talking like that, like you know what's going on."

"Don't tell me what to do and how to talk." Galina almost snarled at him. "Who do you think you are? I'm not your wife, so you don't snap at me every time something goes wrong."

He shrugged and handed her the feathers. "You figure this one out then."

Galina studied the feathers on her palm, tilting it sideways to catch the light from the window in the end of the hallway. She looked as perplexed as Yakov felt, and he had to suppress a smirk of satisfaction. "A charm or a spell?" Galina mused. "And do any of you remember any fairytales with feathers?"

"Just with flower petals," Sergey said. "Remember the one about the seven-colored flower?"

Galina grinned. "Sure do. 'Fly little petal from east to west, from north to south, and come back around, make my wish come true when you touch the ground.'"

"That's the one," Sergey squawked, pleased. "Think it'll work?"

"Not the chant," Galina answered, "But let's see what happens when they touch the ground." She loosened her fingers, and all three of them watched as the feathers drifted down to the floor and came to rest, the fine silken fibers wavering in the gentle draft coming from the window at the end of the hallway.

They waited a while; the feathers remained motionless.

"Screw this," Yakov said. "Let's get out of here, find Koschey, and see if he knows what that's all about."

"We can't leave," Galina said, and pointed at the door. As if he were stupid.

"Sergey," Yakov said. "Can you get to the lock?"

"Hold on," the rook said, and waddled outside through the slot in the bottom of the door. They heard it scraping and panting; an occasional thud signified a fall.

"I can't reach it," Sergey informed them, poking his head through the opening. "If you could give me a boost—but even then I don't know if I'm strong enough."

"I am," Yakov said, and lay down on the floor. He squeezed his arm through the opening and waited for the rook to step on his open hand. Once the clawed cold bird fingers wound around his thumb, he turned on his right side, bending his arm upward.

"Just a bit more," Sergey instructed. "There. I'm touching it with my beak." There was more scraping and clanging of metal. "Can't do it—the lock's too strong."

"Put your beak next to the tumbler," Yakov said. "Does it go right or left?"

"Left," Sergey said. "Just be careful."

Yakov grasped the bird's legs and put all the strength of his arm into forcing the internal tumbler aside. He worked blind, and his heavy breathing was the only sound in the cell. Sergey was a trooper—Yakov could feel how stiff the rook was, how hard he tried to remain motionless and rigid.

A sharp crack startled Yakov—at first, he thought that Sergey's beak had broken. Galina jumped to the door and pushed it outward, and it gave. Yakov released the bird, picked up the magic feathers, and jumped to his feet. "Are you all right?" he asked Sergey.

"Fine," he answered from the outside. "Just a little sore. Come on, I'll show you the way."

Yakov was not fond of violence; he approached it as something one needed to be stoic about, never deriving either pleasure or distaste from it. He tried to maintain the same perspective once they rounded the corner and encountered one of the Napoleonic soldiers; this one was French. He looked at Yakov with very round, very pale eyes, and his mouth mimicked their round shape. He reached for his musket, but Yakov knocked him to the ground with a single economical punch before he could level his piece.

"What should we do with him?" Galina said, looking at the soldier with a worried, almost pitying expression. "We are not going to just leave him here, are we?"

Yakov shrugged. "What else can we do? I'm not carrying him." He stared at the soldier's waxen face, his concave closed eyelids shot through with a multitude of veins, fine like cracks on a porcelain cup. "He'll be all right." In truth, the soldier didn't look like he would be all right—none of them did. They all looked deader than dead, and that didn't sit well with him. Everyone else was alive in here—or at least they seemed to think so. What if they weren't, though? What if he were dead too?

Yakov shook his head and smiled, and followed the rook, which danced and hopped impatiently, down the wooden hall. He wasn't dead; this wasn't some stupid story they used to tell as kids by the campfire, during the blue and endless nights at the summer camp. He still remembered them—stupidities and non-sequiturs, man-eating furniture and menacing but unforgivably dumb serial killers. And dead people who didn't know they were dead until someone told then that they were, and then they crumbled into dust. Even as an adult he remembered the chilled shivers that crawled down his collar then, induced not so much by the stories themselves but by the darkness and the overall mood of joyful conspiracy, the conspiracy of being voluntarily scared, of faking the emotion until it became true.

"Here." Sergey stopped in front of a door, and Yakov looked back, dismayed to realize that they hadn't traveled far, just turned the corner and gone a bit down the corridor that seemed to run around the entire perimeter of the palace.

"You knew they were here the whole time?" Galina asked. "Why didn't you give the feathers to them?"

Sergey puffed out his bird chest. "'Cause. You're people, you're my folk. These fairytale things—not so much."

"You're a fairytale thing," Galina said. "You're a talking bird."

"Regular birds can talk too," Sergey said. "Besides, I'm not really a bird."

"Your feathers beg to differ," Yakov said. "Come on, get in there."

The slot on this door was located higher than on the one that imprisoned them previously. Yakov picked Sergey up and unceremoniously shoved him inside; he looked through the slot, but could see only darkness and dilute shimmer. A weak scent of grass and milk told him that Zemun was indeed in there.

"Look," Koschey's crackling voice said, "it's that reanimated corpse from the surface."

"Don't call him that," said Zemun. "Don't you think one might not want to be reminded of one's mortality?"

"I wouldn't know anything about that," Koschey said with an audible sneer. "What do you bring us, rook?"

"Feathers," Yakov said, pressing his lips to the slot in the door. "From Alkonost and company. Do you know what to do with them?"

There was some gasping and whispering inside.

Yakov sighed and fiddled with the lock—a simple thing, easily overcome with any narrow tool. "Do you have any pins on you?" he asked Galina.

She dug through the pockets of her jeans—the same ones she'd been wearing when they first came here; Yakov realized that his own clothes were also filthy, and wondered why it bothered him so little.

"Here." Galina offered a slender bobby pin on the open palm of her right hand.

He studied it a while, a thin black piece of metal nestled into the deep furrow of her life line. It seemed so out of context here, it didn't belong. They were in a wooden corridor in some medieval palace, with nothing but pale unearthly light for company; they were underground, in a place that was below the river and the subways and secret KGB bunkers, the place that was so far below as to not exist, for all reasonable purposes. Bobby pins did not belong. Still, he jammed it into the lock, shifting the tumblers inside—easier this time, since he didn't have to work blind. He stuck out his tongue, self-consciously, because he remembered since childhood that it helped. Breathing heavily, tongue out, he concentrated on his work until the tumblers shifted and Galina tapped his shoulder.

"What?" His voice came out more irritable than he meant.

"Look," she whispered.

He did. More soldiers, of course, and one of them carried a child on its shoulders—a horrible malformed child that grasped the soldier's neck with its claw-like hands, its heels cruelly digging into the man's sides, bunching his uniform. Yakov recognized him for the legendary Zlyden. The group exuded the smell of old ash and sour milk, and Yakov never wished for anything more than to be away from them.

The horrible child whined, kicking the soldiers and urging them on. It flailed and bit the ear of his visibly annoyed mount.

Yakov felt something shift inside his soul at the sound of the child's crying. Why wouldn't it stop, why wouldn't it just shut up and be quiet, why did it have to mete out the dull torment of its sniffling and sobbing, fits and starts, deceptive and momentary silences that were quickly displaced by resumed crying? And the only thing that was stopping him from crying out now—Shut up, shut up, or I'll—was a sudden unexplained fear that the voice would fall silent in compliance with his unsaid wishes, and . . .

"Do something," Galina hissed into his ear before he could complete the terrible thought, and the threads fell apart again, like the pieces in a kaleidoscope, nothing but trash, ghastly bits of the soul-crushing toy he would never buy for a child.

A strong shove from behind sent him sprawling under the soldiers' feet—the door he had forgotten about hit him in the back as it swung open, and Koschey and Timur-Bey stood in the doorway, ready to quarrel.

Yakov curled up, covering his head with his hands, expecting a blow. Instead, the soldiers rushed past him, and the only kick he received was accidental. He rose to his feet, just in time to witness Timur-Bey reaching into his wide sleeve and pulling out a long shining blade.

Koschey stood next to him, exceptionally tall and thin and straight, with a grey feather held in his bony fingers. His hollow cheeks puffed out in a mockery of a breath; he blew on the feather, all the while drawing symbols in the air with his left hand.

Yakov had no sense of what was happening; he only knew enough to rush past the soldiers (he tried not to look at Zlyden), to grab Galina's elbow and drag her away. He wanted to cover her wide eyes with his palm, to spare her the sight of the wide flashing arc of Timur-Bey's saber, the dull glint of the bayonets, and the dark swirling of the air where Koschey agitated it with his hand.

He pulled her to the wall by the now open cell door, pressing flat against the wooden planks that still—all these centuries—retained a faint smell of cedar and pine, a frail and resinous scent. "Don't look," he whispered.

She looked, and why wouldn't she? She was a grown-up, not the imaginary child Yakov was—had been—protecting, in his muddled imagination; she didn't need to turn away when the bayonets and sabers stabbed and slashed, leaving the febrile blooms of red carnations in their wake; she was perfectly capable of watching the air thicken into a gray cloud, Sirin's spell rumbling inside it with brief lightning flashes, charging the air with the smell of ozone, heating the wall under their backs and making it breathe forth an exhalation of resin and summer and wild strawberries.

The cloud surrounded the soldier who carried Zlyden and grew solid—it seemed a porous resin, a roughly hewn chunk of cement. As it solidified, the rest of the soldiers, many of them bleeding, stepped away from it, confused. There was no sign of Likho, and Yakov sensed that without their guardians the soldiers were timid.

Yakov stepped forward, holding up his palm to the fray. To his surprise, even Timur-Bey stepped back and wiped his saber on his sleeve. "Citizens," he said to the soldiers, "you're under arrest for disturbing the peace. Please surrender your weapons."

"No," one of the soldiers said. "Why should we listen to you?" His gaze traveled to one of his comrades bleeding on the ground, his blood, surprisingly real, soaking into the green wool of his uniform, staining it black.

How many times could the dead die? Yakov thought. *A lot*, the answer came to him. The dead always die, every time the living think of them dying, like the child crying in the crib who fell silent and resumed again—he died over and over, killed by the mere thought, only to come back to life and cry and die again. Just like the soldier of the long-ago war who kept falling, in slow motion, under the bayonet, under the bullet, under the blade of a saber; the soldier who slipped in his own blood and fell among the red carnations, again and again. He only lay still when one pinned him with a gaze.

Galina gently nudged him aside. "You should listen to him," she said, "because Zlyden and Likho are not here to be listened to. You traded your luck away, and ours. I'm just looking for my sister and I don't know if I can find her without any luck, and if you won't help then at least let us go."

"Or you'll end up like him," Koschey said and pointed at the grey blob half-blocking the corridor.

The soldier opened his mouth to answer but his chest exploded in a loud blast—not carnations but a cavernous red mouth opened in his chest, fringed with white rib fragments like hungry teeth. A slow wet hiss came from between his suddenly white lips, bubbling forth with pink foam. His knees buckled and he fell forward, folding on his way like a lounge chair.

At first, Yakov thought that Koschey's magic had done it to the soldier; but Koschey's face expressed as much surprise and shock as Galina's. Even Zemun and Sergey edged out of the cell where they were wisely waiting out the altercation, looking for the source of the blast and the deafening silence that followed.

A careful scattering of footfalls came from behind the grey boulder that was blocking most of the view; military boots, Yakov guessed. He gripped Galina's elbow; Koschey's hands knotted into fists, and Timur-Bey reached for his saber. The confrontation forgotten, the Napoleonic soldiers turned to face the unknown danger, their shoulders brushing against Timur-Bey's sleeves and Koschey's outstretched hands, their backs turned on Yakov as if he was no longer a threat but an ally.

"Don't anyone move," a female voice said, and the muzzle of a shotgun peeked from behind the gray boulder. "What on earth is that thing, anyway?"

Galina shook off Yakov's hand, and rushed forward, pushing between the soldiers. "Elena!" she called out. "Is that you?"

The Decembrist's wife stepped into view, her black velvet dress stained with river mud, and the fingernails of her small white hands marked with half-moons of dirt. She dropped the shotgun she was holding to her chest on the floor and extended her arms to Galina. The two women hugged and laughed, oblivious to the blood on the floor.

Elena had not come alone—from behind the gray boulder of Sirin's spell, several rusalki shod in heavy military boots filed out, followed by two soldiers circa 1917 or so—Yakov pegged them for Budyonny's cavalrymen, Cossacks or outlaws (not that there was much of a difference) all. Revolutionary and war heroes, led by the class enemy and several drowned girls. Yakov decided not to contemplate further.

"Why did you shoot him?" he asked Elena.

She shot him an irritated look—clearly, she wanted nothing better than to gab with Galina. "They're traitors," she said.

"That is not true!" one of the surviving soldiers protested.

"Of course it is, Poruchik," Elena said. "Burned during the retreat, imagine that! You're forgetting that my husband was leading your regiment. I know why you stayed behind; I know why you burned—the city couldn't stand your presence, the deserters. It would rather lose a building than let you remain inside it. You've abandoned your commander."

The poruchik straightened, his white eyes almost glowing with anger. "You should talk, you bitch. You were the one who betrayed him, you didn't do as a good wife was supposed to—

you were meant to go to Siberia with him, so you too deserve to be here in the blasted underground, you too . . . "

He didn't finish—Elena picked up the shotgun in a fluid motion and leveled it on his chest. Yakov took it for bravado, just like everyone else—the soldiers on Elena's side smirked, the ones opposing her murmured discontent. A shotgun blast came unanticipated.

"What are you doing?" Yakov yelled as the poruchik fell into the arms of his comrades, thrown back by the force of the blast. "Have you lost your mind? He wasn't doing anything!"

Elena shrugged and rested the shotgun on her naked shoulder. "It wasn't a self-defense killing, Yakov," she said. "It was a revenge killing. They killed Berendey and they cost my husband his health and his soul—he was a broken man after that war; Siberia couldn't do worse than they."

"They also fed Likho and Zlyden," Zemun interjected.

"You can't just go killing people!" Yakov said.

"Sure she can," Timur-Bey said. He was so quiet until then, Yakov forgot that he was even there. "We have no cops here. And we do not like traitors."

"I hate to interrupt the spirited debate on the nature of justice," Koschey said. "But I think that perhaps we should take care of Alkonost and her sisters, and worry about these fried fleshbags later."

The three remaining soldiers obediently went into the cell vacated by Zemun and the rook; the lock was busted, and two stoic-looking cavalrymen stayed behind to guard them.

"Wait," Galina said. "What about my sister? What about the rest of the people turned into birds?"

Koschey twirled the white feather in his fingers. "I can help them, but we need to get them to the surface first. I don't want all these tourists stuck here."

"Isn't this place supposed to be connected to Kolomenskoe?" Yakov said.

"Yes," Sergey squawked. "Slava always met them there, and there has to be some connection. And I think the tower in the east, that's where the exit is. The birds are in the western one."

"We'll check everything," Elena said, and motioned for her small but intimidating army to follow. "Your other friend is on the surface, and if Father Frost hasn't imagined things in a drunken stupor, he and his girlfriend were planning to visit Kolomenskoe. Come on, let's get Gamayun and the rest, find the exit and round up the birds."

"And find One-Eyed Likho," Galina added. "Funny you didn't run into it—him."

Elena nodded, smiling. "That's a lot of things to do," she said. "Let's get a move on."

18: Birds

Fyodor did not expect the bear made entirely of rats to be helpful for much longer—it seemed to work more as a distraction, a quaint way of buying time. If only he could do something with the time they bought—running seemed superfluous now, and the only thing that occurred to him was to shove Oksana into the nearest snowdrift, to protect her from harm that now seemed inevitable.

Unfortunately, the bear made of rats misinterpreted his intentions and turned toward him, raising its arms silently and protectively.

"What the fuck is that thing?" one of the maroon jackets said.

"It's a bear of some sort," another answered. "A transformer bear."

"Oh yeah," the first one said, brightening up. "My kid has one of those—imported. Good toy."

They watched as Fyodor retreated up the path, the jackdaw Vladimir hovering over his head. Slava remained silent, but his hand reached inside of his jacket and Fyodor cringed at the thought of what it would extract. He never liked guns, was fearful of them—even when his stepfather went hunting he preferred to stay behind and never looked at the glassy-eyed birds and rabbits he brought back. Now, he imagined his own eyes turning into expressionless glass marbles, clouded with death.

Oksana, now between him and the thugs, got to her feet. She spat out snow and whistled to the bear, redirecting its slow shambling attack. Fyodor thought that it was getting embarrassing; it was the only reason why he ignored the glint in Slava hand and instead charged him.

He was too far and the path was too slippery. Slava saw him move and raised the gun. His gray eyes squinted, aiming a heavy long-nosed Luger at Fyodor. The bear moved closer and Slava hesitated and changed aim, as his bodyguards stepped off the porch and walked toward Fyodor.

A shot rang out and the bear tottered and fell apart. The rats scattered, leaving one writhing and spraying blood onto the blue-streaked snow. Oksana cried out and fell to her knees to pick up the injured rat. She cradled it in her hands, oblivious to the danger.

Fyodor took an awkward swing at the thug who'd reached him first, but the man just waved Fyodor's hand off, as one would a fly, and his round rubbery fist slammed into Fyodor's jaw, dislodging something important and filling his mouth with salty blood. He staggered backward a bit but remained standing, watching the blood drip from his lips, searing small black-cherry red craters into the packed snow of the path.

The other thug stepped forth—there was no hurry in his movements, as if he were going to take his sweet time beating the trespasser. Fyodor found himself sympathizing with the thug—how often did this man have an opportunity to pummel someone in peace, in the middle of the snow-covered forest at sundown, where there was no risk of interruption or discovery? At the very least, their attention was diverted from Oksana. Even Slava put his Luger away and watched the beating.

Another punch, and out of the corner of his swelling eye Fyodor saw a streak of motion—a dark blur in the blue twilight, and realized that Oksana lunged for Slava. She knocked him off balance, and the two of them tumbled into the cabin. The last thing Fyodor saw was Slava pushing Oksana away from him with one hand, and reaching into his jacket with the other.

Fyodor strained to follow them, but two thugs cut off his route, reluctant to let go of their forbidden amusement, like a bulldog with an imported leather shoe. One of the thugs grabbed his coat at the chest to hold Fyodor up, and the other deposited slow, methodical blows to the face and sternum, calculated to inflict the maximum amount of pain and remorse for ever having tangled with Slava's goons.

The blows stopped and Fyodor looked up out of his one working eye, waiting for the inevitable sounds of Oksana's scream and a gun shot. Instead, there was a flapping of wings and birds poured into the darkened air, coming seemingly from everywhere—the windows and doors of the cabin, from between the clouds, even flying up from among the rats that ran on the ground.

Fyodor was let go, and his knees buckled; he dipped, staggered but stood up, as the air churned around him, black with wings and eyes and beaks. There were reptilian clawed feet touching his face and hands, there were soft-as-butter feathers of owls brushing against his bruised and swollen face. Rats climbed up his trousers and sleeves, seeking protection from the air that suddenly became a whirlwind of predators.

Neither the crows nor the owls showed much interest in the rats—instead, they landed on the trees, the path, the roof of the cabin. There were hundreds of them, and the thugs stared at them, open-mouthed, not yet sure if it was to be their reckoning—if all the people they had turned into birds by their slow-witted, cruel magic had come back to exact revenge.

Fyodor used their consternation to break away and to run to the cabin, muttering, "God please let her be alive" with his split and bleeding lips that stung in the cold air. The cabin was darker than the outside, and he couldn't see a thing; he blundered inside blindly and immediately stepped on something soft and bumped his elbow against something hard.

"Oksana?" he called into the darkness.

"In here," she replied, her voice surprisingly calm. "Just wait a second and let your eyes get used to the darkness."

Slowly, like a photograph in a vat of developer, the inside came into focus, black and grey in the darkness. He discerned Oksana—unharmed, thank God—standing by the wall; the soft thing by his feet was Slava, alive but lying prostrate on the floor, with the barrel of a shotgun pressed against the nape of his neck; Elena was the one holding the shotgun. She shot Fyodor a friendly smile that flashed white in the darkness. "Hi," she whispered. "How many of the others are outside?"

"Just two," Fyodor said. "And a shitload of birds."

He squinted into the darkness, and as his eyes adjusted to the twilight he realized that the fourth wall of the cabin had been subsumed by a gray fog that stretched somewhere far, into unimaginable dimensions. The swirling fog cleared and condensed again, allowing him only brief glimpses of the shadowy figures inside of it.

He stared into the fog as one would into a snow globe—the concerns about the thugs and the questions about Elena's unexpected presence melted away, leaving him charmed, entranced by the unfolding spectacle. The figures inside appeared distorted, as if one was looking through a soap bubble, but he recognized their long gray coats and the red stars on their hats, their military boots striking the ground in unison—the legendary First Cavalry, the product of propaganda and folklore in equal proportions; they passed through the bubble, each of their faces briefly magnified and distorted, and disappeared again into the fog.

Fyodor felt his throat tighten as he realized that he was not seeing real people but an entire epoch passing into realms unknown—all his childhood heroes, all the revolutionary soldiers he had been conditioned to admire as a child became irrelevant and disappeared into the mist. They did not look at him as they passed—perhaps they couldn't see him—but stared straight ahead. Their horses followed, with a subdued clip-clopping of shod hooves, their heads lowered, their eyes pensive, all of them bays with a white star on the forehead.

The vision passed, and the fog swirled again.

"What was it?" he whispered to Elena.

She shrugged, never letting go of the shotgun's stock. "Another era has moved underground."

"But those were not real live people."

"Of course not. They were symbols. Now, if you're done with asking irrelevant questions, will you give me a hand?"

He shook his head and winced—every movement resonated with a sharp pain in his skull. "What do you need?"

"The two men outside," she reminded him. "See if the birds are done with them."

He peeked through the doorway. It was completely dark now, but on the snow he saw two large dark spots, motionless and bulky like two beached whales. "Yes," he said.

"Good." Elena moved the shotgun away from Slava's neck, and motioned for him to stand and move against the wall. "Now, let's get this thing over with."

The walls of the cabin dissolved in a mild yellow radiance around them—Fyodor felt like the four of them stood on a stage, the audience hidden from them by the glare of footlights. But he could feel their presence in the undifferentiated glow, he could hear breathing and voices.

"All clear," Elena called into the light. "Come on out."

Koschey was the first to emerge, his lips pressed close together in a habitual sour grimace of general disapproval of the state of things. In his bony hands he held two feathers—one black and one white—with the air of a stage magician.

"Bring out One-Eyed Likho," Elena said to him. "I don't want him underground."

"I'm pretty sure they don't want him on the surface either," Koschey said.

Elena shrugged, her milk-white shoulder dipping out and back into her black dress. "I can live with that."

Oksana touched Fyodor's sleeve. "One-Eyed Likho," she

whispered to him by way of explanation. "It was in here, talking to him." She pointed at Slava. "When it saw me it ran through the wall, but I guess they intercepted it."

Koschey allowed a small satisfied grin to light his hollow face. "It was quite convenient. Likho stole your friends' luck, see? And what is the worst luck if not running into Likho? They are practically designed for attracting misfortune. Too bad for them, but here we are."

"Where are they? Galina and Yakov, I mean?" Fyodor said.

"They're coming," Koschey said. "Apart from loss of luck they are all right."

Likho was the next to emerge from the glow—a slavering, wild thing that cast about with its hungry single eye, and Fyodor took an involuntary step back. It growled at him, so unlike the dry scratchy voice he had heard previously. Likho strained and fought, but a rope around its neck, held by several rusalki, kept him secured.

Yakov and Galina followed close behind. They both smiled and nodded at Fyodor, and he smiled and nodded back, unsure of the protocol. Were they his friends? Was he supposed to hug them or at least shake hands? He decided to remain aloof, and just hung in the background listening to Elena explain the situation to the new arrivals and introduce Slava to the gathering. The white rook who sat on the Tatar-Mongol's shoulder squawked indignantly.

"All right then," Elena said. "This is everyone. What do you think, Koschey, what's first, the curse or the charm?"

"The curse," Koschey replied and stuffed the white feather into the pocket of his long black jacket. "Fun stuff first."

He tossed the black feather at Slava; he ducked but the feather followed him like a target-seeking missile. It attached itself to Slava's head, and he cried out in pain as black, tar-like substance oozed from the feather, spreading over his face and his now screaming mouth.

Likho watched the happenings with its single eye burning. It swallowed often and looked around, as if searching for escape routes, but as the tar kept pouring and dripping, forming long streaks like melting candle wax, Likho's gaze focused on Slava, as it were drawn to him with some inexplicable force.

The rusalki loosened the bonds, and Likho strained toward Slava, now just an amorphous mass of tar. They let it go, and Likho bounded to its victim, claws extended and mouth slavering. In one long low jump Likho reached Slava, wrapped its scaly arms around him and clung, suddenly submissive and content.

"What's happening?" Fyodor whispered.

"A curse," Koschey explained. "Likho will stick to him now. Whatever he attempts, he won't succeed."

"You're not going to kill him?" Fyodor asked.

Koschey turned to face him; in the twilight his cheeks were dark hollows, and his eyes barely glistened from under the dark heavy eyelids. "I'm not a merciful entity," Koschey said. "They call me chthonic. They call me Deathless, but death is my realm, and I want nothing to do with his kind. Let him walk the earth forever, like accursed Cain with a red brand on his face, let One-Eyed Likho follow him for all eternity."

"You're going leave this thing here?" Fyodor said.

Koschey shrugged. “You heard the countess. Better you than us.”

“But I thought . . . ”

“What you thought doesn’t matter,” Elena interrupted. “As long as you’re on the surface, you’re not a friend. You have your problems, we have ours. You dumped enough corpses and spoiled magic underground already. Let’s see you deal with your own problems for a while.”

“She’s not a benign entity either,” Koschey said, and a shadow of affection snuck into his old brittle voice.

The tar had thickened around Likho, making it into a shapeless lump—Slava looked like a hunchback, Likho just an ugly growth now. The tar started to melt and soon was absorbed, leaving only a few unclean stains and drips on the cabin floor.

Slava shook—shuddered, even, with strong convulsing spasms. Likho became just a bump on his back, smaller than before, but certainly disfiguring and prominent enough to split open the maroon jacket along the seam. His gaze cast wildly about, as if it were Likho looking out of his wide eyes.

“Go,” Koschey motioned. “Go and don’t ever come back to Kolomenskoe, or you’ll regret it.”

Slava hunched over, eyeing them all like a cornered wolf. “I know where your death is,” he howled to Koschey, and bounded through the lights into the surrounding darkness. There was a crunching of snow and a snapping of branches, and Fyodor exhaled in relief.

Koschey sighed too. “Everyone knows where my death is,” he said, addressing the direction of Slava’s flight. “What no one understands is that it doesn’t matter.”

"How do you mean?" Yakov said. He had remained silent until then, his head cocked to one shoulder as if he was listening to some distant whispers rather than the goings-on. "Why doesn't it matter? Aren't you afraid that someone will find it?"

Koschey took the white feather out of his pocket. "They can find it," he said, "but they can't destroy it. How do you destroy a negation?"

"Metaphysics," Elena interrupted. "Come on, turn the birds into people."

"Wait," Galina said, anxious. "Are you sure they are all there?"

"As sure as we're going to be," Elena said. "The mermaids and the First Cavalry scoured every corner and shooed them all here."

"I thought you said they were symbols," Fyodor said.

Elena tossed her head impatiently, letting loose a long serpentine coil of her smooth hair. "What does that have to do with their ability to scare up birds?"

Koschey stepped to the lights that now burned brighter. The white feather in his fingers trembled and stretched, shooting long tendrils of blinding-white fog that stood against the darkness around the cabin like the flares of the aurora borealis.

The birds, invisible in the black branches of the trees, rose as one to meet the wrapping of the tendrils; the fog spread until Fyodor saw nothing but white, and then he had to look away.

When he looked back, he saw people like any others. Their feathers turned into black and gray and brown clothes with only occasional splashes of color. They looked around them as if waking from deep sleep; Fyodor tried to imagine what was it like for them—were their lives as birds just vague ghosts now, things one remembers in a dream? Did they wonder how they got there? And, most importantly, what was it like, waking up back in one's body, and finding oneself in Kolomenskoe at the very break of dawn?

He tried to imagine it now—their lives, their dreams. They were just like everyone else; Fyodor thought about the time when everything changed. He was glad then that he'd chosen to live in the streets, painting the overly-expressive gypsies and sentimental landscapes, and not having to deal with the shifting economic and political climate. He could ignore the fearful glances of the people who suddenly felt that the very fabric of reality had been yanked from under them as the oil industry became privatized and classified ads bristled with scary and foreign job titles—copywriter, realtor, and manager. The techy kids, marked from childhood by their glasses and pasty complexion for the engineering careers, dropped out of colleges and opened their own programming companies, while the engineers, suddenly finding themselves on the brink of starvation, sold cigarettes through the tiny clear plastic embrasures of the subway kiosks.

Fyodor remembered the conversation he had overheard in the street once. Two men, both small, slender and unremarkable—likely engineers or junior researchers—stopped by Fyodor's paintings. Not to buy (he had a pretty good instinct in that regard) but to stare at the inviting cloudless azure of the summer sky on one of the canvas.

"I have to take another job," one of them said. He looked the epitome of the Soviet engineer, a gray harmless creature, timid to the point of invisibility. "Sveta wants to privatize the apartment, and Grandma is ailing and her pension only pays for the fish for her cat."

"You can work for me," his companion said. "You can sell shawls—we have a joint venture with those folk-masters from Vologda. Nice lace too."

"Sell?" his interlocutor repeated with a note of candid fear in his voice. "I can't. I don't know how."

"There's nothing to know," his friend reassured. His distracted gaze slid over Fyodor as if he were as inanimate as one of his paintings. "Easy; just hold those things up and be loud."

"I don't know how to be loud," the presumed engineer said, desperation edging into his voice.

As Fyodor watched the group of people outside, as they looked at each other and shook their heads, trying to remember, and cried silently, he realized what they had in common. The bird people were the ones who did not know how to be loud, in any sense of the word—they only tried to carry on as best they could, holding to the memory of a dignity that didn't seem to be allowed in the new capitalist jungles that sprouted around them, lush and suffocating and seductive but blocking the view of everything but themselves. He felt acute pity for their voicelessness, for their inability to adjust or to turn back time.

He watched as Galina and Fyodor stepped outside and mingled with the crowd. Oksana nudged him. "Do you want to go to them?"

"Why?" Fyodor said. "What can I do?"

"It doesn't matter," Oksana said. "Can't you see? They need someone to tell them it's going to be all right."

Fyodor followed her down the steps of the cabin, which seemed to have reappeared from the dimmed lights, outlined anew against the gray dawn sky. He promised himself never to go back to this place, to avoid every memory of Peter the Great and his blasted cabin that harbored rather more than he was willing to take on. He wondered if it was possible to simply forget such things, and smiled to himself lopsidedly—his drinking would surely take care of that, and who needed a liver anyway.

Oksana approached an older woman, her head covered by a kerchief patterned in lurid red roses, a wide-mouthed handbag clutched in her hand. Oksana whispered to the woman, and it must've been something soothing because the woman's shoulders relaxed and her crooked fingers lost their desperate bone whiteness.

Fyodor looked around until his gaze met that of a middle-aged woman. During her ordeals her eye makeup had smudged, giving her a battered, haunted look. Fyodor stepped closer, noticing the fresh stitches on the seam of her light coat and her old-fashioned shoes with square toes and heels and that orthopedic look one usually associated with much older women.

"I'm Fyodor," Fyodor said. "Are you all right?"

"I'm not sure," the woman said. "What happened? I was going to work, and . . . "

"Where do you work?" he asked.

"Biryulevo," she said. "Meat-packing plant. Where are we?"

"Kolomenskoe," he said. "You'd have to take the subway back."

"And a bus," she said, looking straight through him distractedly. Still, he had a feeling that talking about routine matters grounded her.

"Route 162?" he asked.

She nodded. "There are a couple of new ones, too. What am I doing here?"

"Don't you remember anything?" he said.

"I remember a man," she answered. "The man who followed me to the plant. And then . . . " She ran her hand over her face. "I had strange dreams—I dreamt of flying through the water, through a dark black river, and white pale faces stared at me—and I remember the city's rooftops—as if I were looking at them from the air."

"It sounds like a nice dream," he said. "Do you have anyone waiting for you at home?"

"Just my daughter, Darya," the woman said and smiled a little. "Good girl, very clever. Says she wants to be a mathematician. Want to see her picture?"

"Sure," Fyodor said and waited as the woman rifled through her roomy handbag, shuffling combs, compact cases, coin purses, plastic baggies, scented handkerchiefs and whatever other arcane objects female bags of such size contained. He was surprised at how calm everyone appeared—no one seemed to have gotten hysterical or distraught, like the woman before him. Her movements seemed sluggish, as if she just awakened up from deep sleep (he supposed she did), or if she deliberately avoided any thought that would make her panic. He also thought that a crowd of people had to be reassuring, even if she didn't remember how she got here. Out of the corner of his eye he saw some of the former birds take off down the path leading to the exit, and he sighed with relief. They would get home and find some way to explain the dreams and the missing time.

She finally fished out a small black and white picture mounted on cardboard and covered with a clear polyethylene sheet, taped at the edges. The girl in the picture appeared utterly unremarkable, but Fyodor nodded and made an appreciative noise. "Cute kid," he said. "Listen, maybe you should head home, to tell her you're all right? She must be worried sick."

The woman looked around her, perplexed. "It's winter?"

"No," he said. "Still October. Just a really fucked up one."

He heard Galina's voice calling out, "Masha, Masha!"

"Excuse me," he said to the woman. "Let me see what's going on there."

She nodded, already looking after the people heading down the path. "Don't worry about me. The subway must be open already, so I better go. Beat the rush hour." She smiled. "Thanks for stopping to talk to me."

"My pleasure," he said, and turned to see Galina, panicked now, running from one cluster of people to the next. She looked anxiously into women's faces, grabbed sleeves. Yakov followed behind her.

Fyodor caught up to them. “What’s going on?”

Galina mopped her sleeve at her tear-filled eyes. “Masha . . . ” she whispered, all fire gone out of her. “My sister. She isn’t here.”

19: Masha

THE SILENT PARK CAME ALIVE WITH THE CHIRPING OF BIRDS as the sun's first rays filtered through the naked black tree branches that stood against the watercolor-pale sky. Galina listened to the sounds absentmindedly—these were small ordinary birds, tits and nuthatches and wrens. She heard the cawing of crows off in the distance, but no Masha. She snuggled into the snow, finally exhausted, and hugged her knees to her chest. Everything had been useless. The transformation of birds back, hundreds that went home to their families—just now, before her very eyes—did not matter. Masha was not here, and everything was pointless. She couldn't fathom returning home, and she thought with indifference that she could freeze to death, die here in the snow, and it would be as fitting an end as any.

Yakov sat down next to her. Her heart fluttered for a moment when she saw a bird in his hand, and slowed down just as quickly—the bird was an ordinary crow, who cawed at Yakov demandingly.

"Imagine that," he said by the way of explanation. "This crow was the only real one in the whole bunch—my Carl."

"Your pet," she remembered.

He didn't argue. "I'm so sorry," he said. "Elena said they would search underground once more."

"What's the use?" she said. "The charm is gone, and Alkonost has no more feathers to give."

"Koschey . . . " Yakov started.

"Can't do anything without the feathers," she concluded, determined to wallow in her misery with as much abandon as she could muster in this low-spirited moment. "And how do you know she wasn't on this side, somewhere?"

Yakov remained silent, his fingers caressing the crow's shining black head absentmindedly. "I'm sorry," he said. "I know how it feels—but really, you shouldn't sit in the snow, you'll freeze."

"That'd be just fine," Galina said darkly, but couldn't help but feel ridiculous and small, and her eyes grew hot again with unbidden tears.

"Come on," Yakov said and nudged her to get up. "It's warmer in the cabin."

Galina sighed and followed him inside.

Elena smiled at her, but stopped once she noticed Galina's face. Elena gave her a quick warm hug. "I so wish I had some tea here," she said.

Galina nodded. "Tea would be nice."

Oksana, Yakov, Fyodor and Koschey stared at them, and Elena wrapped her arm around Galina's shoulders and turned her to face the window, their backs to the others. "Don't pay attention to them," she whispered. "They mean well, but they don't know what to say. Frankly, neither do I."

"Where's Zemun?" Galina said. "And Timur-Bey?"

Elena waved her hand. "Underground. You can come back with me, if you want. It's not so bad there, and you can forget things you want to forget. If it's especially bad, you can always give it to the boatman."

"I know," Galina said. "Yakov met him; he didn't seem too happy."

Elena shrugged. "It's funny how it goes. But the boatman, he can help you, really. And it is—quiet. It'll be quieter still with Likho and Zlyden gone. We can drink tea and talk all day."

Galina nodded. "It sounds nice." Better than the alternative, she thought. She remembered the story of Sirin, of the power of her voice to lull people into quiet contentment that was worse than death—at least, so the stories went, but they never explained why it was so bad. The heroes were meant to struggle and persevere, to fight, to not give in. But after the fight was done and one still lost, why not let the contentment take over? There was nothing for her on the surface.

She heard Yakov and Fyodor murmuring behind them, and turned to see what was going on. She had decided to abandon hope because hope would only hurt more, but she couldn't help it.

Fyodor was showing Yakov and Koschey a jackdaw, and Sergey, still in the body of the white rook, looked on skeptically. Galina's heart squeezed in a painful spasm.

"No," Fyodor said quickly. "It's not your sister, sorry. It's that guy, Vladimir—or rather his soul, see? It was in another one of those glass spheres, Oksana's rat stole it from Slava—so we jammed it into the jackdaw. Koschey said that he might be able to bring Sergey back, so I thought maybe he'd help Vladimir."

Vladimir the jackdaw gave a strained squawk. "Are you really Koschey the Deathless?" he asked Koschey.

"Really," Koschey said. "And yes, I might be able to help you, only I would need a suitable body."

Yakov and Fyodor exchanged looks.

"What?" Koschey said. "I can't make something out of nothing. Soul-trading is one thing, but making bodies out of thin air is an entirely too metaphysical a proposition."

"But those birds . . . " Yakov started.

"Those people were turned into birds by a magic I don't have," Koschey said. "I reversed it. But how do you suppose I could make a human body out of a glass sphere, or a stupid jackdaw? Haven't you idiots ever heard of conservation of mass?"

Yakov and Fyodor nodded, silent like guilty children.

"Let's take a look at what you've wrought with this jackdaw here then," said Koschey, and took the jackdaw from Fyodor's hands. "Uh-huh—wait . . . what is this?"

"What is what?" Oksana said. "Did we do something wrong?"

"You mean, besides ramming a glass sphere down an unsuspecting bird's beak?" Koschey scoffed. "Yes, actually you did. This bird—this is one of those cursed ones."

"Why didn't it turn back to human then?" Yakov said.

"Because you stuck another soul into it," Koschey said. "Fucking amateurs." He studied the jackdaw for some time, and finally turned to Galina. When he spoke, his voice was careful, calculated. "Darling," he said. "I have good news and bad news for you."

Galina swallowed with a dry throat, the sound of blood in her ears deafening. Through its roar, she barely discerned Koschey's words.

"The good news," he said, "is that I think we've found your little sister."

GALINA REMEMBERED THE TIME MASHA HAD RUN AWAY FROM home. Unlike most children who come back around dinner time, Masha had kept walking; the police apprehended her ten miles away from their home, well beyond the circular highway that surrounded the city like a snake swallowing its own tail and gagging on its own noxious exhalations of gasoline and tar heated by the sun. When the policeman brought Masha home, her dress—pink roses on pale-yellow background—smelled of gas and exhaust, and she could not provide a cogent answer to the grownups' questions—why? What were you trying to do?—and just stared past the worried faces of their mother and grandmother. And only when they left her alone and Galina asked her the same thing, she shrugged. "I don't know. I just wanted to be away."

"Aren't you happy here, with us?"

"I am." Masha smiled, her usual sunny disposition returning. "I just wanted to see where else could I be happy."

Where else indeed. Even her rebellion was good-natured, not a denial but an attempt to affirm more, to embrace more of the world. Galina envied that capacity for love—when she had run away as a child, she had come home before dinner, after wandering through the neighborhood streets and indulging in the fantasy of her mother's grief and remorse until she grew tired and hungry; past that point, her sullen indignation could not sustain her. Masha taught her that love and curiosity was a more enduring force.

She looked at the jackdaw sitting in Koschey's palm. "What's going to happen?" the jackdaw said. "To me, I mean—Vladimir."

"We'll have to find you another vessel," Koschey answered. "I fear that we only have some rats available."

Vladimir did not look thrilled. "A rat?"

"Don't worry," Fyodor said. "I'm sure we'll find you something more suitable underground. Maybe a rook, like Sergey."

"I don't want to go underground," Vladimir said.

"Neither do I," Sergey confirmed.

"Well, it doesn't look like you have a choice now, does it?" Elena said. "Unless you want to stay here—but you know what they say about white crows. Besides, underground there are no cats, except Bayun."

Galina heaved a sigh. "What about my sister?" she said. "Does it mean she will stay a bird forever?"

Koschey shrugged. "That's my bad news, dear. I can't turn her back, but I can transfer her soul into another woman's body—if you can find one, that is."

"You mean for her to live someone will have to die?" she said. The idea did not seem monstrous to her—after all, just a few minutes ago she contemplated freezing to death. Petulance was not enough to compel her. But love . . .

"No," Koschey said. "Not die, exactly. Just trade places with her, become a bird."

"Like these two?" Galina pointed at Sergey and Vladimir.

"Not quite," Koschey said. "They act human because their souls are separated from birds' bodies, wrapped into glass.

They are like hands inside puppets—they animate them, but they are not the same. Without the protection of glass, the human soul will become a bird's soul."

Galina nodded. "I'll trade with her," she said. "Gladly."

Elena shot her a worried look. "Galina—do you think this is really a good idea?"

Galina smiled. "This is the best idea I ever had. Just let me tell her something, while I can still talk."

Koschey grasped the bird and extracted the glass marble with Vladimir's soul from the bird's crop. Galina cringed at the unceremonious manhandling of her sister, and looked away. She only looked when the green glass sphere lay secure in Koschey's narrow palm, ridges of bone running parallel along it like barrel staves.

Galina cradled the jackdaw in her palms, carefully as if it were a fragile Christmas ornament. The jackdaw looked at her sideways, its head tilted, its expression roguish. Galina stepped outside.

"Listen," she said to the jackdaw, "when you remember all this—and you must, you must—please don't feel bad. Sure, this body is older than your own, but this is the best I can do. Remember—you have a baby, and mom is your responsibility now. Don't tell her what happened. Just be yourself."

She looked at the naked trees, delicate and yet stark against the sky like a painting. She searched for words to explain to the carefully listening bird. "She won't like you at first, but soon enough she'll realize that you aren't me. Just do what you always do. I wish I could make it easier, I wish you could come back to things like they used to be. You'll be a spinster aunt to your child, but it is better than not being there at all. And your husband will come back from the army and grieve for you, and you won't be able to tell him the truth, no matter how much it rips you up—just like that story, remember? No signs, no telling about the curse, or they'll lock you up and you won't like it. I leave you with my liabilities.

"But also, my advantages. You have a job—you'll just have to brush up on your English, and Velikanov will forgive you for missing work, and he'll cut you every break. Maybe you'll even like him.

"But most of all, remember this: I will try and visit you sometime. I don't know what it's like, being a jackdaw, I don't know if I would even remember, but if I can hold onto anything, I will hold onto this. And one thing I'm asking of you: remember that you had a sister once, a sister who loved you more than forty thousand brothers."

Galina swallowed and thought of something else to say. She wanted to talk about love and how strong it was, about how Masha ran away all these years ago and surely, if it was strong enough to take her away it was strong enough to bring her back. She wanted to tell her to be kind to their mother even though she wouldn't be kind in return—not at first at least, not while she still thought that the woman in Galina's body was Galina, the same damaged creature. But Masha knew all that already, and if anyone could win their mother over, it was her.

Galina returned to the cabin, the jackdaw perched on her wrist. "We're ready," she told Koschey. "Just let me say my goodbyes."

Yakov nodded at her awkwardly.

"What are you going to do?" Galina said.

He made a face. "I'm not going back underground, that's for sure."

"What about your grandfather?"

"I'll send him a note, I guess," Yakov said. "But my mother—she needs me more than he does. And there are things I need to take care of here."

Normally, Galina wouldn't pry; but right now coyness seemed superfluous. "What things?" she asked.

He jerked his shoulders, making the crow that perched there flap its wings and caw. "I want to talk to my ex-wife, for one. I need to know what happened—do you ever think that there are people you should've been kinder to?"

Galina nodded.

"Same with my ex," he said. "There are things we need to talk about."

"Good luck," Galina said.

"Same to you," he said. "It's really nice, what you're doing for your sister."

She was grateful that he didn't argue with her decision. "Thanks," she said. "Good luck on the surface."

"I'm staying underground," Fyodor said. "It's much nicer there."

"Yes," Oksana added. "I only came to the surface to help, but I can't wait to get back—Sovin will be so mad at me that I got one of his rats killed."

"It could've been more than one," Galina said. "You did well. Thanks for helping."

Oksana shrugged. "I suppose."

Timur-Bey didn't say much and just shook her hand.

"I'll be seeing you around the underground then," she said, and turned to Elena. "And you too."

Elena pouted a bit. "That's not what I meant. But you're welcome to stop by any time—even though jackdaws are poor conversationalists."

Galina was flattered by the disappointment so evident in Elena's voice. "I'm glad to have met you," she said. "I really would've liked to be friends with you."

After that, there wasn't much else to say and she looked to Koschey. "I'm ready, I guess."

"I haven't done this one in a while," he said. "It's not at all like putting one's death into a needle."

Galina wanted to ask what was the difference between a soul and a death and how did he learn to do these things, and what was his relationship to Baba Yaga. But there were too many questions—she would never ask them all, and now was her last chance. It seemed better to descend into silence without asking them. Let Masha figure out these things.

"Here we go," Koschey said.

He ordered Galina to stand still while looking into the eyes of the bird perched on her wrist. Out of the corner of her eye she could see Koschey plucking thin translucent threads of magic from the air, weaving them together. She felt a nudge form within, a momentary vertigo, as if she were falling into a well. The jackdaw's eye became black and huge in front of her face, like a black moon, like a starless sky, like the bottom of a well.

The giant eye shrunk into a pupil, and was now surrounded with a hazel iris, crosshatched with golden and brown streaks. As she pulled away, her field of vision widened to the view of a pale face with blue smudges of shadow under tired, heavy-lidded eyes and a bloodless, tormented mouth. It took her a while to realize that the face she was looking into was hers.

The woman's eyes focused, and her mouth opened in the expression of childlike surprise and wonder. "Galka?" she whispered.

"Yes, Masha, it is me," she wanted to answer, but her mouth—her beak, made of hard bone and horn—opened in a loud, jubilant squawk.

It is me, the jackdaw Galina cried, *and this is you, and oh God, I'm so happy to have found you. I'm sorry it is not as perfect as I wanted it to be. Go now, go, hold your child, tell Mom that it'll be all right, visit grandma in the hospital. Just go, just go.*

She felt restless itching in her arms (wings), and she spread them wide. She circled the cabin, faces of people around her barely registering, until she found the open door and flew outside. There were other birds there, but there would be time for them later, and she circled over the cabin, rising higher and higher into the air.

She saw a woman and a man, both looking familiar—the woman tall and hunched and pale, the man squat and blocky—exit the cabin and walk down the path. As she rose higher into the sky, they became two black dots slowly traversing the great powdery whiteness below, the black tree branches weaving a delicate net above them. The river, still free of ice, snaked in its wintry desolate blackness between its white banks, and a white church stood almost invisible on a white snow-covered slope, only its onion roof golden with captured sunshine.

She spiraled downward, to take another look at the small wooden cabin tucked away in the very heart of the park, and watched a tall, skeletal man exit the cabin and crane his neck, shielding his eyes from the sun. A woman in a black velvet dress holding a shotgun stood next to him, watching Galina like he did.

She also saw a small gypsy girl, surrounded by an army of rats, make her way to the river; a tall lanky guy followed her, not quite with her, not quite separate. They sat on the bank, the rats spread around them like a living blanket, and watched the smooth river surface.

Deep inside the jackdaw knew that sometime soon she would find those people again, follow them by flying through an imaginary window or a reflection of a doorway in a rain puddle; a part of her had an inkling of other birds underground, and a fond memory of a white cow glowing with warm bluish light and spilling stars like milk. But not yet—she had things to attend to here, on the surface, first.

She rose high enough to see the streets beyond the park, animated with a slow churning of crowds and smells of fire and exhaust; she saw the squat tomb of the subway station and its slow disgorging and consumption of the dark throngs. There was ringing of trams and heavy sighs of the kneeling buses that carried tourists and honking of automobile horns; there were smells of fresh bread and beer and ash.

She headed north-west, where more golden domes lit up under the sun, and the clock on the Spasskaya Tower announced the time with deep hollow beats; she circled over the Tsar-Bell and Tsar-Cannon, both blue with patina and gigantic, ludicrous in their excess. Her wings clipped the air into even, turgid fragments as she swooped down over Red Square and the blue spruces by the Mausoleum, as she flew over the river again, perching for a rest on the guardrails of the humpbacked, ornate bridge. She circled over the New Arbat and took a cursory swoop down Gazetniy Pereulok.

There was a sense of significance to her flight, as she remembered that these places were important somehow. But her human memory was receding already, leaving behind only the keen intelligence and the cunning instinct of a bird. Only a few images lingered behind, and in her mind's eye she saw the tall woman walking through the snow-covered park, the woman with hazel eyes and bewildered frown. Galina did not remember how or why that woman was important, but she thought about her with the warm regard one afforded to kin.

"She's going to be all right," the jackdaw thought. And that was all that mattered.

Biography

Ekaterina Sedia, a Moscow native, currently lives in Southern New Jersey with the best spouse in the world and two needy cats. Her short stories have sold to *Analog, Baen's Universe, Fantasy Magazine*, and *Dark Wisdom*, as well as *Japanese Dreams* and *Magic in the Mirrorstone* anthologies. In addition to *The Secret History of Moscow*, Prime Books will be publishing her novel, *The Alchemy of Stone*, in late 2008. Visit her website at www.ekaterinasedia.com